THE LIGHTROOM

A H PILCHER

First published 2022 by Backleg Books UK
ISBN: 978-1-8382090-2-5
Copyright © 2022 A H Pilcher
All rights reserved

The rights of A H Pilcher to be identified as the author of the work has been asserted by him in accordance with the Copyright, Design and Patents Act 1988. All rights reserved. This publication may only be reproduced, stored or transmitted in any form, and by any means, with the written permission of the author. A catalogue record for this book is available from the British Library.

This is a work of fiction and characters and incidents are fictitious. While some towns and villages in West Sussex and Dorset- which have provided inspiration to the author - are identified, the names of others have been changed.

Backleg Books, UK
ahpbackleg@gmail.com
@ahpilcher

Book and cover design: Macaulay Design, Hampshire

The Lightroom

The Lightroom

The Lightroom

**A good life is a big life;
often in so many small ways**

The Lightroom

Chapter 1

It was just after 6pm. With luck, he would be back about 8.30. Heading down the lane, the darkness was deeper without streetlights. Passing the fields and scattered cottages, he soon joined the by-pass and headed west. Realising he was low on fuel, he made a mental note to pull in at some stage. The dual carriageway stretched forwards into endless fields of darkness, punctuated only by ripping lights of the occasional traffic. Some way later, he took the slip road leading to the motorway, heading to the capital. An on/off drizzle started and he flicked the intermittent wiper a few times before the rain gave up. As the van gained the higher ground, he passed banks of housing on both sides, then they too slipped back as he moved on. With the heater on, he was warm and cocooned, the journey was lost in the memory of a good day. His thoughts moved to the coming week and work. Although he had seen the advanced notice of the filling station, its coloured lights came fast onto him as he crossed the rise. Pulling up under the canopy he found a vacant pump and positioned the van as close as he could. Opening the door and getting out, he went around to the other side and flipped open the fuel lid. He removed the cap, repeating the word 'diesel', picked out the fuel line and pushed the nozzle into the throat of the tank.

Squeezing the trigger, the task of filling began. It always seemed to take longer than it should. Swapping hands, he leaned on the back panel thinking what a great day it had been seeing Helen, and walking by the sea with her dog. Eventually, the pump clicked, signalling the tank was full. After replacing the nozzle in its housing, his hand automatically searched his trouser pocket for his wallet. Opening it as he walked to the forecourt shop, he removed a card in readiness and, passing the now empty newspaper flip stand, the double doors opened automatically in front of him.

It was one of those mini supermarkets with a food franchise inside, and he joined the queue snaking its way between roped poles to a row of tills. A man wearing a turban took his transaction and passed him his receipt, giving and receiving a simultaneous 'Thank you.' Outside, Max paused, folding his receipt and putting it and the card in his wallet. As he pushed the wallet into his pocket, he glanced in front of him to see someone leaning out of a 4x4 car window directly behind where he was parked, shouting something in his direction. His senses picked up as he walked towards his van. Then, as the big man shouted again, he heard very clearly: 'What took you so long? Get your fucking van out the fucking way.'

Max frowned and open his arms a little showing his palms. The man leaned out of the window again, his heavily tattooed arms on show. Max, who was almost in front of him then, said, softly: 'What did you say?'

The man sneered and threw back at him: 'You heard, you cunt, now move your fucking van. Don't make me get out.'

For the briefest second, time hung. Then Max hit him through the open window with the force of a jackhammer. The driver had tried to turn away towards his passenger, but the blow landed directly on the side of his head. At the same time, Max grabbed his hair, pulling with a downward motion, and smashed the man's face with all of his strength on the edge of the door frame. The driver's badly-cut face exploded blood. The door was wrenched open, and as his body weight shifted, his leg slipped over the door sill. Max then slammed the door with as much force as he could muster, putting all his weight behind it. Staring at the car's passenger, he spoke quietly: 'Don't get out.'

Max, breathing heavily, fished out his keys, saying to the woman parked opposite: 'I'm very sorry you had to see that.'

He got into the van and drove away.

He had been provoked. He knew it was probably all on camera, plus several people would have witnessed what had happened. But, at this moment, he didn't care. He was massively pumped up. The rising, the compression, the explosion of anger burst a damn in him, shocking him with a return to the past. Seeing a turning off the motorway within a mile, he took it and on reaching the roundabout at the head of the slip road checked his mirror. Breathing deeply to calm himself down, he set the sat nav for a route across the remaining countryside to the suburbs. He felt shuttered in like an animal and angry with himself for the loss of temper that had caused him to break a promise made a few years ago. He had returned to a place in his life he hoped he had left behind. After the tension in him subsided, he reasoned there was a fairly good chance the driver he had hit would probably let it rest there. His 'type' have their pride too, and even if he were to consider revenge, it wouldn't be in a courtroom.

Driving the last of the country roads, Max headed into the suburbs. This was the forever time, the stop-start of endless traffic lights; but none of it could dislodge the feeling of remorse and shame that bore down his spirit. The man at the garage may well have deserved a sharp response, but Max wished it hadn't been him that had given it. Trying to push his thoughts away, he decided the best path was to keep quiet; tell no one what had happened. Recognising the streets as his own, he reached out and disconnected the sat nav and unclipping its body, dropped it onto the passenger seat to put away later. The last traffic light turned green, it was just another 100 meters and he was home. Finding a parking slot close to the flat, he drew in and turned off the engine. His body sagged into the seat for a second, then he looked at his mobile phone for the time, but the battery had gone. Turning the ignition on, the clock lit up as 8.25. Taking the keys out, he put the sat nav away in the glove compartment and sat back, allowing his head to stay on the headrest. He knew he needed help. Help is a cry from without.

He was without hope, understanding, friends and - finally - time. Picking up his hat and jacket, he got out of the car. Reaching the door, he pressed the key fob and the lights blinked back at him. Once inside, he drew the curtains, put the heating on and the kettle. Then he remembered to plug in his mobile. By 10.15 he was ready for bed and by 10.25 he was asleep.

He woke just after 3am sweating, his body hot, thinking he must have left the heating on. By the time he returned to bed, his feet were cold and he lay in bed prone, awake, and alert. Sleep stood little chance of taking him back. His mind started to replay the previous day, showing how the barometer of life can change as suddenly as air pressure. Turning over, he curled in the foetal position and settled. At first it was only a tear, a single tear running at a quickening pace down the side of his face towards his ear, then it rushed on. It wasn't sobbing, it was crying as in some way, some uncontrollable way, to wash away the tension and disappointment. He just couldn't cope. When the wave had passed, he moved, and using the back of his hand, wiped his face. So quickly had his anger burst the defensive gate yesterday, he knew that he would have to get help. This pattern of slipping backwards into a hole couldn't be covered over any more, it had to be confronted somehow. As his body regained its warmth, his breathing grew deeper and more regular until he slept again. Awaking before dawn, he had been within the edge of a dream just out of his grasp, pleased to be awake for fear of returning, and he lay waiting for the sun.

Getting up was hard for Max, he would have preferred to stay where he was and hide. But there was no choice. After washing at the sink, he walked back to the bedroom, put on a clean T-shirt and work clothes, and headed into the living room. Turning on the radio, he realised he had missed the news headlines and the interviewer was questioning a government minister hard, continually nudging him to make a mistake over yet another incentive for the NHS.

The subject was a familiar turkey that everyone wanted a slice of, the reality of it was that there was barely enough to go round. It prompted him to reach for his phone on the worktop. Unplugging it, he checked to make sure the doctor's number was in his directory. Then he looked at the missed calls, there were none he recognised. So he left them, moving to a single message from someone who obviously thought about his home improvements on Sunday and rang, expecting him to jump on that day too. Opening the fridge, he saw there were no eggs and not much of anything else. He bent and opened a lower cupboard for a cereal packet. Involuntarily shaking it, he poured the remains into the bowl, dumped it with milk and, bending towards the bowl, shovelled it in. To him, breakfast was just re-fuelling. The sports reporter was talking on the radio, so he turned it off. He didn't 'do' sport like other men. Pints in a pub watching a communal screen, or an afternoon of beer and football from the sofa just wasn't for him. It was the watching bit he didn't like. He would much rather be doing it - at any standard - like swimming. It was the feeling of fitness, his body working, driving forward to reach an objective, and claiming the endorphins in the process. That's what did it for him. He used to run regularly, but that had stopped because of a knee injury, which sometimes still troubled him at work. It was time to go. Outside, he brought the van to the door, loaded a selection of tools and the paint kit he thought he might need, and drove to his first call. It wasn't too far, maybe a couple of miles. He had been given special instructions by a woman, covering where to park, as it was permit parking only. Pushing through the traffic, he was just arriving as the phone rang. It was the woman he was driving to, who asked, covering possible disappointment with uncertainty, whether he was still coming. He let her unwind before telling her, with a smile on his face, that he was just outside, parked up, now. With clear relief, she said she would bring him out a visitor's permit straight away. The next call was from a roofing contractor with a problem.

In most cases, they themselves were the problem. Three roof trusses were proud, and the tilers were in the next day. Someone else's mistakes; the usual story. When Max said he could come around midday, the contractor asked him immediately about the cost. It was day rates only, and still he tried to manoeuvre. He was clearly the sort of bloke whose nature it was to beat every pound down to 80 pence. 'Take it or leave it,' said Max, as he saw a smartly-dressed woman waving a piece of paper at him through the van window. He held up a hand to indicate he would only be a moment, then heard the contractor say: 'OK.' He noted the address, logged the name and number and then got out of the van to apologise for what may have been construed as rudeness. Thanking her for the parking pass, he slid it on to the dashboard on top of all the flotsam that somehow washed up there.

Turning back, she was already walking back to the house. Expensive clothes, mid 50s maybe and with stylishly-cut short hair. The house was part of a beautiful, early Georgian crescent-shaped terrace, the whole terrace exterior was well maintained, probably under one contract. The front boundary wall and dividing walls of the houses were of low brick, topped with continuous coping stones, and the heavy spear railings were sunken and bedded in with lead, in the traditional way. All the gates were matching, and this gate was open. He was led up the stone slab path, past a miniature box hedge maze and three steps up to a landing with the same railings beside it. Before him was the oversized front door. Doric columns supported the narrow continuous balcony above this, with French windows opening on to it from, perhaps, a drawing room. There was one more floor, with skylight rooms above that and a basement below where he stood. All of this made a remarkable, beautifully-balanced exterior. Sheets had been put down for him in the hall and lower part of the stairs; she wasn't taking any chances.

He had been called on the previous Friday and asked about replacing and painting two broken banister spindles. She didn't ask how much the work would cost; she just wanted it done quickly. She waved a hand and said: 'Call me if you need anything.'

Max felt he was being treated in an offhand manner now that he had arrived, but it didn't matter because he was the one being paid. He had brought with him two larger, pre-primed spindles that he expected to plane down to size. After carefully removing the two broken rails, he cleaned their settings with a small chisel, ready to take the new ones. The mobile bench was set up on the front garden path and in a short time the spindles were planed to the correct size and in. He spot-glued and panel-pinned them tightly, leaving only minimal areas to fill with a wood filler. Next, he gave them a coat of thick undercoat, then he thoroughly cleaned up with his vacuum cleaner, shaking her sheets outside then replacing them either side of the stair rails ready for the gloss coat. Looking round the hall from where he stood, he saw three modern paintings all hung in unusual frames. A small ceramic, decorated glazed pot, Picasso style, possibly the real thing, sat on the narrow Jacobean hall table, a statement to its owner's way of life. There were no pictures of any children. He was aware the woman wasn't far away all the time he was working, but no tea had been offered. Putting the paint brush in a plastic bag, he twisted it so the paint wouldn't dry on the brush, and called out to her. A door opened all too quickly at the end of the hall, and she appeared. Explaining that he would be away for a short time while the paint was drying, he walked back to the van and loaded all his tools, wrote out the bill in readiness, then locked the doors. His next job was to call the doctor's surgery. The person who answered was surprisingly understanding when he outlined his problem and he was given an appointment at 8.30am in a few days. Was it a cancellation or an emergency slot? He didn't know, but he was surprised to get in so quickly.

Covering some 50 metres while walking during the call, he looked up to see he was now outside another house in this magnificent crescent. It was practically identical, apart from the door colour. What caught his attention immediately was the white statue at the side of the raised landing in front of the door. The statue was of a serene ballerina en pointe, holding a large, open fan. Perhaps it was symbolic that the dancer was secured to the railings, with a bicycle lock through and around her ankle. Perhaps there should have been a similar ankle lock in the place he was working. The moment he had seen the two spindles, side by side and broken in the same place, he thought an angry kick must have caused the damage. Yet there seemed to be no one in the house apart from the woman who had hired him, and she had mentioned her husband was away on a business trip, returning in a few days. What would make a woman like her do a thing like that – Max thought. Behind every curtain lies a different story; perhaps she had an unfulfilled life, like his? He walked back to the job, gave the two new spindles a gloss coat, and washed the brush of its water-based paint in the cloakroom. On hearing the running water, the woman came into the hall. He explained the paint work wouldn't be an exact match, as the hall paint had faded a little. That was unavoidable. He then handed her the hand-written bill. She appeared quizzical, by raising an eyebrow, but didn't comment. Fetching her bag from the other room, she paid him in cash. He thanked her and left.

Driving to the South Circular next, Max turned the heater up and knew he would be pleased to have the jacket and scarf in the back. He made the site in about half an hour and, luckily, managed to park outside. Going to the back of the van, he put on steel-toed boots, a high-vis safety jacket and hard hat. As he stood up, he heard a shout from the scaffold: 'Come on up.' It was only three storeys up to where a short, bald man greeted him with a broad grin, the site foreman probably. 'Thanks for coming over, here's the problem.'

Max spotted it straight away. One end of three consecutive trusses was proud by about 20 millimetres. The trusses had been craned up and laid, placed by several pairs of hands in the upright position. Spars and guides had been fixed to keep them permanently fixed before the tilers covered them. It looked to him that they might be sitting on tiny wedges on the plate itself. The only sure way to find out was to lift them, but it would take a crane, and that takes time and money. Max felt sure the site foreman had not seen the mistake until after the chippies had been and gone. Why weren't they still here? He didn't ask. He suspected the foreman realised his mistake, and needed a scapegoat to either sort it or take the blame if things went badly wrong. It was worth a go. Using timber off-cuts as levers in the confined space and his van jack, he wound up the jack under the lever to raise the truss just far enough to clear the tiny wedge with the flat edge of his set square beneath the first truss. He removed the wedge and then lowered the jack again. Using a spirit level on a long, straight-edged baton, he checked the level of the truss against the good ones, it was spot on. It had been a gamble, as it could easily have cracked the truss or collapsed it, but as it wasn't his, he wasn't too concerned. The other two worked well. It was over and done within an hour. The site foreman was pleased his problem was solved, but didn't like parting with the money. It was still only mid-afternoon. Max should have been riding high as he had done very well today, but he was tired and felt strangely vacant about it all. He headed home.

The doctor's appointment came round, and Max decided to take the tube as it wasn't far. Leaving himself plenty of time, he walked the familiar road with his hands in his jacket pockets. There had been an early frost and it was cold. As the footfall increased on the pavement, it had started to wear away the slippery surface.

It took about five minutes to turn the corner and head into the mouth of the station, where he joined the swelling numbers funnelling down to feed the tube. Scooping up the free daily paper without losing step, he waved his card through the reader and passed on. The escalator took him deeper. He could hear a train, the rushing of warmer air as people compressed on the platform and became ready to move onto an already crowded train. Standing still in the carriage, he realised he should have taken the bus. He felt hemmed in, being in such close proximity to so many people. That noise, a hard rattle, continuous, as the train hit points or a join in the rail. It seemed to get inside his head. Soon it was over and he was emerging into the street again. Looking both ways, as though checking his bearings, he moved on, turning off the main road and immediately arriving at the surgery. He stood on the pavement for a moment, wondering how all this was going to go. The surgery was a multi-practice, purpose-built place, with an open plan design, and decorated in plain colours. He followed an elderly couple, bent by time, towards the desk. She fumbled for, perhaps, an appointment card and he was gentle with concern. This small scene touched him. He was early, it was just 8.20, so after registering, he sat among the waiting patients. Taking out his free paper, he looked at the headlines. Syria, what a complex mess of suffering, with so many other countries trying to enforce their foreign policy. He thought they should substitute the words 'foreign policy' for 'best interests'. He didn't settle, so he folded the paper and put it inside his jacket. Leaning back on his chair, he started to take a look at the people sitting around him. Some say they enjoy people-watching when they are static themselves, perhaps in a street café, or an airport. They say this as though it's some kind of personal skill, only gifted to the few. But in reality, it's a compunction for all to watch the masses in front of them, but few remember the details. The frown on one

The Lightroom

face in that crowd, for instance, the lowered head; signs that mask the pain of life.

Max's name was called, with instructions to go to Room 12. Getting up, not looking at anyone else, he passed through the swing doors and followed the numbers until he reached the correct door. He knocked and waited. The response came and he went in. The doctor, about ten years older than him, waved him to a chair and asked how he could help. Max started slowly. He was embarrassed and stumbled along with his problems - the depression, the uncontrollable crying, the anger, the short fuse, the wanting to hide from life, not wanting to get up some mornings, and - finally - the despair of it all. The doctor listened without interruption, and when Max found himself again on the edge of tears, the doctor touched him gently on the arm and told him he was experiencing a breakdown. The severity of which could affect him for the rest of his life. The doctor explained how the breakdown leads to a chemical imbalance within. This can be rectified, to some extent, by drugs that he could prescribe, providing Max would stick precisely to the course. He was asked whether he has tried to harm himself in any way or had thoughts of suicide. Max slowly shook his head. Then, having looked at Max's medical history on the screen, the doctor turned back and suggested that his symptoms could probably be traced back to the horrific accident several years back.

Max could hold it back no longer. He had wept about it many times, but always tried to keep his tears hidden from others. He told the doctor he had bathed in his own sorrow for what might have been. Max took the prescription that was offered, nodded to further instructions and the offer of therapy. Then, shaking the proffered hand, and with a single 'thank you', he left the room. Not looking at anyone, he left the building. At the bus stop, under the arc of glass, he tipped up a seat and sat with his eyes shut, thinking. He realised that for him to rise above all this would require more than kind words and sunshine.

What was needed was a warm draught of self-belief; knowing that he belonged, and that there was a purpose to his being. He pulled himself up from his slumped position, looked at the arrival board, and waited for his bus. As he reached his own neighbourhood, he looked out of the window at a vast area of land, either derelict or covered by low-level industrial units and estates that were fast becoming one of the biggest redevelopment sites in London. Most of these buildings had already been demolished and some re-siting was still underway. The very structure of such fundamental change taking place here would completely re-shape this area for ever. Cranes were dominating the ever-growing buildings around them. Millions of square feet were being built into the sky, offices and flats and all manner of other use classes. Max regarded this as a double-edged sword. Change and progress went hand-in-hand, so councils hoped and developers believed. But what of all the 'small people' and their daily lives? What was the size of the housing association allocation of these new buildings? Would they face another wall, or be around the corner from the flats being globally touted by smart city agents? What kind of community would they have, or would that vanish too, like the previous landscape? Rents would soon rise and carry on rising as certain as the sun would come up tomorrow. Even in his area, small local shops like the open-all-hours Asian fruit and general store, and the small offices, laundrettes and taxi firms would eventually disappear; allowing restaurant chains and retailers to brand their way across our psyche, filling in all the spaces. Is it cities that shape people or people that shape cities, he wondered. He felt some small guilt as he walked toward the new 24-hour supermarket that had recently opened. Once inside, the vast, brightly-lit space was alive with colour - giving its customers everything they didn't know they wanted. All of it pre-packaged for their (but whose?) convenience. Looking at the ceiling, he idly thought of the hundreds of flats above him at that very moment.

All those people in their personal living spaces and having little or no idea of their neighbours. He paid on the self-service till, a physical echo of his thoughts, and, without speaking to anyone, left the building. Carrying his bag of groceries, he walked slowly toward home. Days passed, and he kept them to half days for work, wherever possible. He was on strong medication now: two types of pills, which meant he was not supposed to drive or operate machinery. But that was impossible, given his job. The side effects included tiredness, a lack of energy, some dark dreams and no interest in sex. He was like a man from the desert walking around an oasis, but not drinking. One night, he slept deeply for almost twelve hours, without dreams. The calendar rolled.

The party on the weekend of November 5th, on the rooftop garden at Lily and Niall's house went well. Alcohol fuelled the conversation while fireworks filled the sky. Plus there were stunning backdrops from the big shows up and down the river. He met and made a mark with Lily's friend from work, Nadia. She was slim and dark, a good looking, confident woman, and he enjoyed their conversation. They went out a few days later, walking in the park, with a gallery visit afterwards and then stopping somewhere for food. The following week, he cooked a meal for her at his flat and she stayed over. This lasted for a few weeks. It grew more difficult, and then she stopped taking his calls. The affair, or perhaps more accurately, the arrangement, was over and its ending seemed to disappoint her less than him. For him, it was the transience of it all that grated most. It was as though the peacock was out of a job. The pills the doctor had given him seemed to ease some of his symptoms, and he now felt calmer, but he suffered with a sense of detachment. He got the expected form through the post from the doctor's surgery. It was box ticking really, giving each question a score from 0-10. He filled it in and sent it back. The stand-out question was about suicidal thoughts. He hadn't had those, but he knew that others with his symptoms did.

Armistice Day fell on a Sunday, symbolically, as the last leaves fell from the trees. For the past few years, Max had walked to a memorial in the park near his flat, to remember the relationship he had lost. He rarely talked about it, but the thoughts lived inside his heart. That day, as before, wearing his poppy with pride, he remembered those that had died for the freedom we all now enjoy. Standing well back, not singing, he listened to the sound of a brass band, then hymns and a short service. He watched the small crowd, which was mainly elderly people, but not all.

At the end, as the people started to drift away, he noticed an old man walk to the memorial and, with some difficulty, place a poppy cross at its base. Starting to move away backwards, he faltered and sagged to the grass. It started with a whimper and then the tears came. He must have been crying for those he once knew, and perhaps for the simple thanks for his own survival. People stepped up quickly, helping him to his feet again. Watching him go, Max turned in the opposite direction and walked towards home, lost in his own thoughts about what had happened to him, some six years before.

The Lightroom

Chapter 2

It was about six years ago. The pub they had chosen was busy. Full of the vibrant sounds of conversations and laughter. A table vacated right in front of them. It was immediately theirs. The other two slid into the chairs and he went for the beer at the old Victorian bar. The queue was two people deep and, looking at the long mirror behind the bar, he saw the reflections of the faces in front of him. Reaching the bar, waiting, and without thinking, Max ran his hand along it, curling his thumb under the bevelled edge of the mahogany, imagining for a moment another pair of working hands in another age.

'What can I get you?' He snapped back into it with a jolt. 'Two pints of Summer Lightning and one IPA, please.'

Before his request was finished, the barman's arm, with a rolled-up sleeve, was pulling the pump for the first golden beer. After paying, he trousered his change and, taking the small tray that was offered, gently placed the three brimming glasses on it. Turning and holding the tray at waist height, he moved forward. Experience had taught him that an 'Excuse me' wasn't always enough to clear a path, so he added a gentle touch with his knee at the same time to anyone in the way. Back at the table, the conversation was embedded in football. Putting the tray on the table, he passed out two glasses and then picked up his own, and holding it slightly above eye level examined its clarity briefly before topping it. Time after time, the beer was clear as a bell. What must it be like to be a brewer, an alchemist, a magician producing such joyous pleasure? Settling at the table too, he waited for the subject of football to ease back before springing the two with a question about the current railway strike. This was always entertaining. Watch a working bloke get wound up when it affected him head on, no support for the brotherhood then.

Jimmy was one of the few commuters doing it the other way, living in London and commuting outside, as the software company he worked for had moved to Crawley. He always joked that he should have a London allowance for living, but not working, there. Seb, though, worked right in the West End in a jewellery business. He was a smart, softly-spoken link between charming and charms, rings, necklaces, and anything else he could sell. They had met when they were younger, playing football. The football had long since finished but not the companionship that continued. A few beers together every couple of months.

They called it The Old Boys' Club. They had a shared history and that was the glue that held it together. He turned from his friends because he heard her laugh. It was, perhaps, a hen party or a work celebration. The women all got up to leave the crowded bar, helping one another to stand and walk, looking as though they had all had rather too much to drink. Pushing through between the tables, Max stood to allow their path, and as they passed, he watched her back; shaking his head and smiling, too. The bar door closed on the last frame of that small scene. It was when he turned back that he saw the red purse she had been carrying lying on the floor under the chair. As he bent towards it, he heard someone say: 'Thanks mate, my wife just dropped it.' Looking across at the approaching man, he saw a smiling face. 'Bad move,' responded Max, and without taking his eyes off the other man, he retrieved the leather purse and placed it in the centre of his table. The chancer disappeared back into the crowd and the group of women were long gone. Max's two friends laughed. Seb said: 'Bloody thieves, they're everywhere. You saw him off though.' He smiled and replied: 'I just hope she gets home safely.' Meanwhile, he fingered the red leather, noting the long silver clasp with tiny hallmarks. He could tell this was expensive. With a deliberate movement of his thumb and forefinger, he snapped the clasp open to reveal a note and card case on the side. Inside were several cards, both debit and credit, a small bunch of £20 notes and some Euros. The card case contained four thick business cards with a smart logo. Under that was the name, 'Benson and Coren', and beneath that 'Stephanie Handley' and two phone numbers. After talking briefly to the others, he checked the business card against the credit card to be sure of a match, then sent a text to the mobile number: 'Purse found, contents in situ. Will call you tomorrow morning for delivery or collection. Max'

His battery was very low, so he turned the phone off. Both Seb and Jimmy hit him with a few jokes about how pleased she would be to see him tomorrow, but he shouldn't take advantage and so on. He laughed it off. The consensus was to step out for food. He was led by the other two, turning first into one side street, then another until he wasn't sure which way was north. They had made it to a narrow-fronted Ethiopian restaurant the other two seemed to know. The front was a deli with a long glass display unit on one side. It reached from the floor with a curved front top counter and, even at this late hour, the colourful display was enticing. An apron-clad woman behind the counter was packaging food into cartons and she waved them deeper into the building. The sound of various languages grew as they approached the eating area.

One man stood up from a large table and said: 'Welcome, welcome,' and picked a single sheet menu from a shelf and handed it to them. They chose one of the four vacant aluminium tables with matching chairs upholstered in yellow vinyl. The large fan next to the strip light was turning slowly. In these plain, yet comfortably relaxed, surroundings, he chose a mezze and a glass of water, while the other two chose lamb tagine, with beer. Two small bowls were placed on the table with an open palm gesture. The food came later, served by an older woman, who smiled to cover the fact that she spoke little English. The conversation was sparser now and, eventually, thoughts of home crept into the edge of their minds. The bill was split and what was left from the rounded-up total was left on the table. With thanks and a wave they made their way outside. Back in the street, they only walked a short while, when they emerged alongside the train and coach station just north of the river. Here, after shaking hands, they parted.

As Max walked on among the late-nighters, he reflected on the people he called friends. There weren't many, even though he had known several of them for years. But if his storm came, his tent would be ripped from the ground. The pegs scattered, nowhere to be seen. Maybe it was like this for everyone, he didn't know. He walked on, heading south. Picking out the bus stop for the night bus, he stood waiting. The night lights clashed with the neon signs all around him and the traffic lights. What would it be like, to walk under a dark night sky, looking at the stars with silence and stillness? Someone alongside him moved and he saw the bus open for them. Using his card, he then climbed the stairs, pulling himself up the hand rail. The top deck had a heavy spattering of people, mostly quiet among their own thoughts. He chose half of a bench seat. An older man alongside him turned his head slightly, examined him through bifocals and then turned away. Max watched the streaming light across the window faltering in tune with the stops until the bus finally crossed the river and he got off.

The Lightroom

Chapter 3

Oh My God. What a hangover, what time is it? Rolling over from her back and holding tight to the covers so as not to lose any warmth from the bed, Stephanie slid an arm out gently. Fumbling, she brought her arm back into the warm cavity, locking the duvet around herself with a twist. Again, her head throbbed. She was desperately tired and wanted sleep. Somewhere far back she knew it was the weekend, which, in some strange way, seemed to help, and then she slid back to where she had been. It must have been the sound of the cistern flushing that woke her again, but now it was light and the clock had moved on about three hours. Her hands came to her face and with them came a deep frown. Sliding her fingers to her temples, she started slowly massaging. This, she knew, was a reaction rather than a cure, and she was feeling the price of last night's drinks. It all came back to her soon enough. The night before. She had no difficulty in recalling the events; it was the end detail she was now lacking. The celebration had started well. The Famous Five from university, as she liked to call them, had met at Bennie's, the cocktail lounge, straight from work. The plan was to make a splash for Esther's birthday. It began with several colourful drinks each in those bright, brash surroundings before moving on to a table she had booked. The tapas bar had a long Spanish name she could never remember, but, what shellfish! It was a small place, tucked away up an alley off the fashionable side of Fulham. There was usually a long wait for the food, but they didn't care, and just drank more wine. After the meal they decided to round off the evening by calling into a pub for a quick nightcap, then a taxi home. Taxi? Oh fuck. It was as though a light was turning on and off repeatedly in her head, and she had failed to notice. She slid to the side of the bed, and on the floor was her leather bag with its strap lying on its side, discarded from the night before.

Dragging it to an easier reach position, she flipped it open. She had the freefall moment, the one we all have when something is not right. Her phone was there, but her purse wasn't. Out of bed now, well aware of the consequences, she had her phone in her hand and saw the red line of a powerless battery. Rather than throw it across the room, which was her immediate thought, she plugged it in. All of this had side-lined her hangover for a few minutes. Deciding on a shower, she reasoned that having only just discovered her purse was missing, any damage to her bank cards had already been done. The real loss was that purse. It had been a gift from her father on her last birthday. It was Mulberry; it really was special. Getting out of the shower, she opened the cabinet door and took down the paracetamol bottle. At first, she couldn't get past the safety cap. Then with more effort, she took two tablets with some water. Standing straight, she heard the closing of a door, probably her flatmate going out. That was irritating, she had planned to use her flatmate's phone to cancel her bank cards. Drying herself, then wrapping a large, warm bath towel around her, Stephanie went back to her bedroom and picked up the hair-dryer. This done, she put on jeans and a T-shirt and shoved her feet into trainers. Now, she thought only of her phone. As she picked it up, she saw there had been a missed call from an unknown number while she was in the shower. It also showed a text, sent last night. She read the text and couldn't quite believe it. After looking away, she looked back to read it for second time and wondered what sort of person was this? Realising the missed call and the text message were probably connected, she pressed the return call button, taking an involuntary breath as she did so. The phone rang twice and the man who answered said a single word, 'Hello'.

'Is that Max?' she asked.

'Yes, and who are you?'

'Stephanie Handley,' she paused before going on. 'You kindly called me and sent me a text. You have my purse?' Trying very hard to keep the relief from her voice.

'Yes, I've got it here. Whereabouts do you live?' he asked, hoping it would be somewhere central. She felt slightly uncomfortable about giving her address to this stranger, regardless of his apparent kindness. She changed tack and said: 'Close to East Putney tube station. If it's not too far for you, there's a café opposite the tube entrance. Polish, I think. We could meet there.'

There was a slight pause while he thought through what else he had to do during the morning, and then he said: 'That's fine. I think I know how you must be feeling right now, and you'll be anxious to get this back; so, shall we say an hour from now?' Stephanie agreed and thanked him. She followed this with: 'How will I recognise you?'

He said: 'I remember you.' And, with that, closed the call. Was he smiling when he said that? Was it something she had said or done last night? Or was he just speaking from a position of strength, knowing he held the purse? She wanted it back. The sound of a key being turned in the lock made her look towards the hall door, as it opened and her flatmate came in. Marli was holding a plastic bag with something in it, and the edge of a newspaper sticking out. She twisted slightly, shutting the door with the flat of her hand, then, turning back, laughed. 'The party girl's back in the land of the living then?'

Stephanie started to give her the details. Sitting at the small table, drinking tea, the story of the whole evening unfolded. It ended with Stephanie asking for a £20 loan. She went to her room to pick up a sweater from the back of the small nursing chair. She put it on, and then, reaching over her shoulders with both hands, flicked her hair out of the neck of the sweater.

As an afterthought, she opened a thin, top drawer in her chest of drawers and put her driving licence in her pocket, just in case he should ask her for ID. Unplugging the phone, which was now fully charged, she checked the time and then put it in her pocket. Perfect she thought, if she went now, she could be sitting in the café, watching people coming in and not feeling too uncomfortable. Passing her flatmate, she said: 'Wish me luck,' and with that she was through the door and heading for the stairs. It was only a few minutes' walk, so she hadn't bothered to take a coat. She went out of the gardens that surrounded the low-rise mansion flats and into a partially cobbled street, passing the now empty school playground. On reaching the main road, with the tube station on the corner, she looked across at the café. A few more quick strides and her hand was on the long chrome bar, pushing open the heavy glass door. It was the heat after the cold she felt first, then, feeling in her jeans for the £20 note, she looked up and saw a man to the left holding his hand up, as though in a classroom. She just pointed at him and he lowered his arm, smiled and nodded. As she approached, he stood up, and pulled back a chair for her, giving her little option but to accept. She looked at him. 'Hello, Max, thank you'.

She sat down and waited. A server had come to the table. Whether this was simply attentive service or Max had beckoned her, she didn't know. Max asked for another cup of tea and then asked Stephanie what she might like. She got the distinct feeling he had done this on purpose, in order to encourage her to stay a little longer. By then, he had unzipped his jacket and taken her red leather purse from an inner pocket. He placed it on the table, and looked at her directly. For the very briefest of moments, she stalled, then picked up the purse.

Without thinking, she opened it. He said: 'Don't worry, it's all as it should be.' He was right. Her coffee arrived.

She relaxed, telling him how grateful she was; how lucky it was that someone like him had found it, that sort of stuff. Then, he said something that stopped her in her tracks. 'Honesty may only be a trait, but our consciences will be with us forever.'

She was so surprised, and unsure what to say. It was then she started to really look at him, and wonder what sort of a man he was. The hangover swept over her again, her face crumpled a little as she lowered her head for a moment. 'Are you alright?' The concern was obvious. 'Ah, last night,' he said. Realising that she was at a disadvantage, she ploughed on. The previous night had been, well, much heavier than she thought it would be. 'We were on a girls' night out. We went to more than one place. I'm sorry. I don't know where you fit in, because I have no recollection of you, or anyone else we may have spoken to towards the end of the evening.' This wasn't entirely true. Soon after arriving at the tapas bar, they had seen two very good-looking City boys in smart suits. With the confidence that comes from being in a group, the women had enjoyed a rather too loud discussion about them.

'Have you ever tried the Polish dish, Zurek? It's their renowned hangover cure,' he suggested. 'Right now, I'm suffering so badly I would try anything.' When the server came over, Max asked, nodding towards Stephanie, if they had Zurek. They always had Zurek! Stephanie carried on talking about the group and where they had gone last night. She was aware she was doing most of the talking, when a wide bowl was placed in front of her. It was a sour rye soup with white sausage, potatoes, and vegetables with two boiled eggs, halved yoke side up.

'This looks interesting.' It was her way of being questionably non-committal.

'Go on, try it.'

So she picked up the spoon. The taste really surprised her. Just as she was getting well into the soup, his phone rang.

'I'm sorry, I meant to turn it off, please excuse me.'

He got up and moved between the tables to go outside and was talking for some time. Returning after a few minutes, he went straight to the counter and paid the bill, then walked back to Stephanie. 'I'm sorry. But I have to go.'

She got up and walked with him to the door, which he held open for her. Once outside, she said: 'I really can't thank you enough.'

It seemed weak and ineffectual. 'I hope the cure works for you,' he said and held out his hand. With just the single word 'Goodbye' he turned and walked away. She watched him for a moment, to see if he would turn and look back, but he didn't. Feeling the chill in the air, she folded her arms, dropped her chin a little and headed back to the flat. Using her key fob, she let herself into the stairwell corridor, ignoring the lift, and walked quickly up the stairs to the second floor and her flat. Once inside, she took a deep breath. Things had worked out OK; she had got the purse back, but something was troubling her. It was him. Marli called out: 'How did it go? Would you like tea?'

As she reached the kitchen, Stephanie held the purse in front of her, almost like a trophy. 'So, how did it go?' This was Marli's invitation for a debrief. 'Well, it was successful as far as the purse was concerned. Money, cards, everything still there. It could have been some nutter, but it wasn't. I expected an older man for some reason, maybe because on the phone he had such a deep voice. But, what can you tell from a few words on the phone?'

Marli interrupted: 'So, what was he like then?'

Stephanie took another deep breath and carried on: 'Tall, fair hair. He had presence, he's obviously honest. About my age, maybe a bit younger, and he had strong hands.' All of this was just one tiny imprint, but it still left a mark.

'Sounds like he made an impression.' Marli was fishing now, but she didn't answer. By early afternoon, Stephanie had completely recovered from the hangover. Perhaps due to the Zurek.

She had been contacted by her friends from last night, all suffering damage of some form. She also found out the taxi had been paid by one of them as a result of a rash bet earlier in the evening. This explained why she hadn't missed the purse earlier. Normally, some of Saturday was a 'tidy up and clean' day for her, starting with the laundry and then the ironing. The basket never seemed to stay empty. After putting the washing machine on, she started some ironing. Maybe because it was quiet, her mind kept going back to this morning. The 'what if' questions started. What if he had looked back? What if he rang later? What if she rang him; after all she had his number. What a ridiculous idea, dismissing it immediately. The ironing failed to hold her and soon she gave up and put everything away. The afternoon wound on. She was going out to meet some other friends at her sports club in the early evening. The annual membership was not cheap, but she loved the classes and the pool. Occasionally, the gym too. The club had a long, elaborate bar set in a wide space, with a small area used as an occasional dance floor, fully banked by the restaurant. It was casually separated by tubbed palms, some sofas and small coffee tables.

Further up in the building, there were large studios with sprung floors, sided with mirrors. The space had been designed so that the onlooker saw the sport. Glass walls on the ground floor shielded the pool, tennis and the gym areas, with occasional panels blanked with wave markings, adding a sense of style. It was the sort of club that attracted people who want to see as well as be seen. They didn't play tennis that evening, it was just a glass or two of wine and sofa talk, with intermittent glances raking over the other evening drinkers. Time passed and she returned home in a taxi, feeling secure in the knowledge that each group of her friends never overlapped. She managed them well. The next day she was to visit her parents, or folks as she called them, for lunch. They lived in what is often called, quite misleadingly, a mews cottage.

It was a cobbled mews and the front of the house was unchanged. It was built in red brick with two pairs of wooden coaching doors, a centrally placed doorway and three ground- floor windows. Above them, five more were symmetrically placed. All of the windows had matching sashes. In the early Victorian years, it had been the coachmen's quarters, housing two coaches and their horses on the ground floor, with all of their tack, for the grand house behind. The coachmen had lived above, next to the hay loft. Now, things had been reversed, in so far as the grand house was luxury flats and the coach house was many times its original size. It had been worked over yet again by some award-winning architects, who had taken a good slice of the garden from the main house, giving it privacy as well as a small roof garden. It was, by any account, a skilled and stylish quality conversion, with no expense spared. Indeed, a magnificent house. The interior gave the visitor the idea of carefully chosen antique pieces, displayed with many modern bright artworks mixed with older, eclectic material. The reality was somewhat different. Practically every piece of the interior had been placed by design, in the same way as the building, by experts. Although her father was fond of art, he had been directed towards these pieces by his art investment advisor. It was there to see for all who visited. But of course, few things in life are what they seem.

Her father, now in his 70s, had not been around much for Stephanie and her younger sister's early years. He had been on the board of a private bank and his work had often taken him on overseas assignments. It had been thought best that the family should stay in one place for the stability of the two girls, and - other than a holiday home in Suffolk, which was rarely used now - the girls, had known no other home than this. Although there were five years between Stephanie and her sister, and their lives were quite different, the two were still close. That day, her parents were looking forward to seeing Stephanie. She didn't seem to visit so much, since her break up with Dan six months earlier.

Nobody had seen that coming. Her father had high hopes for them as a couple. They had been together for more than six years and had seemed perfect for each other. They were both 30 when their relationship began, and when a stratospheric career in banking opened up for Dan, there had been plenty of travel, often at very short notice. When he was working it was full-on; he was often away for weeks at a time, following a similar pattern to her father's working life. Her father liked him because he fitted, but when Dan ended the relationship abruptly, it had seemed brutal. Stephanie had hoped their future would be together but, one day, they had a row that had escalated, and when she came out with: 'So, where are we going?' He reminded her that when they first met, he had told her marriage wasn't for him. 'Seriously, I told you I was never going to be the husband and father type. I'm never going to give up my freedom, I thought you knew that,' he snapped.

All those years when she thought they were a couple and he would change his mind had just gone, like steam out of a window on a cold day. Stephanie was lost for a while, then started to realise how controlling he had been; commenting on what she wore, arguing over where she went and who with. Yet, looking back, even though he had appeared possessive, he had obviously never cared deeply for her. Her parents found it difficult to accept that Dan wasn't the man they thought he was. But they realised they couldn't always pick her up after a fall and make everything better. Parents can't always catch their children the second before their faces hit the gravel.

Stephanie would be arriving soon. Her father had moved into his impatient mood. He was dressed quite formally for a Sunday, but that was his habit. As he paced the open hallway, his shoes produced a dull click on the limestone floor. The thumb and forefinger of his left hand were in the open pocket of the waistcoat, while the remaining fingers drummed on the cloth.

Suddenly, while in thought, he felt a sneeze starting. Fumbling for his handkerchief in his top pocket, he wiped his nose before pushing it back into the same pocket. Stepping up to the circular mirror on the wall beside him, he adjusted his tie. With that there was a loud double knock on the door. Opening it with a broad smile, he greeted 'Number One daughter', who was more casually dressed in jeans and a puffer jacket. Once into the hallway and with the door closed, they hugged. Stephanie spoke first: 'Hello Pa, are you good?' He nodded twice before giving her a wink. Then, he called out loudly 'Number One's arrived,' and they both went through to the vast kitchen, where her mother was just putting something on the large inset electric stove. She took off her apron and stepped up to Stephanie, saying: 'Your timing's perfect, darling.'

Leaning forward, Stephanie kissed her mother on the proffered cheek. Her mother was a tall, elegant woman, but sometimes a little insular. Lunch, even though it was Sunday, was a simple affair. A small plate of risotto with a bottle of white wine, followed by cheese and fruit, eaten at one end of a long table that fronted the glass expanse of this part of the house. Stephanie sat as she looked at the garden with its soft pea shingle paths leading to unseen seating areas and the giant vase that showcased it. The array of coloured grasses, even at this time of year, fulfilled the chosen expectations. Her father asked about her work. Was there any sign of faltering in her market? She thought for a moment and said: 'Not really, we are always busy, and my team are more concerned with the individual needs of clients on both sides in order to get the contracts right. Anyway Dad, this is boring stuff on a Sunday.'

The talk at the table turned in many ways, covering a wide range of topics before the meal tailed off. Still sitting at the table, on her own now, as her father had wandered off and her mother was making coffee, Stephanie examined what was left in the bottle before pouring it into her glass.

With nobody watching her, she tilted the stem sharply and emptied the contents in one go, thinking how far a single bottle of wine went in her parents' house. Putting the glass down, she stretched her legs under the table and then crossed them at the ankle and folded her arms. Thinking of nothing in particular, she saw a few last plane tree leaves cartwheel over the marble patio, one catching by the stem in a crack, wavering as if helpless. Turning her head slightly on hearing the sound of cups and saucers being placed on a tray, she got up to carry the coffee into the sitting room, with her mother following her. When they went in, her father was fiddling with the gas look-alike log fire. He always talked about there being nothing to touch a real log fire, but the unlikely image of her father in workman's clothes, splitting logs would have verged on comical. Her mother poured the coffee then said that while she was in Liberty's during the week with one of her friends, she bought two silk scarves for Stephanie. It was supposed to be just one, but she couldn't choose, so she had bought two. Although her parents weren't trying to outdo one another, this sort of behaviour was very common. Stephanie loved the scarves. She asked her mother if she had heard from Ellie.

Her sister had married one of her university friends shortly after finishing her degree, and lived in Yorkshire. They had very quickly started a family, and had a ready set, with twins; much to the delight of her parents. There had always been healthy competition between the two sisters, but, fortunately, never spilling over into outright rivalry. Her mother chose her words: 'Not this week,' and left it there. Two cups of coffee and Stephanie was ready to go, or she would become wallpaper. With goodbyes, she was back in the street. The door shut. She thought she saw a shadow in one of the downstairs rooms, but couldn't be certain. Leaving the mews and joining the high street, she picked up the first bus heading towards the underground station. She stepped smartly up to the top deck, and using the hand grip, swung into an empty double seat, settling at the window.

She put away her card in a side pocket and zipped it safely shut, then she turned her attention to the stiff, elaborately monogrammed paper bag containing the scarves. There was always an unexplained small thrill, setting aside the thick, coloured rope-like handles and parting the stiffened top of the bag, designed to stay shut in transit, to reveal its contents. Taking the scarves out, she put them on her lap, while examining them. She felt the silk soft between her fingers. On impulse, she picked one, looping it around her neck then pushing the looseness beneath her jacket. The other scarf was folded twice, then put in another pocket. She folded the bag for the bin when she left the bus.

Looking out of the window at people on the pavement, she noticed that it was starting to drizzle. The buzz from the gifts evaporated almost as quickly as it had arrived. She walked through the busy streets, with tourists taking endless photographs. Fragments of their different languages caught the wind and carried over the traffic. Her plan was to take a short stroll and stop somewhere for coffee rather than get the tube straight away. She stepped off the street into a small bar and found herself a stool and shelf table at the very back, away from other customers. Taking out her phone, she first automatically checked her messages and her mail, and then thumbed the directory for her sister's number. Then she pressed the call sign on the number that had come up. Raising her arm while involuntarily shaking her head, she placed the phone to the side of her head and heard it ringing. It rang several times before being picked up and Ellie's voice bounced in. It must have been the background noise she heard first. Children shrieking, music, the voices of adults, a sort of mayhem in the making. 'Hey, Steph.'

'Wow, sounds crazy there, what going on?'

Ellie spoke quickly: 'It's a kid's party at a friend's house. Utter chaos. The entertainment is about to start and jelly has just hit the wall. Can I ring you later?'

Steph was laughing now. 'OK, that's fine I'll be back at the flat by then.'

Finishing her coffee, she left. It was colder now. Zipping up her jacket and tucking her scarf in, she set off, widening her steps. She was thinking about the week ahead. Had she at that moment looked across the road parallel to her, she would have seen a middle-aged woman being pushed in a wheelchair, with no movement, no plans; waiting only for science to set her free. But Stephanie hadn't seen her. She opened the communal door to her building using her entry card and crossed the small lobby. Passing the stairs, she went straight into the open lift. Turning to face the control panel, she prodded the number of her floor. The doors closed with a rushing sound. A brief delay, then the lift juddered very slightly under her feet as it started to move upwards. Parting her hair with her fingers, she leaned slightly closer to the mirror on the back wall and smiled into it, perhaps in some way to seek the smallest reassurance. The lift slowed as she straightened in time to spin on a heel and face the doors as they opened at the second floor. A man was standing in front of the open door, and he stepped aside to allow her to pass. She thanked him, then walked a couple of steps. Then a thought struck her, and she turned and looked back as the lift doors shut. That image was gone. He was middle aged, with a grey rim of hair, glasses, and was wearing a short coat. She had never seen him before. She had lived in this flat for nearly two years and had hardly spoken to any of her neighbours. She had no idea what most of them even looked like. Walking the short distance to her door she took out the keys from her pocket. The flat was quiet and in semi-darkness. As she closed the door, she stepped from her shoes. Crossing the living room, she put her keys on the table between the two small sofas, and removed her jacket, placing it on the arm of the nearest one. Then, finding the side cord to one of the blinds, she pulled it gently and continuously until it revealed the city view, looking out at millions of people - seeing none of them. She reached and turned on the spotlight, then turned on the kitchen lights, too. Her mood lifted a little.

She made some tea, and began looking through the newspapers left on the sofa. Later, her phone rang. 'Hi Steph.' Ellie's enthusiasm was coming down the line. 'What are you up to?'

'I've had a heavy week, we were particularly busy,' she said, giving herself time to think before continuing, 'Not busy like someone clearing up after a party, hosing jelly off their walls though,' she laughed.

Stephanie liked her job, the role was interesting and challenging, but she was unsure it was a life career for her. She had imagined, hoped even, that by now she would have had some of the hectic simplicity of children, like her sister. Dan had been the obvious choice, but even in these so-called times of equality, it was still the man that did the choosing. And that hadn't happened. The sisters burst through a few subjects, including Stephanie's lunch with their parents, and gossiped about a TV programme they both loved, before Ellie asked Stephanie if she had met any new men recently.

'Well, funnily enough,' and she started to describe the man outside the lift a short while ago, only to hear Ellie melt into laughter at the other end. They both continued laughing, then Stephanie stopped. There was a brief silence, then Stephanie started again. 'Well, actually, I do have an intriguing story to tell about someone I've just met.'

How strange, a bit like the TV series she was keen to get back to, it was that almost tangible feeling, when she knew the character, but with the anonymity of his not knowing her. 'It's extremely rare to find someone so honest, especially in a crowded pub,' commented Ellie.

'Yes, but it was the way he returned it, what he said, his movements, they all suggested someone strong and self-contained, but also caring.'

'Sounds to me that the sticking plaster has finally been removed, after Dan,' said Ellie, 'but watch out Steph, you don't know anything about him.'

They both laughed. The call ended soon after that, and Stephanie was left looking at the light on the phone in her lap. Within seconds that, too, went out. There was no doubt she was intrigued by Max. He made her question what honesty really meant. Not just the meaning of the word itself, but all the other words used to describe it. They seemed to come back to Max. Words like sincere, fair, worthy. All of these led her to that simple short word, trust. Since the collapse of her long relationship with Dan, she had only gone on a handful of dates, and none had led to anything. But she was regaining her confidence, and perhaps the time had come to get back out there and look at the view again. The next day, Monday, was an earlier start than normal for Stephanie. The alarm on her phone sounded while the device vibrated, almost spinning on the glass-topped bedside cabinet. Showering, then drying her hair, she put on her underwear. Taking her make-up bag, she sat on the edge of the bed, and, leaning towards a small mirror, started applying her eye make-up with very careful strokes. The certainty of these strokes would last all day; this easy art form was her own creation.

Still sitting on the edge of the bed, she put on tights. Standing in front of the wardrobe, she selected a tailored dress and a short jacket. She added a silver necklace and low-heeled shoes. The mirror reflected the desired effect. Coffee was next. In the kitchen, she turned on the radio. The shower started again; Marli was getting ready for work too. Turning up the volume a little, she heard of increased new car sales in the UK. Then the presenter moved on to people in Yorkshire protesting about fracking. She poured water into the coffee machine and waited a few minutes before filling her mug. Her liquid starter pack was essential to kick off the day. Then, shouting out to Marli, she grabbed her large tote bag, checking it contained her purse and umbrella as she made for the stairs. Getting into her stride, she cut round the side of her block and started the short walk on the winding tarmac path across the gardens.

The flowers had died back now, but the shrubs still held their shape and form. The few scattered white barked birches reached up like upturned country broom sticks, their leaves all blown away on the early winter winds. How fortunate she was that her father had bought the flat for her a few years ago. The value of it had burst through the skyline since then. It had given her financial freedom. Letting the spare room to Marli was for company as much as for the rent. She passed a near-empty bicycle rack, followed the stone steps to a heavy wrought iron gate and emerged from a passageway that most people missed, into the street. Crossing the road in sections, first to the keep-left island in the middle, then diagonally to the station, she joined the growing surge of people heading down into the station. Once on the escalator, it always seemed more orderly, but on reaching the platform, it clearly wasn't. Glancing over the heads of the now packed platform at the electronic arrivals board, two trains were imminent. Either would take her in the right direction, and when she finally surfaced from the tube, the walk to the West End office would take just a few minutes. She found the 45 minutes' commute more than tiresome. Today, it was 8.15 as she walked through the large double doors and took the lift to the second floor. This large floor was open plan, but sub-partitioned with movable dividers. Stephanie was an associate partner, and was seen by those above her as a rising star, set for a good future, providing she didn't burn out first.

She worked in a tight team of six, with four further people as outriders or stringers. As an investment surveyor, she didn't survey anything, she sold and acquired all kinds of investments on behalf of retained clients. It was mainly retail, but sometimes industrial or land, open storage and similar options. All the investments were let with different leases over varying lengths of time with a diverse mix of tenants; some secure and others less so.

Her team would trawl the market to buy, and if instructed to sell, they would flash flood it, to get maximum coverage. She was good at her job. Pouring out another black coffee, she turned on the computer and got started. Because of the intensity of the work, the day seemed to slide away. Lunch was usually an 'if, or maybe', affair; even though she knew missing meals was not great. When she finally left her desk, it was 7.15 and most of her colleagues had gone. Putting on her jacket, she picked up her bag and, while turning to do this, she noticed the thread of one of the silver buttons on that sleeve was loose and a thread hung down. Narrowing her eyes and using her centre finger and thumb nails, she drew the thread in then tightened the button against the sleeve. With the loose end wrapped around the back of the button, she left the office. It wasn't quite raining but there was that heavy dampness hanging everywhere; typical for a November evening.

She started walking, opened the flap of her bag to get her phone out, and locked the bag again. By the time she arrived at the tube station, she had checked her messages and made two calls. It wasn't until she was passing the shops in the small cobbled street outside her block that she thought about food, and veered, as though guided by an unseen hand, to the small deli. Joining a short queue, she looked over several dishes behind the glass counter before settling for a coronation chicken with rice dish and added, as an afterthought, a couple of olive bread rolls. The food was wrapped, she paid and moved on. At night she preferred to walk the length of the main road to enter her block rather than take the shorter route through the mansion block gardens. Approaching the corner at the top of the road, but without stopping, she stepped into the road to avoid two men outside a small grocery store. They were shouting at one another in a language she didn't recognise. When well clear, she turned to see one of the men pick up something from the ground while the other was walking away still shouting.

In seconds, she rounded the bend, entering the small mansion block square through tall double gates, her door card ready. She chose the healthier option, and took the stairs rather than the lift, climbing two at a time at a steady pace. Then her phone rang. Stopping on the landing at the turn of the stairs, she carefully placed her packages on the low window sill and opened her bag to take out her phone. Recognising the name against the number, Stephanie just answered with: 'Hello, Max?' Leaving him an open field of play.

'Hello,' he said. 'I thought of you. I am going to the Tate next Saturday to see an exhibition, including some works by Picasso and Cezanne. I wondered if you would like to join me?'

Trying hard to sound relaxed, and also knowing she had a tennis game fixed for some time on Saturday morning which, as of now, was a lost match; she said: 'I would love to, that would be great.'

Max suggested going to Borough Market afterwards for something to eat, and she agreed. 'Well,' the syllable hung for a moment, 'It opens at ten, how about I get tickets and we can get in before it gets really busy. I could meet you outside Southwark tube station, at 10.30.'

She was listening to the sound of his voice, wondering where he was. 'Lovely, I'll be there, I'm looking forward to it.'

'OK.' A further pause, then: 'Until Saturday then.'

Still sitting on the edge of the window sill and thinking, without looking at her phone, she weighed it in her hand and smiled to herself. Rising with her packages, she continued up the stairs two at a time as before, but somehow, now she felt a little lighter. The flat was warm inside, the underfloor heating had come on. Flicking the light switch, she almost fell over the sofa with her arms full. She surveyed the night through the open blinds. All those people out there, and yet it had been months since she had been out on a date.

He had found her, when she wasn't looking. How odd this all was. She was keen, yes, but hesitant; perhaps because she knew nothing about him. Moving to the bedroom and getting out of her office clothes, she heard the door open and Marli talking into her phone. The door shut, and Stephanie called out: 'Hey Marli. You OK?' But there was no reply. She knocked on Marli's door. It opened and Marli just stood there with her shoulders and her head lowered. She had been crying. She had lost her job - no notice, no pay, nothing. The company ceased trading during the day and just closed. Staff were ordered out of the building, and doors were locked. Talking to others, nobody knew the details. Senior management had kept them in the dark. Apparently, everyone had been called to a meeting, and addressed by someone they didn't know who said that further contact would be made with each of them through the liquidators. They were not to report for further work. Stephanie listened without interruption until the words ran out. 'Jeez, that's terrible.'

Stepping towards her friend, she hugged her. 'Let me get you a drink?'

Receiving a nod, she went into the kitchen and made a strong gin and tonic with ice, then went back and got another for herself. They both moved to the living room. For a minute, nothing was said. Stephanie spoke first: 'I'm sure it will be OK, something else will turn up.'

Marli responded by simply raising her chin. Later, Stephanie made a meal for both of them, using what she had brought from the deli and padding it out with things from the fridge and cupboard. The alcohol helped to relax them both. During the evening, she thought about the cards of chance. One person is right down after losing her job, while another is right up there, having been asked out on a date for the first time in months. Whose luck would hold, and for how long? Luck, fate, or chance?

On her way to meet Max at the agreed time, the bus halted, but not at a designated stop. The delay lengthened. Perhaps an accident. Or a breakdown. A few more minutes passed and then the bus started to move again, winding its way eastwards parallel to the river. Within 20 minutes, she was getting off almost outside the tube station where they were meeting. Checking her watch again, she realised that although she was five minutes late, he hadn't arrived yet. Looking around among the number of people coming and going from the tube, she grew slightly concerned that he wasn't there. What she didn't realise was that he had arrived before the appointed time, taking up a position on the other side of the road so he could watch her arrive. She first saw him as he came over on the crossing among a batch of people. He was looking straight at her. And then he was in front of her. He simply smiled at her and said: 'Hello again.'

'Hello Max.'

He walked with her through the growing crowd, pausing to listen briefly to a wailing singer trashing the strings of a guitar, then they headed for the steps to take them up on the pedestrian bridge. The air was sharp. She pulled her scarf around her neck, took a beanie hat from her pocket and put it on. At an unmarked spot, they stopped and both marvelled at the startling view. Facing Wren's magnificent architecture, St Paul's Cathedral, and swinging round to Tower Bridge; in front of them at the end of the Millennium Bridge in perfect perspective, the Tate Modern. As they walked, they discussed the building's design and the slab effect of the unbroken face brickwork with the magnificent centre chimney, built specifically lower than St Paul's. Crossing the courtyard again, they entered the building. Inside the turbine hall, both were just stopped by the vastness of the space, with its overpowering height, made possible by the huge roof light box above them. They toured the space with its massive sculptures.

They moved to the boiler house with its galleries, and looked at the paintings, pausing in their own understanding and interpretations. The display of Picasso's early pre-cubism was a surprise to them both. He had been trained as a traditional artist, but had no formal training as a sculptor. Stephanie loved the exhibits for their use of Mediterranean colours and their unusual design and learnt that most of his work had been produced during a 25-year collaboration with two local ceramists. Max felt the two very large sculptures reaching majestically into the display space demanded his attention. Later, leaning on the rail in one of the viewing galleries overlooking the Turbine Hall, nearly touching shoulders, they took in the dramatic perspective of the internal features. Stephanie suggested coffee in the shop below them. Finding a small table away from the draught from the door, they started to talk in earnest about their responses to what they had seen, stopping only to give their orders. Stephanie waited for a pause and, hoping to catch him off balance, asked: 'Max, can I ask you, when did you decide to ask me out?' She leaned forward onto the edge of the table, waiting to measure his response. Smiling, he mirrored her movements, then started from a different tack. 'When I first saw you, you were smashed. Although I told my friends I thought you were attractive, my first thought was to hope you got home safely.'

Sitting upright now, he asked: 'Do you have that same purse with you?'

'Yes'

'May I see it?'

She took it from her bag and put it on the table, pushing it towards him, then withdrawing her hand. He reached forward and very lightly touched it, moving it back to her while looking straight at her: 'To answer your question - it was after picking this up off the floor, when I put it on our table.'

She leaned back, folding her arms as if to give her space from this intensity and laughed, not at him, but with him.

Then putting her finger tips to the edge of the table as if to move on, said: 'Let's find some real food.' They got up and started to walk, talking about their favourite foods. Getting to the market, the street sounds changed and voices in volume took over from traffic; it was a total profusion for the senses. Cooking and colour were all around them. They literally walked into the arms of it and were enveloped by it. Starting on the street food with mini kebabs, he ploughed on with Balkan bites, and Spanish omelettes for them both. Walking slower now, he pointed to the cheese counters, a yard high with a choice as wide. He bought her several cheeses to take home; she bought dips and olive bread for him on other counters. Finally, they stopped again for coffee, perching on a narrow bench away from other people. She looked at him carefully, taking her time and without any embarrassment, before saying: 'Tell me about you, where you live, what you do.'

'That's not too difficult. I live in very small flat out at Southfields, I would like to move to a more central area as most of my work is here. I'm a self-employed carpenter; but please - don't define me by my work alone.'

'Are you married?'

A bit surprised, he said he wasn't and never had been. This answer cleared the air for her. She carried on: 'Sorry about that one, but some people are not honest; it complicates everything.'

Wanting to get things back on track, he stood up and offered his hand to her, she took it, not letting go immediately. They walked out of the covered market a little way; it was cold and getting dark. Tightening the zip on her jacket and putting on the beanie again, she repositioned her bag and linked arms with him, saying: 'Let's look for a bus, shall we?' Reaching the stop, a bus came, and they found a seat together downstairs towards the back. Feeling light in each other's company, they continued to peel back bits and pieces of the picture of each other's lives. Her stop came quickly. He stood and moved back to let her out.

'I'll see you home.'

'That's OK, you're going on.'

With that she touched his arm at the elbow, reached up and kissed him on the cheek. 'Thank you for a great day.' Adjusting her bag again, she continued: 'Will you ring me?'

He nodded and she walked away to get off the bus. In one movement, he slid back into the seat and was close enough to the window, and just in time, to see her smile, raise her hand and wave before the bus moved away, leaving her behind. Stretching his legs a little, he clasped his hands and let them drop to his lap. The image of her had just become a memory. Looking at his hands he noticed a small mark on his jeans, probably a food stain, he scratched it twice and then, after a quick brush of the hand, looked around.

There were several other passengers, but the only sound apart from the engine seemed to come from a mother holding the bar of a buggy, with a small boy whining loudly at her side. She got up, saying something to the driver that was lost to him, then manoeuvred the pushchair and the boy to the door and got off. It wasn't until the doors had snapped shut and the bus started to move again that he saw the miniature teddy bear lying on its side near the driver's enclosure. He realised only then that there must have been two children not one; and no one had helped her. His stop came and as he passed, he picked up the toy and wedged it in the handrail as he got off. Walking quickly, it took 10 minutes before he turned into his street. The large Victorian house where he lived had originally been a merchant's house on the end of a terrace, with the benefit of a handkerchief-sized garden at the side. Many years ago, this had been built on to give it a small garage with a flat-roofed extension above it. The mineral felt on the roof was peeling at the corners and lifting a little. Like the rest of the house, it was nearing the time when proper money would need to be spent.

There was just room for his van, with all his gear, to be off the road and backed hard up against the doors, as the garage was used only for storage by the landlord. Squeezing between the wing of the van and the low privet hedge, he joined the short, tiled path to the front door. He could hear music coming from inside somewhere: not loud, but loud enough. The house had been converted into four flats. His, although at the top of the stairs on the second floor, was the best of them because of the clear views over the lower terraces from the two main rooms. When he moved in the previous year, he had re-decorated and re-carpeted the flat, re-fitted and tiled the shower room. The landlord paid for most of the materials, and the arrangement worked for both of them. It was small but comfortable. Letting himself in, and pushing the timer for the landing light, he climbed the stairs to his own flat and, with another key, opened the door into the living room. Turning the light on, he removed his jacket and let it drop on the back of the sofa before stepping into the kitchen area and getting a beer and glass from the lower cupboard. Opening it, pouring most of it slowly into a glass to avoid too much froth, he took a large mouthful and then poured the remainder of the bottle into the glass. Lowering himself to the sofa, he gazed for a moment at the night sky through the large bay window, thinking of Stephanie. He hadn't met someone remotely like her for a very long time. She just seemed to make him feel good. She had asked him to ring her; that was unusual. Normally, that was only implied in some way at the end of a date. He tried to be rational about it, but the fact was - he was excited by having met her. Taking another pull at the beer, then moving his open book on the box in front of him, he fingered a coaster. He put the glass down on it and stood up to lower the blinds. Finding a small tray of curry in the freezer, he put it in the microwave while he cooked some rice. After he'd eaten and cleared away, he picked up the phone, and looked at the messages. Most were about work, so he put the phone in his pocket.

He couldn't settle. He would ring her but not too soon. Turning on his PC for distraction, he looked through the list of films he could watch and started what was to be a long evening. Monday morning, he was up early. He wanted to be on site at first light with Janusz, an older man he had linked up with for two-man jobs. Traffic was unusually heavy for the short journey, and when he arrived, Janusz was already there, holding a parking permit for him in the side street. 'Where you been, Maxi? You took too much time.'

The permit was passed through the open window. Parking up, he scratched off the day and dates before adding the van number then putting it in the windscreen, clear of the other papers. He wanted to check the power was on and the extension leads were long enough to get to the work platform first. He and Janusz were there to hand cut an odd-shaped roof. The timber was supposed to be delivered first thing, after being loaded the previous night, and much to his surprise, the truck then appeared at the end of the street. Slowly edging its way between the rows of parked cars, it pulled level with their scaffolded corner building. The driver left the engine running and swung down from the cab in one easy motion. 'Hello Headroom, how's it going, mate? Where do you want it?'

Dropping the hydraulic stabiliser legs, at the last minute the driver slid an off cut of timber under each of the legs with his foot. Then, climbing the short ladder at the back of the truck, he fingered a control box slung from his neck. This started the hydraulic telescopic lifting crane mounted on the back of the truck. With his spare hand, the driver looped the strops into place, ready to swing out the pile of timber. Max was now pointing to the inner edge of the pavement, and the first of the three large piles was duly swung round and soundlessly lowered to the ground. When this was completed, Janusz released the strops. The driver wasted no time in packing everything away.

While this was happening, Max bent to count the lengths, using his middle and forefinger to march over the ends of all the stacks before signing the delivery note. Then, with a thumbs up sign and a 'See you next time', the driver was in the cab and pulling away. The two men started the heavy work, manhandling the long lengths up the outside of the scaffold, laying as many as they could on either the scaffold walkway or the ceiling joists. Their work platform had been set with two 8x4 sheets of shuttering ply, laid side by side with the bench ends set ready. Before climbing the ladder himself, Max went to the back of the van, unlocking the double locks, and took out his tool bag and nail gun. He shouted up: 'Have you got the skill saw up there, Janusz?'

'Yes, but we need the chop saw and two hand saws.'

After locking the van again, Max managed to carry all the tools to the bottom of the wooden scaffold ladder. Meanwhile, Janusz had come down to help him and between them they carried the remaining tools to the platform, two storeys above them. With the power on, Janusz put two lengths on the bench, and plugged in the circular saw in readiness while Max laid out the plan and checked with his scale ruler the roof apex height. This was the critical starting point. This first pair of rafters were fixed with the ridge board in-between and extending away to the end of the extension. That, in turn, was fixed temporally with a single post. The first pair were set back for the hip end to be cut in later. The rain held off, perhaps because of the breeze. They worked on until about 11am, before stopping for some tea from Janusz's flask. Max phoned the contractor, just to let him know he hoped to finish in a couple of days. While he spoke, leaning on the safety bar, he saw a woman walking away at the top end of the road, and he thought of Stephanie. He pictured her standing by the side of the bus. It seemed so remote now. Finishing the call, he started to turn back again when he saw beneath him an elderly woman, with a cane, hovering on the kerbside.

Without thinking too much about it, he went down the ladder, introduced himself and said he was happy to help. He took her by the elbow to guide her over the busy road. Feeling good about his actions, he returned to the platform to be met with: 'Not bad, but maybe she did not want to cross the road!' They both laughed, then hacked on with the work.

The difficult angles were cut by hand but, with the help of the different power saws, the roof started to take shape. As the light faded, all that was left was the short angle fillings, which he would sort out the next day. Standing for a moment, he could still smell the cuts of the softwood timber and, resting his hand on the rough rafter, he thought about the satisfaction of having done a good job for the money. For him, this always added to his sense of self-worth. After stowing away all the gear, he paid Janusz, slapped him with a handshake, and they parted.

Sitting in the van before leaving, he moved his hand on the wheel and could feel tenderness on the last two fingers of the hand he had been sawing with. He could see the purple stain of an extending bruise that swept down the inside of two of his fingers after he pinched them behind the back of the rounded edge of the scaffold ladder earlier. It was like a hot pulse to remind him of his carelessness. Pushing the indicator down, he let the vehicle drift out into the evening traffic. It had started to rain; that hard drizzle that soaks. The windscreen wipers thumped rhythmically in front of him while pools of light from street lights marked out the route back to his empty flat. In the early hours of the morning, well before dawn, he snapped awake. His T-shirt was drenched in sweat. He had had a nightmare. His whole body was alert. He lay there, telling himself it was just a dream, but it had seemed so real. He worried if he shut his eyes he would go back there. Slowly, his body relaxed and his eyelids dropped again. The dream had been that he had lost Stephanie in a crowd, and it was the look of fear on her face that woke him. At breakfast, she was on his mind again and he knew now that she was upsetting his circadian rhythms. He would ring her during the morning.

Stephanie had arrived at the office that day knowing a lot was resting on the second meeting she had with clients. She was dressed, smartly but simply, in a navy suit with a white shirt, low heels, and a fine gold chain around her neck. She went over the strategy presentation again, having already prepared examples in comprehensive detail on her laptop. At 10am, she was buzzed by the receptionist to say the clients had arrived. They were shown into the conference room, settled and seated with coffee. As Stephanie entered the room, they both stood and came around the table to shake hands politely before returning to their seats. The two brothers, both in their

60s, were acting as trustees for a second-generation trust. Her presentation was mainly to show examples of the sort of investments that would help them spread their investment strategy further into more long- and short-term fields. She was putting the case to be further retained, and to purchase and manage on the trust's behalf, selective blocks of strategic farmland which was not yet at its full growth potential. She was also suggesting increasing the trust's immediate income stream with national covenants attached to larger convenience stores on longer leases. After nearly an hour, they seemed satisfied with her presentation, and the meeting was wound up. They said they would be in touch the following day. They all walked to the reception area together and, after shaking hands, they left. Stephanie went back in the conference room, feeling confident with the way it had gone. Retrieving her laptop, she then took her phone from her pocket and switched it from silent mode. She chose the stairs to go back up to her office. Right on the dot of midday her phone rang. Looking at the screen, she could see it was Max. She was on her feet, walking to the swing doors leading to the corridor to find a space that would be a little more private, as she started to speak. 'Hello Max.'

'Hello. I'm sorry I haven't called earlier. I wondered, would you like to come out with me again.'

'I'd love to.'

'How are you fixed for evenings this week, or perhaps the weekend?'

She had thought about him many times since she had seen him last, and suggested Friday. Whatever plans she had for Friday had just gone on hold. The call was brief.

He suggested drinks, then something to eat. They arranged to meet at 7pm outside the tube station near her flat. She spent a moment thinking about the short simplicity of that call, and how it had caused a massive rush of wellbeing within her. It was the feeling of joy. Hearing the sound of someone sneezing, she glanced towards the door opposite before walking back to her desk. The remaining days of that week passed quickly and as Friday was drawing to a close, she took her coat and bag and headed out of the office. While walking to the tube, she called her sister for a catch up. When the phone was answered, Ellie sounded tired and a little harassed, explaining that the kids were fractious and were soon going up for a bath. They talked about Christmas getting nearer and the preparations that had started. Stephanie was walking under and surrounded by Christmas lights as she walked. She said that other than noting the few empty cards that had arrived - the ones with no message, just the name of the sender - she had done nothing yet. She expected there would be one mad shop and a big wrapping session quite soon. Dropping into the conversation that she was going out that evening with the man who had found her purse, Ellie said: 'This is so intriguing. I'll phone you to catch episode two.'

They both laughed and then the sound of a door slamming in the background drew the call to a close. When Stephanie got home, she showered and spent some time choosing what to wear.

She smoothed down the bed, picked up items of clothing and went to the bathroom to put them in the washing bin. She looked around and, without thinking, straightened the towels and brushed her teeth. Walking into the sitting room, she was now ready, and watching the clock. At four minutes to 7, she left the flat. She saw him from a distance first, casual, wearing jeans. Again, he had his hands thrust into his pockets, and was leaning against a wall with one knee bent, braced against the wall; a bit like a stork, waiting. He was looking the other way as she approached, and, slipping her arm through his, his reaction was instant, not arrogant though. He swung round very gently, at the same time taking his hands out of his pockets, drew her to him and kissed her, then, taking her hand for a moment, pointed to a pub. Again, in some small way, he had surprised her. They walked the short distance and went in. It was thick with people, a few still in suits, taking the long way home, but mainly people like themselves, starting their evening. She'd asked for a gin and tonic. Although in a queue, he was served quickly enough and with his pint they edged through the mass to a corner with a long shoulder-height shelf on the wall already full of glasses. He shifted some together, making room for theirs. Their corner was crowded, they were much closer than they would normally have been, and while talking loudly, he watched her relaxed, easy laughter. He had noticed several men look longer than they should have, but she had made no effort to look over her shoulder. This in itself, was unusual, he felt. When they finished their drinks, she suggested a restaurant further down the road. Once outside, she pointed the way, and then locked arms again with casual normality. It was a branded chain Italian restaurant, which she seemed to like. Max pushed open the heavy door, and as soon as they entered, a young man came over to ask if they had booked. 'It's just two of us,' said Max. 'Do you have a table?'

They were shown to a table near the window. He was amused by this, as he had read somewhere that it was window dressing to put good-looking people in the window tables. She would certainly fit the bill, even if he was questionable. After asking her, he ordered some wine, which came quickly, and having looked at the menu for a few minutes, they both ordered. While waiting for the food, she asked about where he grew up. His forearms rested on the table, one hand lightly clasping the other wrist while he talked. She watched him. She saw his rough hands. She was intrigued how someone like him, who was clearly an intelligent, deep thinker, and with his background, had found himself where he was now, so obviously fulfilled by his work as a carpenter. He was so unlike Dan, it was laughable. But he unsettled her at every turn. They touched on politics and current affairs, and each time his sharp reasoning and breadth of knowledge came through. Plates of food came, plates of food went; still they talked. He asked about her ambitions, and what she was passionate about.

For her, it all seemed to be about earning enough money. She was confident and funny, making him laugh. She was light, he was rather intense perhaps, but it was a good balance. After coffee, he asked for the bill, which he paid, despite her protestations. As they moved to the door, he checked the time. It was just gone 11pm. Pushing open the door for her first, they stepped onto the street and she, without realising, turned like a homing pigeon for her flat. He put his arm around her shoulders, giving her a hug, then allowed his hand to drop and loosely take hers. She didn't let go. Still talking, they crossed the main road and walked to the gate that led up to the garden, stopping only to allow others to pass, then took the steps onto the tarmac path leading to her flat. They were coated in a growing dampness, suggesting a mist would rise before the sun. As they reached the entry door, she asked if he would like to come up for coffee. She seemed hesitant, perhaps for the first time with him, unsure.

He put his arms around her, drawing her close, and just said: 'Not this evening, maybe next time. I don't want you to regret that it was me that found your purse.' Adding: 'Can I call you in the morning, to make sure you, um, got home ok?'

He did call the next day, and they arranged to spend the following weekend together. On Friday they went to see, at his suggestion, an award-winning Spanish film at a small art house cinema in Brixton. They had burgers and a beer first, at a place with long tables, side by side with others. Graffiti covered the walls and Reggae music played continuously. It was full of noise, but they were lost to each other. He saw her home again, taking a direct bus that snaked slowly to the main road near her flat. They sat upstairs, he with his arm around her, and the late evening lights streamed them home. At the entrance to her flat, he stopped.

This time, she said to him: 'I want you to come up for coffee.'

Stepping back from him, she opened the door and held it for him; then leading up the stairs, she opened her own front door and they went in. Stephanie's flatmate had found another job starting in a couple of months in

North London, and had moved home to save money in the meantime, so the flat was just hers again. Once the door was closed, she waved an arm across the living room: 'Make yourself at home, and I'll fix the coffee.' He started to take in his surroundings. A modern corner sofa dominated the room with a small, low G-plan statement table in front of it. The blinds were up and, from where he was standing, he could see through the sliding glass doors across a small balcony and the edges of two, pale blue folded campaign chairs. Beyond that was an open view of the communal garden. Turning, he took in two oversized modern pictures. They weren't prints. He removed his jacket and sat at one end of the sofa. Directly in front of him on the wall was a large mirror with a small red light in the bottom corner, betraying its true identity as a television.

There were several Christmas cards, and in one corner of the room was a pile of Christmas presents, wrapped and tagged perfectly, as though by a professional hand. As Stephanie reappeared carrying a small tray with white cups and saucers, he realised what was missing in the flat. There were no books. As she put the tray down, one of the cups tilted and spilt a little into the saucer. 'That one's mine,' she said. Then, flipping the blinds, she slid along the sofa to him. He stayed that night and they slept well, eventually.

He woke by habit at dawn. Getting out of bed quietly, he put on his jeans and went to the kitchen. Resting his hands on the edge of the sink, flexing his toes, he looked out of the window at the sunrise. It was a flaming, rolling, slow unfolding rage of splintered light. First, behind the cloud bank and then, through and into the open, like a promise that never lets you down, came the full sun, giving them the new day. He took it all in with a slow, deep breath. Not wishing to wake her he found a pan and holding it sideways like pouring a bottle of beer, he turned on the tap slowly, then with a lid put it on the stove to boil. Opening most of the cupboards, he found what he needed, and two mugs of tea were soon ready. The underfloor heating must have been on a timer, as his feet felt warm on the tiles as he crossed to the bedroom again. He placed a mug on her side table. She roused, and turned over to his side just as he dropped his jeans and climbed back into the bed. And so their relationship had begun.

Both were going to their parents' homes for Christmas and Boxing Day, but Stephanie had arranged to go to her sister's home in Yorkshire for a few days over New Year, and she wanted Max to join her. He was initially unsure, but was brought round by gentle persuasion. While talking through their plans, Stephanie added that months ago she had booked a skiing trip with her tennis friends. She would be away around the end of January, but now she wished she hadn't booked it.

He was disappointed to hear she was going away, but enthusiastic for her. Like all fires, it starts slow then burns hot.

Christmas came and went. Max told his mother that he had met a woman he really liked and had been seeing her for a few weeks. They were enjoying their time together, but he didn't give away too many details. Stephanie did the same with her parents, but she told her sister much more. They spoke on the phone late on Christmas Eve just after she arrived at her parents' home.

It was almost an unloading, saying she couldn't wait for her sister to meet him soon. It all came up fast enough. He was thinking about driving his van but decided to rent a car, not wanting to make Stephanie feel uncomfortable. The drive was hard. On the way out of London, it seemed everyone was on the same road out of the city. Ellie's home turned out to be a large, mellow stone farmhouse set back from the road on the edge of a village, complete with a five-bar gate and gravel drive. Max's first impression was that wealth gives its owner another window of opportunity that otherwise would be bricked up. He felt immediately at home in the building, noting its idiosyncrasies and the quality renovation works at every turn. He took to both Ellie and her husband, Will, and made a special bond with the five-year-old twins. Stephanie and he exchanged presents on New Year's Eve rather than Christmas Day, and they had bought a wigwam for the twins. Spending time with them, playing games under the table, hide and seek around the house, and giving them piggy back rides, Max won them over. Ellie watched him, glancing at her sister from time to time. They walked together, ate together and drank the New Year in. At the stroke of midnight, the bells of the village church started, fireworks burst in the night sky and everyone went out into the streets. They felt their star had turned. Then the holiday passed, and they headed back down the same roads, back to their other lives.

Over the next couple of weeks, they saw each other most evenings and stayed at each other's flats regularly. She remembered the first time Max had shown her his flat. It was when he said he had left his phone at home. He had left it behind on purpose, believing that if she visited his flat casually the first time, it might break the ice for when she stayed over. She had not been sure what to expect. The area, to her, appeared shabby; and she was not used to the long terraces, the carelessly left bins in the forecourts, and the litter. However, when they climbed the stairs, she didn't think about the décor, just that this would help her find out more about Max. He opened the front door and let her go in. Her first impression was how small it was. Then she saw more. One alcove was floor to ceiling with books, the kitchen area was neat and clean with a row of pans on a shelf, cooking knives in a row on a magnetic surface, and there was a wall spotlight at each side of a small sofa. While he put the kettle on for tea, she moved to the wooden box in front of the sofa and turned the open book over, it was a novel about ageing, apparently by one of America's greatest 20th century writers. Putting it down gently, she saw other books and magazines on the restoration of antiques and open water swimming. It wasn't until they had left the flat that she realised there had been no television. She knew he had taken her there on purpose; to open up a little of his world to her. When the ski trip came along, he accompanied her to the mainline station where she would get the airport express. She wished she wasn't going, but he reassured her she would have a great time and teased her that once she was with her friends, she would forget about him. He remembered how she moved her head sideways against the fur collar of her coat and said she would never forget or regret anything about him. He, at that moment, rested his arm around her shoulders while pulling her case in the other hand, and they headed towards her train platform.

At the barrier, she took the offered handle for her case, and after checking her bag one last time for passport, tickets and purse, she secured the bag, then kissed him goodbye. He watched her walk among the other passengers to the second carriage. Folding the case handle down briskly with the flat of her hand, she turned and raised her arm high as if in salute and then disappeared from view. Instead of turning away to hurry forward with his own plans, he walked to a row of seats just back from the platform entrance. Choosing one away from other people, he lowered himself first to perch on the edge. Leaning forward with his elbows on his knees, he thought the trajectory of life doesn't leave much time to really see the small details in front of you. If life were a book, you would read every word. Then, stretching his legs, he sat back with his hand behind his head, before dropping them to his lap. He was focusing on the fact that the images had changed quickly; time had slipped another notch, she had gone and he was again alone. Oblivious to the movements around him, he thought about her and how they had already started to talk about a future, and where a life together might take them. Hope was the word that came to his mind. Standing suddenly, he re-tied the woollen scarf around his neck, tucking the ends into his buttoned-up jacket, then, sliding his hands into his pockets, walked towards the tube entrance.

Ten days can seem a long time, but he intended to work hard and keep busy, to try and make up for all the time off he had taken over Christmas and the New Year. Having to 'make' the money by the end of a given week had been a worrying insecurity when he had first started out, but now he knew the work would come in again soon enough. In the meantime, he had an expensive kitchen to help fit in a house near the Common. He had promised this would be his first job after Christmas. What he would really have liked, but was impossible to find, was a workshop with room for all his tools. He could then build doors and box sashes, maybe try the finesse of intricate furniture restoration.

But he knew finding a workshop he could afford was highly unlikely in London. Fitting the kitchen kept him busy for a couple of days and then it was ready for the specialists to fit the marble work tops and up stands. By then he had moved on to hang seven new doors, with all their door furniture, in a neighbour's house. A return call from someone he had worked for before gave him five days, with 14-hour shifts, with a shop and pub fitting company. The job was a pub re-fit in Hertfordshire. The money was good and he was paid on the nail when he finished. It was tough, as the company was on price work with a finish date. He managed the five days, sleeping on a camp bed in an upstairs room with others, surviving on take-away food, mainly pizzas, before returning to London with his gear. Max was worn out. It took 12 hours of deep sleep, and then he was revitalised, and he started the day with an oversized mug of tea. He put the washing machine on and set about cleaning the flat thoroughly. His last job was to clean the shower while he was in it. Pleased with the results, he went out to get a paper and have an all-day breakfast. Stephanie would soon be back. It was early evening when they arrived back at the airport. Stephanie looked tired when he saw her coming through the arrivals gate, pulling her case with one hand and carrying some smart, duty-free bags in the other. He made her laugh, though, by holding up a card sign saying: 'British ski team' which had a drawing of a ski rack and a photo of her on it. He took the case and gave her a proper welcome hug. 'How did it go?'

She started to talk. The skiing was great; the evenings very long, she missed him. She had wished he had been there and the last few days had dragged. If it hadn't been for the late-night texts they sent each other, she might not have lasted the whole holiday. Talking more on the bus to the car park, he searched for the exit ticket. Growing agitated, he finally located it in an inner jacket pocket. Knowing he would be picking her up in the van, he had cleaned the interior thoroughly.

After putting her case in the back, he held the passenger door open, and lifted the edge of her coat away from the sill as he shut the door. Beside her again, he said: 'I really missed you so much.'

Then they drove down the lanes of cars and finally exited the airport curtilage to join the dual carriageway back to London. Once inside her flat, he said he would get food sorted and checked what he needed before going out to the nearby convenience store. There was no hurry and she started to run a bath, then unpacked her bag and put the case away in the wardrobe. Nipping back to check on the bath, she added her favourite oil and swirled the water with her hand, gauging the temperature. Satisfied, she turned off the taps, returned to the bedroom and removed all her clothes. Picking up her laundry from the holiday as well, she stepped smartly to the kitchen and put it all into the washing machine. Back in the bathroom, checking the water temperature again, she flicked on the hot tap for a last boost, then tentatively stepped in. Using both hands she lowered herself slowly. Feeling the warm water move slowly up and over her body, she relaxed completely. It was then she started to think. During the last few days of her time away, her period should have started. She was late. She was surprised more than anything. For most of the time she had been with Dan she had been on the Pill, and when that relationship collapsed, she had stopped. The first couple of times Max stayed over, she hadn't even thought they were taking a risk. Since then, they had mostly used condoms; they both kept them. Stephanie had good reason to want to avoid an accidental pregnancy. She had told no one, apart from Dan, about the abortion she had during their time together. It was the feeling of shame and sadness, it never left her. It was out of sight to everyone but her. She remembered the discussion with the doctor then, about the complications a termination could have. Now, here she was, in the same street again. But maybe it was a false alarm. A week or so and she would take a test.

A shout and the closing of a door distracted her. Bending forward, she pressed the plug to empty the bath and then reached for a towel to drape around herself. Wrapping another around her head, she returned to the bedroom. He tapped the bedroom door and called out: 'When would you like to eat?'

'About 15 minutes?'

By the time Stephanie came out, Max had set the small table in the kitchen and poured a glass of wine for her, which he put in the living room with a small bowl of mixed olives. He had fixed a salad and was oiling two thick tuna steaks with pepper and ground coriander ready for the hot griddle pan. Bringing back her glass, she sat at the table saying: 'You are wonderful' - just as he drained the asparagus. They sat and ate. Topping their glasses afterwards, they moved to one of the living room sofas, him with his feet on the table and her curled up alongside him. They watched the TV news until it was late, then went to bed.

A couple of weeks later, with an over-the-counter pregnancy kit, Stephanie tested positive. She decided to get medical confirmation and called her doctor's surgery to make an appointment. As a private patient, she was given a time the following day. She was asked to provide a urine sample before waiting on one of the long sofas in the reception area. The doctor came out and greeted her, leading Stephanie into her consulting room. After an introductory conversation, the memories of the time before started to unroll. She experienced that detached, not quite *happening to me again but it is*, feeling. The doctor examined Stephanie and then left the room briefly. Returning after a few minutes, she confirmed that Stephanie was around seven weeks pregnant. The doctor began: 'You will be booked onto our system, and we will call you in for a 12-week scan.'

Stephanie said: 'I'm not sure. Not sure what I'm going to do. I need some time to think about this.' Feeling stronger at the sound of her own voice, she went on: 'How long do I have to make a decision either way?'

The doctor made immediate eye contact with her, as though to read her thoughts, before stating: 'Around 23 weeks is probably the outside edge. But most women make this decision quite early; within the first ten weeks.

If you decide that route is the best way for you, we can offer advice. Meanwhile, we will book you in for the scan I mentioned, to see how things are progressing. You may start to experience nausea and tiredness, which is to be expected. However, if there are any significant changes to your health during that time, or you're worried about any aspect, call me straight away and you can come in and see me.'

Stephanie stood, holding out her hand, and said simply: 'Thank you.'

She left the surgery. Walking away, she was surprised at her own uncertainty. Normally, she was so purposeful and strong-minded, and yet now she felt without direction. Her task was just to get home. Moving to the kerbside in the one-way street, she held her arm up at an approaching cab. It slowed, then stopped for her. Climbing in and giving her address, she sat back in the seat. Her first thought was the ease at which the cab could transport her home, reminding her that if you have the money to make a choice, life can be so much easier. She had arranged to meet Max and some of his swimming friends later in the evening, at their pub. It was a bizarre situation to be in – here she was, about to meet Max's friends for the first time, after only knowing him for a couple of months, and here she was – pregnant. She decided to keep this to herself. Max told her they would be in The Red Hat pub by Stockwell tube station by around 8.45. It wasn't too far from her flat. It was just after 9 when she put her hand on the long brass handle of the pub door. Pushing hard, it opened into the suddenly noisy space. Looking around, she spotted them standing at the far end of the horseshoe-shaped bar. Working her way across the crowded room, she joined them. Max turned to her, touching her arm as he did so, a cross between contact and endearment. He was about to introduce her to the others when he sensed that she was not quite on kilter.

'You OK?' he asked. 'You look a bit -' He was going to say 'tired' thinking she must have had a difficult day at work. His question hung in the air, and Stephanie, with a slight hesitation, said: 'Yeah, sure, everything is OK.' Smiling now, she ploughed on: 'Aren't you going to introduce me?' She didn't wait for a reply. She had her audience. "Hello, I'm Stephanie. What are you guys discussing in the corner? Are you plotting something?'

'It's football. Millwall are playing Queen's Park Rangers in a few weeks and we're trying to work out if we can all make it. It's a grudge match, and we're all keen to be there.'

Max's voice came over her shoulder, above the conversation. 'Steph, can I get you a drink? A glass of wine?'

She leaned on him a little, as a show of affection, mainly for the others to see. She did feel completely worn out. She smiled and shook her head. She didn't stay long, excusing herself by saying she'd had a complex day with some clients, and left feeling a little adrift. When she got home, she lay in the bath, and let the water soak up her doubts, thinking over and over about what she should do. She realised that fate had given her a chance to have a child, and that – whatever the outcome with her relationship with Max – was a gift. It may not happen to her again, she was 38, nearly 39. A small voice deep within her urged her to think carefully. Max had said he would come to her flat within the next hour, but he was late and a good deal more relaxed than he had intended. Over the next couple of weeks, their lives continued, though not quite as before.

Chapter 4

Stephanie surprised Max when she mentioned one of her work friends was moving house with his partner and had invited them to a gathering – not really a party - in their new home in Surrey. She really wanted to go. It wasn't far from London, just an awkward place to get to; so they decided to drive there. She pointed out that they couldn't go in his van, it wouldn't really be appropriate. So he hired a car. That decision to go, then, and to that place, changed his life forever.

The accident happened on a dual carriageway, when an estate car joined from the slip road. It was travelling very fast, and the driver, it transpired, had been seen looking down, maybe at a mobile phone. He misjudged completely the manoeuvre to join the traffic. He drove into the passenger side, forcing Max's car into the side of an overtaking lorry. The sudden impact forced their car into the lorry's underside. First, a single smash; then the noise, the shrieking, tearing sound of metal and glass ripping over the sounds of traffic. The rented car's elegant lines were transformed in the blink of an eye. As the lorry braked and slowed, the front end of their car was caught and began to turn into the lorry's wheels. It was thrown against the lorry like a vibrating tuning fork. By the time the vehicles were stationary, the scene was carnage. The perpetrator of the accident had rebounded away sharply, over-compensating and running off the slight embankment, coming to rest on its side in the bushes a few feet lower than the embankment. The traffic just stopped and immediately started to back up. Two or three people ran from their cars to offer help. Within minutes, the police were there, followed by the Emergency Services.

The police secured the area, four ambulances arrived separately, and then the paramedics sedated those they suspected of having concussion injuries. The fire service worked with specialised jacks and cutting equipment to release them. While this was happening, the paramedics attended to the badly shocked driver of the estate car and the lorry driver, and they were taken away in an ambulance. When Max was released, he was carried, sedated, to another ambulance, which then left. Stephanie was transported in the last ambulance, all with blue lights flashing, as they made their way to hospital.

Meanwhile, a collision officer was visually recording the scene and preparing for a computerised survey, plotting skid marks, debris and taking relevant measurements. Statements were taken from witnesses and, after three or four hours, the site was cleared, cleaned, and traffic moved again across all the lanes. The passing motorists, looking to see what had caused the hold up, knew nothing of the lives that had been broken. For them it was just a momentary distraction. When Max eventually opened his eyes, the first person he saw was the first person he ever saw; his mother. It was nearly dark, he was drifting. He thought he felt her hand on his with the lightest pressure, then he drifted again. The next time he woke it was still dark, dimmed lights in the corridor at the end of the ward gave enough light for him to see his mother asleep in the chair beside him. He couldn't move, he slept again. Finally, he woke. It was daylight and he saw the bright, hi-tech surroundings. A nurse came over, took his pulse, smiled and went away again. He could only remember scattered details of the accident and had no sense of how long he had been in hospital. Then a doctor came. Max asked for news of Stephanie. It was the short silence that told him. Then: 'I'm so dreadfully sorry. We couldn't save her. And of course, the baby was far too small to have survived.' Turning his head away in shock, Max said he had no idea that Stephanie was pregnant.

Screwing his eyes tightly shut, he felt the time they had been together roll up against him, like a weight. Why hadn't she told him? He felt the pain and the anger of it undermining what little strength he had. He wept without any sound, at the thought of what might have been. He was examined, then the doctor left. Alone again, he looked out of the window at a clear blue sky, just making out two tiny crosses at the front ends of vapour trails, hundreds of people going somewhere. He shut his eyes and allowed his head to sink deeper on the pillow. Another doctor came by later. How much later, he didn't know. He learnt that he had a break to the femur in his right leg and two cracked ribs, as well as bad cuts and abrasions to several areas of his body. They had carried out an operation on his leg, the swelling would recede and, unusually, he would then be given a full plaster cast. He also learnt that he suffered suspected concussion, and because his body had suffered trauma, he had been sedated initially. He was alive. He would mend. He felt exhausted. Later, hearing footsteps reach the side of his bed, he opened his eyes and saw his mother. He tried to tell her about Stephanie, but it was so hard, he just buckled. She just listened and, simply by being there, started the long process of drawing out his hurt, emotions and pain. The nights were worst.

To wake suddenly, sweating, then to lie still for long periods before drifting to sleep, only to dream a dream of replays, over and over. One evening after the cast had been applied, he was moved from intensive care to another general ward of similar size. He felt somehow detached from everything. Like someone in the audience, unable to leave the play. Over the next few days, he started to recover some strength, but movement, however limited it might be, was painful. The physiotherapist made sure he was taking a few steps using a frame every day, to avoid complications. There were several visitors. Two police officers came to take his statement, but Max could only really remember what led up to the crash.

He was told there would be an inquest, and the verdict was likely to be accidental death. It was likely there would be criminal charges against the driver who caused the accident that took Stephanie's life. It was a miracle more people had not been killed.

Helen, Max's mother's closest friend and a constant presence in his younger life, came in several times. He found conversation difficult, but it was the comfort of having her there that consoled him. Later on, one of his swimming friends came in, and he also had a visit from two men he worked with regularly. One of them carried a bunch of grapes, looking uncomfortable and ill at ease. Then there was the completely unexpected visit that lifted him more, for unknown reasons. Jay, the rubbish-clearance man that Max had used for some time, had heard about the crash, and taken the time to find him. He wore the same grey tracksuit bottoms and stained T-shirt that he usually wore, topped with an odd-looking anorak, shambling across the ward in his unlaced trainers. Everyone who spent time with Max offered him the hand of hope and help. He took note of who visited, as well as those he had expected to come and see him, but didn't.

Max had plenty of time to think, but it always started with Stephanie and he always collapsed a little inside. Her death was so unreal, and it was so difficult to fully accept that it had happened. He knew that if his injuries meant he couldn't work, he couldn't pay his rent, so his flat would have to go. His savings were meagre, so he would have to move back home. If there was to be an insurance claim, he knew it would - like the inquest – take a long while. Matters were out of his hands now. He tried to rest. Breathing deeply, exhaling slowly through his mouth, the sound of trolley wheels hitting a ridge in the floor somewhere came to him, then, he slept again. It took nearly four weeks to recover sufficiently to be discharged. He had been booked into the fracture clinic at the hospital near his mother's home for two weeks after his discharge.

Further X-rays would be necessary to check the healing process. His mother had already made the decision for him, saying that he should come home. She had cleared the small dining room in readiness and asked a neighbour to help move the divan bed downstairs. Recovery would happen quicker, she reasoned, with her to look after him. Max felt a little stronger now, as the physio had been teaching him specific exercises. She had also shown him how to use his crutches correctly, once he was strong enough to abandon the walking frame. The day before he was due to leave the hospital, he had a visitor he had not seen before. The man entered the ward and spoke to a nurse who pointed towards the corner where his bed was. As he walked towards him, Max heard the soft click of leather soles which brought the visitor to his bedside with even strides. He unbuttoned his sports coat and held out his hand to make a physical contact with Max's undamaged arm saying: 'I'm David Handley, Stephanie's father, may I sit down?'

Max nodded and waited for him to continue. David backed towards the small armchair, placing both hands on the wooden arms and lowered himself into it. Taking time, he chose his words. 'I owe you an apology. I should have come to see you much earlier.' He paused, took a breath, and then started again. 'This has been hell for us all, I've handled things badly. I needed to blame someone other than myself. It's the guilt I feel now that's overtaken me, because I really didn't know what was going on in her life. When she was growing up, I was always working. I was often away from home. I'm sure she told you this. I didn't know anything about you, apart from the briefest of details she gave us at Christmas. You obviously know about her long relationship with Dan? It was Ellie that told me Stephanie had been seeing you for a while and that you made her happy. Ellie, as you can imagine, is heartbroken. So is the girls' mother. We all are.'

His voice tailed away, then he started again. 'I wanted to blame you, even when the facts of the accident said otherwise, but that was wrong of me.

'I'm so sorry.' He used his arms to push himself up from the chair. Straightening his back until he was upright, he leaned forward, touched Max's arm and added: 'I had to come, you understand? There was a cremation service, just for the family.' He then looked directly at Max, before walking away. When David had disappeared from sight, Max realised this was a sort of closure for Stephanie's father, and from now a boundary would separate them as surely as bars. Max couldn't imagine what Ellie and Stephanie's mother were going through, and there would be no room for him in their grief. The twins were probably too young to understand. He thought about David's relationship, or lack of it, with Stephanie throughout her childhood. But Stephanie had seemed fond of her father and bore no resentment. So perhaps he had been a better father than he realised.

It was on a dark, damp and grey morning that he was released from hospital. After the doctors' rounds, he waited impatiently, sitting in a wheelchair holding his crutches. Leaving the ward, he thanked the nurses, and then a porter wheeled him firmly through the long corridor towards the lifts. The noise and the number of people came at him like a barrage; the cocoon of the ward was past. The lift juddered first before starting its short, smooth downward journey. When the doors went back, his chair was swung at right angles into what seemed like a rush of humanity, mostly coming towards him. They passed a coffee shop, a small convenience store and a charity bookshop, all awash with people, before reaching the main reception. The porter brought the wheelchair to a halt as his mother approached.

'You'll be OK now,' he turned to Max. 'Just take it really easy and rest. Good luck, man.'

'Thank you,' said Max, and almost as an after-thought, added: 'Thanks, yes, thanks for everything.'

His mother put her arms around him, saying; 'This is the start of your road to recovery. I have a large taxi waiting just outside.' She released the brake on the wheelchair and pushed him towards the automatic glass doors of the main hospital reception. They opened with a slight popping sound, then slid back from his path. The outside world greeted him with a sharp gust of wind. 'It's the blue one, just there,' said his mother as they moved across the pavement to the taxis. The driver had the sliding door already open for him. 'Here you go mate, I'll put the crutches in. Rest on my arm, that's it.'

Max manoeuvred himself several times, eventually letting out a gasp at his efforts, and sank back on the seat. His mother returned the wheelchair to reception. As the taxi door slid shut, Max's eyes locked on to the strange sight of a row of people just away from the main doors with coats covering their pyjamas and robes. They were smoking. The juxtaposition seemed to him absurd. He was grateful for the blanket handed to him by the driver and he could feel the warmth of the heater too as the taxi started to move away. His mother sitting beside him, touched his arm saying: 'We'll be home soon.' Gradually the miles fell behind them as the taxi pushed on to the dual carriageway and headed south. When the tyres ground on the gravel drive by the garage, he knew he had made it back to another sanctuary where he could rest and hide. His mother's house was like a haven where he could feel safe. He could lie unseen from life's side swipes. Levered out with help from the driver, he managed to get the crutches in place to edge himself to the porch, where he turned and waited. He could hear their voices, and see their backs, but the wind took away their words. He watched his mother raise a hand in thanks to the driver, then, facing Max, she returned her purse to her bag. Walking past him, she reached to unlock the door. Removing the keys, she pushed open the door with her fingertips for him. The heating was on and the house felt warm and welcoming.

Taking off his coat, Max struggled into the sitting room with his crutches, twisted himself into the lowering position with his good knee, and sat in a chair. His mother lifted his leg onto a low stool with a cushion, then went to the kitchen to make tea. Beside him lay the remote control for the TV with that day's Times newspaper, which had been bought especially for him. He liked this room with its big sofas, the overflowing bookcase. On the wall were familiar pictures, including the fly fisherman on a country brook lost in his art. His favourite was an etching of two men bent over the wheel handles of a pump on the deck of a square rigger in a storm, pumping for their lives. For the time being though, he was no longer part of the turn of any wheel. The TV in the corner was small and almost inconsequential, as you might expect in room with so many books. Looking out of the window from the angle of the chair he could see the horizon, but not the detail that lay in front of it. There lay the irony; in his life it was the opposite. It was nearly five weeks since the accident. People say of bad experiences, if it doesn't kill you, it makes you stronger, but he didn't know what he had to be stronger for. His mother appeared at the doorway with a mug of tea and some buttered toast, 'to keep you going,' she said, then returned to the kitchen to prepare supper for later. He took the paper and turned the pages, unable to concentrate for more than a few paragraphs before finally putting it back on the table. There were so many things that would need his attention. His rent was only paid until the end of the month. Doctors had been told him it could take eight months for him to heal properly, so he decided to get his possessions and his van out of London and store everything here. He would have to give up the flat. It was, he reasoned, the sensible thing to do financially, but it would be a wrench, given how much work he had done on the flat. But, perhaps this way, he could try to leave his memories behind. With the help of his crutches, he was able to move to the window.

Movement on the apple trees caught his eye. Early blue tits were nibbling at the newly formed buds before skipping in flight to another tree. The daffodil leaves were high with centred buds, waiting for a warm day to burst out in their yellow shout. Next door, there were two tall plane trees fanning out the backdrop, flanked by a full-grown Mimosa tree. Fronting these was a hidden fence, lined with an abundance of mature shrubs in his mother's garden. The neighbour had planted the Mimosa as a sapling for her brother, now in a care home. The tree grew, as they do over the years, strong and large with a full roundness. The brother's incarceration in the home was the result of a fall in the street, which left him physically complete, but struck dumb and paralysed, with no memory. A freak chance, the unlucky lottery. Max considered that. A life within a life, but no life. But, every January, the tree flowered in a full burst of colour, sending its unknown message of love to anyone who cared to look in that direction. That tree marked the weekly visits to her brother's empty life. It was welded to hers, and stretched to endless sadness. With that thought, Max felt tears well up in his eyes, and he quickly wiped them away. He tried to rationalise his own position. It was a good time of year, all he had to do was hold on.

It was two days after arriving home that Helen drove up from the coast to see him. It was pre-arranged between the women, but a surprise to him when the sharp shrill of the doorbell rang. By the time he had found his crutches, she was in the sitting room with open arms. She bent to give him a hug and kiss while he patted her arm. He returned a kiss to her cheek. It was wonderful of her to make the journey on his behalf, and, for reasons he didn't quite understand, it brought him to the edge of tears. Later, he would come to recognise it was the onset of depression following deep and traumatic shock. The next few hours were an escape, seeing his mother and her closest and oldest friend talk and laugh together, with such obvious joy for one another's company.

Feeling tired, he dozed in a chair and Helen slipped out, leaving him a note: 'Soon will come the day when you are much stronger, and you must come to stay for some sea air.' It was signed just with an H.

His damaged phone no longer worked properly and, even in his circumstances, the telecoms company made no exception and refused to replace it. Still under contract for a further three months, a new SIM card was sent to him. Rummaging around in a desk drawer, he had already found an old handset and had recharged its battery. With a strange sense of expectation, as though it were linking him to an amputated past, he turned the phone on. The light came on and pressing the directory button, it flipped to the list. Scrolling down to 'landlord', he was relieved to see the number was still there. He pressed it and heard the call tone a few times somewhere that seemed far away.

It was answered with a monotone: 'Hello.'

'It's Max, from -'

His landlord interrupted him: 'Yeah, hello Max, the woman in the flat below told me you've been in some bother. She heard about it somewhere. How are you?'

'Repairing slowly, but I'm going to be out for some time.'

The landlord butted in: 'I see you've paid this month's rent, how do you stand for next month, because I've got bills to pay, too.' No sympathy here, although he hadn't really expected any. Max had re-decorated the flat and fitted it out properly, but the landlord was a straight-talking businessman, and he would now benefit from Max's work. Changing his original plan on the hoof, Max said: 'I will have to get someone to clear the small items. But as you know, I paid for new carpets and the bed and sofa are nearly new. I'll leave them so you can get an increased rent, but I do want all of my deposit back.'

There was a short silence before the landlord said: 'OK, only if you leave the flat clean though. I'll write your new address down now and foreword any mail that looks important to you and dump the rest. I'll also take the meter readings and let the council know you've moved out, then that will wrap it up. When can you get your van moved? I can't get into the garage.'

Max replied: 'I'll find someone to sort it. I'll contact you again when someone needs to be let in.'

'Yeah, fair enough, well good luck then. It will all work out in the end.'

Going through all of his messages, Max texted the same brief response to anyone enquiring about work or quotes for jobs: 'Injured in a car accident. Unable to work or drive for a long period. Sorry.' Then he turned off the answering service, so nobody could leave a message. This would cut his anxiety levels, he reasoned. Gradually, he developed a simple daily routine. Getting himself up in the morning, he used the crutches to get downstairs and use the commode in the loo, then moved to the kitchen and strip washed as best as he could. He got dressed with difficulty, then made tea and toast before lowering himself onto a stool at the work top to eat it. He wanted to be as independent as possible from the start. His mother tended to come downstairs later, perhaps to give him space, he wasn't sure.

Most mornings were spent in the sitting room, reading and passing time to get nearer to the day when his cast would be removed. Just a few more days, and he would make a leap forward in mobility that would take him into the garden and literally down the road with more control. But for now, he was amongst the quiet. Sometimes he would listen to the steady ticking of the old grandfather clock in the hall. He always felt it was like a pulse in the house, passing time with the regularity of waves hitting a beach. There were two calls to make that morning, and both were important.

Sliding his hand over the small table alongside his chair, he picked up the phone. He thumbed through for

Jay's number and called him. It went to answer. Jay called back a minute later.

'Hello Max, how's it going then?'

Max told him he was out of hospital now and had moved to his mother's house. He was in a fix and needed someone he could trust to move his stuff out of the flat. He also needed his van with all his tools in it. He asked Jay if he would take it on as a job, putting his belongings into clean rubble bags, tidying up the flat and then putting the key through the letter box. He gave Jay his landlord's number to arrange access and, after discussing a few more details, ended the call. Max had already checked his mother's garage. It was practically empty and dry, perfect for the task. He felt he was loosening the cord with what had gone before, but also felt more than irritation for his landlord. Like the pith from the orange, his bitterness was just under the skin. He was one of the many grasping individuals exploiting the murky world of property. Max was finding having to make calls and take decisions more difficult. Before, these tasks had been easily done, but now they seemed to require much more effort and he often delayed them. Turning his head sideways and looking out of the window at the horizon, he caught sight of an incoming wave of Canada geese wheeling on the wing, circling downwards to grasslands out of sight. As they disappeared from view, his thoughts of their beauty were interrupted. His leg was throbbing again. This, he had been told, could continue, even after the break had apparently healed.

The days rolled over and then he was outside waiting, ready for the taxi as it turned into the street. He had arranged to go to the hospital on his own, as he wanted to use the time to linger a little. The driver came round to his side. As he slid the side door open, its runners made a crunching sound, then it bounced a little on its stop.

Having passed his crutches to the driver, Max levered his body in backwards, using the front seat as an arm support, then swivelling carefully into the seat. The door shut while he was putting his belt on, then they were moving away. The journey was about four miles and didn't take long. Max didn't bother with small talk; he was focusing on what was going to happen next. Getting out of the taxi was considerably easier than getting in, and he had prepared cash in advance to pay the driver. There were a few spots of rain, but the cloud bank looked high, so it would hold off for a while. Tucking the crutches under his arms, he started slowly to the main entrance. Before him was a red brick façade, matching the older late Victorian buildings alongside, with a more modern, 1980s design at the rear. It seemed very busy as he entered, and, seeing a cash machine in the foyer, he made a note to use it on the way out. Following the signs for the fracture clinic, he headed for the lift. Someone held the door for him, and he squeezed in. When the doors opened, the clinic was directly opposite, and this time an older man stood aside for him. Registering with the receptionist, he sat on a high chair and waited. Unlike downstairs, there were only a few people waiting here and, not expecting his appointment to be on time, he was mildly surprised when his number registered on a screen one minute before the appointed time. Making his way to a consulting room, he was greeted by a doctor who, without more than a glance at him, said: 'We'll send you off for an X- ray to see how things are progressing.' Then leaned towards the computer to make a few notes on his file. Max found the department and, after a longer wait this time, entered the X-ray room.

The radiographer was a slight woman, about 50, wearing a white coat, with her glasses on a decorated cord around her neck. She was crisp and efficient, and seemed soulless. He was told to remove his trousers and lie on the bed. After the adjustments, she retreated while the X- rays were taken, then came her voice: 'All done, thank you.'

Max returned to the fracture clinic and waited to see the specialist, who was pleased with the result. He was then taken, in a wheelchair, by a porter to have the plaster removed. This was an operation that he could parallel to his own work. The setting of the blade to the correct thickness, in order to do the job but no more; and using a disk cutter, similar to one he might use to prepare a wall for re-pointing. He watched it skim across the full length of his plaster, opening it with a neat cut, just as he would, along a pointing line. How strange it felt to touch his own leg again and see fragments of plaster lodged in the hair on his thigh. He put his tracksuit bottoms back on. Passing through departments, as though on a conveyor belt, he left the therapists and receptionists behind, trading his full-length crutches for the elbow type on the way.

After phoning for a taxi, he left the hospital knowing his weekly visits to the physio were booked in. It felt like recovery was reaching for him. Arriving back home, on the kitchen table was a small bundle of letters that had been forwarded from his flat. There was a note beside them. First, he made a mug of tea then, leaning his new crutches against the table, he sat down. His mother's short note read: 'Gone for groceries.' There was an x at the bottom. Opening all the letters, a few were junk mail, and some could wait, but one required immediate attention. It was from the car hire company, referring to the accident. He realised now he needed a solicitor to act on his behalf and advise him about compensation, the coming court case, and perhaps other issues too. He fingered the letter before dropping it on the table.

It was such a short time ago, but his life had already changed radically. How would the relationship with Stephanie have gone? Would it have worked? He just didn't know, but he knew that if he had ever felt love, it was with Stephanie. He wondered whether the bruising would completely go from a memory, given time. The door opened and his mother came in with a couple of bags.

Max greeted her and then said he had opened the mail, and would need some legal advice. Could she recommend a local solicitor?

'Hang on, Max, let me put this shopping away and then I'll give you my full attention.'

She lowered the bags to the kitchen table and rubbed her hip as she straightened up.

'Let me do that.' Swinging open the fridge and various cupboard doors, Max put the groceries away. The wooden shelves in the larder, the cup hooks, the kiln jars tight with summer fruit from the garden – it all brought back memories of his childhood.

'Right, solicitors, yes, I suppose you will need advice on claims for the accident, and maybe the court case.

We've always used one of the solicitors in the high street, not that we've used them very often. I'll check the name, hang on.' She started to walk towards the hall, then turned and said: 'Linnett and Spears, that's it. But I imagine the chap I dealt with last time will have retired by now. You could try them first.'

Max called them later and the woman he was put through to listened carefully to his whole story. She took his contact details in order to set matters in motion, and explained that things could take some time before a conclusion. She ended the call by saying she would write to him formally with her firm's terms of engagement, then matters could proceed on his behalf. He was impressed by her manner and when the call ended, he felt it was the right choice.

The Sunday that Jay was due to arrive with the van, Max got a text which just said 'Should be with you around 12.30.' At just after 1pm, he got another message, saying Jay was outside. Max opened the front door and walked with his crutches down the short path to the street to meet Jay, who had his arse resting on the wing of the van, and his hands in his pockets.

A smile played on his face for a moment, before he opened up with: 'You're looking good Maxi. Where do you want this stuff?'

Max pointed to the garage alongside the house and produced a key, moving to unlock and open the doors while Jay reversed the van up to them. When the doors to the van were opened, Max saw it was full to the gunwales. He noticed all the clothes bags had been rolled at the top and stapled. Jay said he would stack everything, then put the van against the garage doors.

He told Max to go back indoors, and he'd unload as quickly as he could. Within 15 minutes, there was a light knock at the open front door. Starting to get up, he called Jay to come in. Jay removed his trainers at the door, and the two men went into the kitchen. Max's mother had prepared a large casserole with roast potatoes and vegetables. It was her way of thanking this rather unusual man. Later on, when Jay showed signs of wanting to get going, she offered him a lift to the station. Max asked Jay what he owed him.

'Well, it took longer than I expected, everything's clean and tidy, but you know what? I've enjoyed this trip to the country, a chance to get out of London. Call it £80 and that'll pay for the bags and the train fare back.'

Max opened his wallet and gave him £250, saying: 'Jay, you earned it. Besides, you helped me when I needed it. For that alone, thank you.' After a handshake Jay was gone. Max reflected that when people look out for each other, good things can happen. He would return that good deed to someone, another time. Physio sessions, PT classes, muscle-strengthening exercises; they all filled the days as summer progressed. Max grew stronger. Walking was a weight-bearing exercise and he knew it would be his personal path back to fitness, but he was careful not to overdo it. His mother had taken him down to the coast to see Helen on several occasions. Nothing had changed, it was the same as he remembered it from his childhood.

He was well aware of just how much love, care and attention he got from both of these women and how they had been the mainstays of his recovery. It was during one of the days there, when he had walked in stages to the quay shop. It was a windy day, but warm from recent rain. The long black-stained clapboard building nestled with its back against the dunes was open at one end and served as a shop, selling fresh fish from the boats. Stopping briefly, he watched the woman at the counter slap down a side of white fish on the scales. The building alongside was the same construction, with a veranda facing the open harbour. It was known locally as 'the shack', now swamped in summer with trippers and locals alike. He eventually ordered a coffee and took it to a spare table in the corner. He was about to sit down when he spotted a discarded newspaper jammed in the side of the seat, probably left by a customer earlier. The coffee refreshed him, but the newspaper didn't, and was quickly discarded. Standing and stepping away from the table, his phone pinged a text message. Curiosity got the better of him, and he slipped his hand into his pocket, retrieved the phone and thumbed it to flash up the message. It was from Jay, with a photo attached. It read: 'Saw this in the evening paper. You seen it? So sorry mate.' There was a photo, slightly skewed, of the newspaper article.

Peckham man jailed for fatal crash

A 29-year-old man from Peckham was jailed for two years yesterday for causing a crash on the South Circular that killed a Putney woman and severely injured several other people. The court heard how Patrick Walker had been texting while joining the fast-moving traffic on February 26 this year. He admitted losing control of his estate car and ploughing into the Audi in which 38-year-old Stephanie Hanley had been a passenger, pushing the vehicle under a lorry. Miss Handley, who was a commercial surveyor, had been pronounced dead shortly after arriving at St Christopher's Hospital. Paramedics, fire fighters and police had attended the scene of the crash, one of five in the past 12 months that has involved a texting driver.

Max stopped reading. The short paragraph stabbed at him. His stomach rolled over, and his free hand grabbed the edge of the table. Engulfed by a great sadness, he stepped down from the café's veranda to the beach. He then walked slowly to the tide line. It took several minutes for Max to recover his composure before turning and walking between the patches of seaweed to the path that would take him back to Helen's house. After a short while, the land rose a little and in front of him, as the path turned, was a worn oak bench. Resting the aluminium hospital walking stick against the seat, he prepared to sit, realising he was sweating a little. The wind had long since dropped away, replaced with warm sunshine. It was the noise first that came to him and, searching the sky, he saw the helicopter. Its sound is particularly individual; the sound of the blades beating and turning the air, and it grew much louder as the helicopter flew closer. He recognised the red and white colours of the Air Sea Rescue; the side door was open and a winchman wearing a helmet appeared to be sitting or kneeling on the lip. As it came to the closest point, Max raised an arm and waved briefly like many others had before him, having a vague feeling of wanting to identify with the winchman. The helicopter was moving away.

Looking around, he saw no one, but still he felt self-conscious of his child-like behaviour. As the beat of the blades faded, he sat down on the bench and with arms stretched along the back rail, he felt the sun warm his face and forearms.

Going over in his mind what he had just read from Jay, he knew this was one of the many tragedies played out every day, with consequences rolling out with never-ending ripples across the human landscape. The best he could do, was to get fit again and carry on. Cradling his walking stick between his knees, he looked out at the long reach of the harbour as the water was being slowly sucked out by the tide. Further up, a colony of seals would be resting on the warm mud, exposed by the retreating tide.

The Romans had plied their trade coming to the small sheltered ports in these inlets and to the magnificent palace that was beyond the tree line. In the surrounding fields, people with metal detectors occasionally roamed, prodding and turning the land after the plough. Stretching and crossing his legs, he took in a woman with a dog on the far side of the inlet, one minute she was a small splash of colour, then they were gone as though never there. Just like Stephanie.

Chapter 5

It was just at the beginning of autumn, when the whispering leaves started to fall, that he was pronounced fit by the doctor. He decided the time had come to return to London and get a job. He had received a partial pay out from the insurance company during the previous month which helped. Known as a hardship payment, it was well-timed and, in a letter from his solicitor, he was told that the remainder of the settlement would be paid before Christmas. The end of the summer had seen him driving again, which released the static boredom. He started to organise himself, completely sorting through his possessions and re-packing them. Then he moved onto the van. Its battery was out on a trickle charger at the back of the shed while it was laid up, but it was running well. It failed its MOT the first time on the front brake pads and a swing arm bush. These jobs presented no problems for him. He also changed the oil and checked all the levels for a successful retest. Every task accomplished prepared him for the moment when he would leave. His mother had noticed the growing restlessness in him and gave him space for his plans. On his last morning, before he left in the van with some tools and a few possessions, he called Helen and thanked her for her encouragement. He told her she was one of the two supports that he wouldn't have made it back without.

As he drove away, he saw in the wing mirror, his mother give a last wave in response to his touch of the horn. What he couldn't see were the tears that ran down to her chin, quickly brushed away by the back of her hand. By then he had rounded the corner. On a trip to London the previous week, he had taken a room on the ground floor of a house, well south of the river. He had also found a job through an agency to start work in a joinery the following week. His first night he slept badly. It was the bars on the inside of the window that unnerved him.

Even though they were there to protect him, and he had a key to the door, he still felt locked in. By morning, he had resolved to move when his front payment of two weeks in advance came through. Quickly finding a first-floor studio flat further down the road, he transferred, and here he found a certain peace as he attempted to re-balance his life. The job was poor money, but the fixed hours and no responsibility suited him just then. He started swimming again but it was at best sporadic and unsatisfying. His social life revolved round the pub; the more he socialised the more he drank, or was it the other way around, some evenings he couldn't remember. Over a relatively short time, he went with a kaleidoscope of girls, all very different, but always for the same reason.

He changed his behaviour when one girl gave him a harsh lecture and then dumped him. She said he should attempt to sort himself out and make something of his life before it was too late. This made him examine what sort of person he had become, in relation to what sort of person he would like to be. If you get what you settle for in life, then he was in danger of settling for something he didn't want. He resolved to cut back on the lonely nights drinking at home and find more sociable things to do, perhaps in the hope of greater fulfilment.

One early evening in the lead up to Christmas, something went really wrong. It was on Friday 18th December, mid evening. Max left his flat and started to walk between the endless, drab bay and forecourt houses bathed in dank yellow lighting from the streetlights. He hadn't gone far, and was lost in his own thoughts, when he approached an alley between the terraces. He wasn't sure if it was the sound of a man's voice he heard first, or the scrubbing of feet on gravel. Alert, he slowed, and just into the alley he saw a man in his 20s raise his hand and slap a smaller woman and, leaning close to her, said something that made her cry.

The man just smiled, took no notice and stepped away from her out of the alley and onto the pavement. The woman behind him was begging him now. 'Please, give me. Just one wrap I need. I'll have money tomorrow.'

Max was drawn into this circle as if by a greater force from the second he opened his mouth and said: 'Drugs? You bastard,' to which the man just replied: 'They're all just stupid sluts mate, this one's pregnant too, now why don't you just fuck off?'

The woman had already receded into the alley. Max should have walked away, but he didn't. The young dealer just smiled. He was cocky, confident and seemingly untouchable.

'Just leave her alone, OK?' Max said again quietly.

The woman used the opportunity to move further away up the alley, and the young man shrugged his shoulders and started to walk away, saying - without even looking towards him: 'She's beyond help now.'

In that instant, a physical change happened within Max. It was like the gears slipped and the engine turned to full revs. He exploded with anger, grabbing the dealer by the shoulder and throwing him sideways, giving him a glancing punch at the same time. The man's knees bent a little and then, as though some unknown hand had let him go, he fell downwards. First, and for no reason, backwards with a sickening thud. It was like a melon falling on kitchen tiles. His head hit the coping stone topping the dwarf garden wall. The man came to rest with his face against the side of the wall, with one of his legs out behind him. Blood was already staining the brickwork. Max didn't know then, but at that same moment, he had been seen by two other people. The first was woman in an upstairs window almost opposite who was just about to draw the curtains. The second witness was a man coming out of his house, approximately 30 metres further up the road on the same side. He was the one who phoned the police.

They both thought they had witnessed everything, but in fact only saw what had happened on the pavement. The first police car with two officers arrived within minutes. There was, of course, a third witness, but she had vanished. Max knew immediately the seriousness of the situation. He had bent to the man, listened and looked for any sign of movement or breathing. He stood with his racing thoughts, with the slow feeling of panic seeping into him. Onlookers were keeping their distance as the sound of sirens reached him. There were two police cars, then an ambulance, and the road was blocked off. He was cuffed, then searched. His wallet, ID, phone and keys were all taken off him and he was put into one of the police cars. They read him his rights before driving him to the police station. It took only minutes and then they were in a secure, floodlit compound. He could hear dogs barking somewhere, as he was led through a steel door and along a wide corridor. The noise and commotion of unseen people came to him. Another door was opened and he was taken into a room which he rightly took to be an interview room. The mood changed suddenly. He was offered a chair, called by his first name and asked if he would like a glass of water. One police officer stood behind him while the other asked him whether he wanted his own or the duty solicitor present at the questioning. Max said he'd prefer the duty solicitor and would co-operate fully with him, going over the events as they had happened. The officer stood up and he was then taken to a detention cell and locked in.

Sitting on the edge of the solid bed at one end, beneath the high reinforced, frosted glass paned window, he looked for a moment, firstly at his shoes without laces, then at the simple surroundings of plain white tiles covering the walls and a polished concrete floor. High up, well out of anyone's reach was a single inset electric light with what he took to be a CCTV camera point. Standing, he relieved himself into the steel inset pan, remembering how close he had come to that in the police car.

He sat on the bed again, then lay down, shutting his eyes and wondering how this had all spiralled; like a finger that finds its way to a certain tooth, a reflex to pain. That was his memory of the event. It had been a reflex to the abuse; the anger had subsided but the damage was done. You can never go back, can you? When would someone open the door?

The Lightroom

The light was intensely bright, probably on purpose, and Max could hear nothing but the sound of his own breathing and the thoughts playing through his head. It seemed like several hours went by before the key turned, the bolts cracked back and the door opened. A large officer about his age just pointed at him, then pointed down the corridor to another man standing at an open door. On entering this room, Max was introduced to the duty solicitor; a thin man with oversized glasses. They were left alone and Max told him everything. The solicitor nodded occasionally, making a taped transcript of the conversation. Things happened quickly after that. He recounted the details to the police, who also recorded the interview, and had his photo and fingerprints taken, as well as a swab from his mouth. He was then told he was being held, pending further inquiries. Max exercised his right to make a call, to his mother. How he hated the shame he brought to her door. Her only son had let her down again, this time badly. To burden her like this was, in his mind, unforgivable. He gave her only the briefest of details, saying there had been an incident, where he was being held and the solicitor's contact details, but he hedged around the facts. During his call, confirmation was received at the station that the young man had died. This changed matters considerably and Max was promptly charged with Involuntary Manslaughter. He was then returned to his cell to what would be a very long night for him. He lay for hours thinking of what had happened and the ramifications of his actions. What had started as a gesture of support for the woman had gone so far beyond that now.

He drifted throughout the night, with sleep and waking in near equal measure. Eventually it was morning, the door opened and he was given a breakfast of cereal with milk and a mug of tea. Later, he was taken for a video link court appearance, where, after confirming his name and address, was told that the court would adjourn to a future date. He was given bail with conditions, and was instructed to report to the police station weekly before the trial. Then, with his charge sheet in his hand and his belongings in his pockets, he was released onto the street. This was surreal. It was Saturday morning. It had been raining at some point, and low cloud with a vague mist hung over the high street. In an inordinately short time, his life had moved from the utterly predictable, to the utterly unknown. It was like waking from a nightmare, except the scream had yet to reach him. He tightened his scarf and zipped the jacket up a bit more and crossed the road, heading for the first hot food outlet he might come across. Not having eaten anything substantial for hours, he slid with his tray and an over-sized burger meal onto a sculptured, coloured bench behind a table for four.

Moving the paper cup sideways, he opened the wrapped burger and the large portion of chips, and lowering his face a little to make the job somewhat easier, he demolished them. A single wipe with a paper napkin was sufficient to dispense with the tray and move onto a slower and more deliberate approach to the tea. Lifting his head, he saw the people around him. The nearest was a harassed mother with a double pushchair, part-filled with grocery bags and a small child who showed little enthusiasm for his meal. A middle-aged man wearing a three-quarter length gabardine coat was nearby. He was poring over a crossword puzzle, his tweed hat with its finger indent placed flat on the table beside his coffee. Across from him was an older woman, clinging to a single cup of liquid, which, at a guess, had long since gone cold. How strange it was that people gathered together like this to graze, and yet also avoided each other.

Before leaving, he called his mother again. This time he told her the young man had since died, and he heard her shocked intake of breath. He said it had been a dreadful accident, he had a solicitor, and there would of course be a court case. In the meantime, he would carry on working and would be with her, as planned, as soon as possible on Christmas Eve. His parting words were: 'Please don't think the worst of me. I got involved for what I thought was right,' adding: 'At a time like this, I have no one else to turn to.'

The weekend passed. On Sunday he walked to the local newsagents to pick up a paper. Once outside, he rolled up the paper and put it in the deep inside pocket of his jacket before zipping it three quarters of the way up again. Standing for a moment, then changing his mind about walking straight back to the flat, he decided to walk further down the main road and then cut through to the river. As it eased towards 8.30am, more people were out now. It didn't take long, maybe a quarter of an hour, first he passed the locksmith's premises, then, following a tarmac cycle path between two terraces of houses, he came out in a courtyard between several low-rise blocks. Some kids kicking a football shouted something at him. He just waved and walked past them, crossing one more main road until he found himself against the railings, with the river wide and flowing on the flood. Looking over the railings, he was always surprised at how fast and dark this tide flows. This surge of ancient power, feeding life like a lung into this city of the ages. Busy with its own traffic, it seemed immune to all the changes around it. He ran his hand over the top rail, as though to signify to himself this topic was over, and walked on. Far up the river, he could pick out a football stadium that appeared to be backing right onto the river's edge. He wondered if it was possible to kick a ball out of play, out of the stadium and into the river, only to be picked out miles down for a record kick. On the opposite bank, grand Georgian houses sat uneasily with endless modern flat developments, some cantilevered over the river walkways.

The perspective made it look as though all their balconies were touching. He soon took another turning to the left and had to move aside as a group of boys on bikes came towards him. He waved his hand in a slowing motion, to which two of them responded in their own way - 'Fuck off'- as they passed. Anger rose instantly. Max knew it was not worth pursuing, but the pleasure of the walk felt instantly tempered. The next day, he went into work half an hour early to speak with his boss. He, too, was shocked, but covered it by saying that nothing would be said about it until the court hearing. Squeezing Max's shoulder in a small sign of solidarity, he suggested that hard work would keep his mind occupied. Thursday of that week was Christmas Eve and, being a family business, the joinery shop closed at mid-day for a two-week break. They laid on a lunch and drinks in the pub down the road, but Max excused himself politely to the boss's wife and slipped away, convinced he would not be missed. Back at the flat, he gathered some clothes into a small hold-all and put it by the door. After tidying the room, he took a shower in 'the cupboard', as he called the very small shower room, then checking his mail - which was mostly for previous occupants - he left. He went down the stairs and headed for the side street where he had parked the van at the beginning of the week, hoping that it would be still there. With its residents' permit in full view all was ok, it started well and, once driving, he felt more relaxed. The solicitor had given Max various scenarios and likely outcomes, but clearly the fact that Max had admitted the charge would be in his favour. On the wait and see basis, he told no one; quietly retreating into his own space subconsciously preparing himself as best he could for the letter with the court date. The utter contempt that the young dealer had shown to a pregnant woman, even now, seemed to override Max's actions. But you can never go back and rewrite the story. It's out there. No one should have died.

After a slab of dual carriageway, he turned off onto the forecourt of a filling station drawing up level with a pump. Pushing the nozzle into the tank to put in £40 of diesel, he became distracted and the indicator raced past that. It didn't really matter though, as the remainder of the insurance money had now been paid into his account. Lifting the heavy plastic window, he took a copy of The Times and then stood aside from the automatic doors, allowing a woman to pass first.

Receiving the briefest of smiles in return, he then went in and set off down the aisles in search of a cup of tea and a couple of sausage rolls. Back in the van he moved to a parking bay to eat. There was always something simple and satisfying about eating on his own in the van. Perhaps it was the self-contained privacy. Finishing the food, he wiped his hands on the old towel he kept between the seats, then placing the paper on the steering wheel, he read the front-page stories. With the cup of tea stood on the dashboard, he started to relax. Later, arriving at his mother's, he could see immediately that she was anxious and tired, but putting up a brave front for him. He was greeted with a silent, enveloping hug then, standing together for longer than normal, they stood back. She turned slightly, patting his arm several times, and he saw her biting her lower lip briefly before she said: 'Let's start with tea and toast, you go into the warm.'

Hanging up his jacket, he went into the sitting room. It looked like it always did at Christmas. The small, decorated tree in the corner, mounted on the same table with fairy lights shining, topped out with the same star. Holly sprigs and cards were laid out on the side table, just as they were every year. So reassuringly normal. His mother came in with a tray and set it down. She poured the tea and, as she leaned back on the cushion, he began his story. Every painful splinter came out. His mother didn't interrupt or judge, she just listened. He told her what the solicitor expected to happen, and finally when he was done, he added: 'It all started because I wanted to help someone.'

She stood, motioned him to hug her, and whispered: 'You're a good man, Max, we'll get through this.' He slumped back into the arm chair as she continued: 'Helen is coming over for lunch tomorrow. I have called her already, mainly to prepare her. I want things to be calm for a few days, and for us all to gather strength.'

Raising his head in her direction, Max looked at her, putting on the best face he could muster. The evening passed. Soon after supper, he excused himself, explaining he had had such little sleep, and went upstairs. The curtains were already closed. Turning on the side light and then switching off the main, he removed all his clothes except his T-shirt, then stepping away from the pile, he got into bed. Lying on his back, he listened to the rising wind pulling at the slates. The rain started light, then flicked harder against the window. Finally, he fell asleep.

Wide awake and sweating, his phone screen showed it was 03:08. He threw off the damp T- shirt, replacing it with his shirt, and tried to go back to sleep. All he could hear was the sound of the house breathing. The creaking of a plastic gutter somewhere, the hot water still in the pipes and the wind licking at the outside. After an unknown time, again he slept. On Christmas day, Helen arrived about 12, and by then the turkey was in the oven. His mother had everything else organised. He welcomed Helen into the house, getting a brief kiss under a sprig of mistletoe she had brought with her. She had also brought a bottle of wine and some of her own plums, soaked in brandy and frozen from the summer. She went into the kitchen to greet the cook. Getting some glasses ready, Max poured out some wine from the fridge while they talked, briefly. Opening a bottle of Burgundy, he left it on the table, putting out the mats and cutlery. Then he went to hang Helen's coat up in the hall.

He could almost believe this Christmas Day to be the same as any other year, comfortably numbing and normal in a wonderfully boring way, except he knew that everything was set to change. The day was as crazily removed from reality as it could be. Max's mind worked forward to his next meeting with the solicitors. Perhaps by then, a date would have been set for the trial. He knew though, as certainly as five comes before six, that by the time today was over, they would all be indelibly marked by what had happened. He had slid away from time. It was the noise, the movement in the air, the simple syllable of his own name that brought him back.

'Max.'

It was Helen calling. Apparently, five minutes should do it for lunch, she said. Going to her bag in the hall, she produced two wrapped presents; one for him and the other for Katherine, his mother. Taking them with a sign of thanks, he went to put them under the tree. Looking out of the window, he saw the movement first. It was the wings of a small bird, perhaps a wren, he thought. It was a delicate mixture of brown colours, coming to rest on the outer edges of the Hypericum bush. The bird turned, maybe looking for predators or uncertain it had chosen the right spot, before hopping deeper into the shrub and out of sight. What did it know? Was it shelter from predators that it sought, that darker, dryer hideaway out of the wind for a splash of safe time? He looked away towards the garden wall and beyond, drawing in a deep breath and then exhaling the air along with his unanswered questions. Max knew it was all going to get immeasurably harder. He dropped his hand from the sill to the radiator beneath, running his palm along part of its length, feeling the warmth permeate his skin, then lifting it as it became too hot. Looking at his hand for a moment, he had moved on. The wren was forgotten and he heard his mother call: 'It's on the table.'

Returning to the kitchen, it was the noise of plates, the talking, the smell of the turkey, the heat - he was enveloped again in today. Later, after presents were given and received, long after the washing up was done, and a TV film had been watched, Helen went home. He walked her to the car and it was there that she turned and, looking him full on, just said: 'Whatever happens, you've just got to shoulder it. Pain is a heavy burden, but nothing goes on forever.'

With a hug, she was gone. As Max walked back through the front door, he reflected on his feelings of depression and his mood swings. His uncontrollable temper and the outbursts that came from nowhere. These were his full-on, capsize moments and he knew they could lead to a breakdown that would sink him. It was his mother and Helen that were keeping him afloat. He went inside and closed the door. The last day of the year started with the first hard frost of winter. He was up early and out to meet the day. Walking from the back door, his steps crunched over the frozen grass, marking his path behind him. Tightening his scarf and pushing his hands into his jean pockets he dropped his head a little and, hunching his shoulders, headed out of the back gate and down the alley. Coming to the road, he crossed carefully, aware of how easily anyone could fall that morning, and made for a footpath that would take him away from the houses and out onto the heathland. The sound of cracking ice beneath his feet splintering into fragments took him back to when as a child, he and his friends would throw bricks on the frozen pond, only to see them skid away because the ice was too thick. He pressed on past the copse with its lifeless trees coated in frost from the night's mist, then climbing the stile, a few more paces brought him to the heathland. It was mainly scrub with intermittent heather, although in another generation it could have been a plantation, like the areas further to the north. Now it only covered a park-sized plot, wedged between the main roads and the estate.

The great housing spread of the 1950s had smeared its ugly rash across this landscape, bringing a higher standard of living to millions of people like him and his mother. It was all progress, but at a price. The narrow tracks were like rabbit paths, crossing in every direction to save the walker a yard here and there. Eventually, he joined a pavement and turning, headed towards the parade of shops. Approaching the forecourt, he saw a Collie roped to an iron ring in the wall outside the convenience store. Bending, he held out the back of his hand. The dog nosed his hand and Max stroked it, feeling its fine, soft coat lying flat against its head. In another life, he would have a dog.

Buying a newspaper, he folded it inside his jacket and set off for the longer way home, through the streets. The pavements were downhill now, and he negotiated this more with a shuffle than heel and toe. Walking the length of two more roads, he came out in a cul- de-sac which led back to the main road, and eventually to his mother's road. While walking, he decided that he would head back the next day and use what holiday time was left to organise himself before going back to work.

London seemed fast and hectic, even after such a short time away, but he quickly fell into step with it. That letter, the one he knew was coming, had arrived and lay sideways on the hall table between a magazine and junk mail. To begin with, he just looked down at the pile, knowing that the beige envelope was 'the' envelope. There was that feeling, that if he just looked away, he could remain detached from events a bit longer. Finally, he picked it up and turned it in his hand, knowing the words were already written and his future was already taking shape, completely outside of his control. With his other hand, he slid his forefinger into the edge of the letter and then, with a sawing motion, opened it. Unfolding it, he allowed the envelope to fall, while he picked the bones from the letter. His trial was to take place at County Court Central London on 9 March, 2010. Court 27.

The sitting would begin at 10am. Somehow, seeing these words signalled the ball had started to roll. But whatever the courts decided, Max felt he could never learn to live with the fact that a young life had ended that day – because of his actions. Folding the letter and picking up the magazine, he went upstairs to his flat. Letting himself in, he tossed the unopened magazine onto the sofa, then moving to the corner of the room he bent to the floor and lifted the electric kettle from the stained metal tray to check whether it contained enough water before replacing it and switching it on. He sat on the edge of the closed sofa bed, allowing the empty mug to drop from his grip and roll backwards then forwards on his curled forefinger. Again, he had an over-riding urge to kick out; the sheer frustration of his life now. Not for the first time, he wanted to clear the decks, leave London and go somewhere in the country where he could breathe and start again. Thoughts like this were just daydreams now, but he had to keep making an effort to raise himself above the blues line.

Max booked a meeting with his solicitor to discuss the court case, as he had been advised to do, and just carried on working conscientiously for his employer while the days turned until his appointment. The solicitor's offices were in the High Road, near the police station, a tall, impersonal slab, facing the pavement.

The opaque glass on the lower front was like a neat slice of ice from a garden pond. He was amused by the juxtaposition of the cracked paving slab that lay at his feet just outside their elegant door. Pushing on the large chrome handle, the power-assisted plate glass door opened and he entered the reception area, a large brightly-lit space with a long, low glass-topped trestle table. Max told the receptionist of his appointment with Mr McAllister, and he was waved to an area with three small sofas, all facing a smaller table of the same type, covered in a neat row of the day's papers.

'He shouldn't be long, Sir,' was almost spoken to his back. He sat, then smiled at her, and took in more of his surroundings. The light oak floor may not have been real, but it created the desired effect, backed by plain white walls and rows of ceiling spotlights. There were just two very large black ink drawings framed in thin black mouldings: one country scene and one city decorating the walls. The surroundings made him realise why the firm's hourly rates were so high. A sound interrupted his thoughts and the lift door opened near the receptionist.

A tall figure advanced towards him, with the almost obligatory outstretched hand. After the greetings, Mr McAllister directed Max towards a door in the reception area, leading to a plain conference room. They both sat, and Stuart McAllister explained he had taken over the case from the duty solicitor who had initially met with Max when he had been arrested. He opened a file to run over the case facts. Max was told that the deceased, Michael Bashley, was well known to the police. He was also informed the police had located the woman Max had seen with the dealer in the alley, but she had not overheard everything that had been said. The solicitor explained he would instruct a barrister on Max's behalf to review the evidence and put his case before the judge. Pleading guilty was bound to help the case, but it was too early to predict the outcome. However, the sentence was mostly likely to be custodial. He was reminded to continue to present himself at the police station weekly under the bail conditions. On the day of the hearing, he should present himself, smartly dressed, at the County Court, an hour before the stated time for the judge's prognostication. After signing papers that might entitle Max to legal aid, McAllister stood up to signify the end of their meeting. Back in the reception after another handshake, Max was again out, crossing the same pavement and wondering if he stood any chance, or no chance, in front of the full might of the law.

On more of an impulse than thirst, he decided to stop in a café. Sitting by the window, he watched a young woman, maybe 20, walk past. She was wearing a colourful coat, and was talking animatedly into her phone, using her hands and flicking her hair back. He thought she had sparkly nails, he wasn't sure. Then she was gone behind other people on the pavements. Nothing unusual about what he saw, but the thought came to him that this simple, unattached observance of a female – of any age - could soon be off the agenda. Finishing his drink, he turned his coat collar up and headed home. Over the weeks leading up his court appearance, he tried to get fitter. He got back into swimming twice a week, went to the gym regularly and started to go to the cinema rather than the pub on Friday night. The weather grew warmer and wetter through February. March took the leftovers and by the beginning of that month, spring was in a rush. Max tried hard to capture small details, like the Forsythia in early bud threatening to flower behind the bins. Daffodils beside hedges, bending their bell heads to the wind's down draft.

The days before he was due to report and surrender himself felt like a carbuncle that was yet to be lanced. His boss at the joinery felt perhaps it was best if Max finished on the Friday before, and with just a handshake or two, he slipped away from the workshop. It was incredibly hard to organise himself in these last few days. His motivation was like a flag with no breeze, lying limp and close to the pole. Preparing for the worst, he bagged all his possessions, using an office stapler to seal the sacks, and put them into his van. His last item was a soft, light zip up hold-all which he would take with him. This he had filled with underwear, a sweater, his wash bag, a block of paper and a couple of pens, a small battery alarm clock, a new packet of razors and several paperbacks. How much of this he would be allowed to keep was unknown.

For his last task, he wrote a short note of explanation to the landlord and gave his mother's address for any mail.

Having cancelled his standing order, the landlord would be round to the flat soon enough. Then, placing the keys on top of his note, he took one last look around him. It was the smell he would remember, the smell of living in a confined space. It lingered like a damp cloth that didn't seem to dry. Turning and walking through the doorway, he pulled the door shut with a jerk of his wrist and started down the stairs. Once outside, shutting the outer door, Max paused, and drew a long breath. Usually, as one door shuts another door opens; but not in this case. The irony almost made him laugh out loud. Then, without looking back, he crossed the road to his van. His plan was simply to disconnect the battery and store the van, with all his gear inside, in his mother's garage. Pulling out of the parking slot, he took the shortest route back on to the main road and as the buildings on either side stripped away his thoughts, the van headed south again.

Glancing down at the fuel gauge, the needle sat firmly on the quarter line. It would be plenty for his needs. The van was put away in the garage, his suit and tie were laid out ready for the next day, along with his bag. The wait began.

In the morning, he travelled back to London by train, with his mother. Arriving at the County Court, his mother met up with Helen and they disappeared towards the visitors' entrance. Max felt he should be more at ease than he was; he wasn't nervous, just a little tense. He went up the steps that had started out wide, narrowing to the two large, open doors leading to an oversized inner door. This door could be pushed open from the outside, but, he noticed, could be automatically locked from the inside. In front of him was a plate glass screen covering several desks. Away to his left was a line of chairs bolted to the floor, several were occupied including one by a sullen teenager, legs wide and outstretched, with arms folded, his head lowered, but not enough to conceal the dirty scowl. Next to the teenager was a woman about the same age as Max.

He assumed this was the boy's mother, and she was agitated, perhaps with the boy, but more likely with the system. Max hovered in front of the glass, looking for a way to get someone's attention, when the door behind the glass opened suddenly. The seated woman leapt to her feet, like a boxer about to defend her corner. She sat again, slowly realising that the police officer was now addressing Max through the speaker. Max slid the letter through the lowest point of the glass and, after looking at it with no expression, she passed it back. Pointing to the seats, she just said: 'Someone will be with you shortly,' and went back through the door, which sprung shut behind her. Still holding his bag, Max sat in the line of chairs, taking care not to sit too close to anyone and infer the want of communication. Placing the hold-all between his feet, Max was aware of a woman nearby who was already studying him. He looked away. There was a clock high on the wall opposite. It was four minutes to nine. His court session was due to start at 10. The door opened again and a policeman pressed a switch that released a door catch to an interview room. Here, they took his hold-all for safe keeping and he was told to put all the belongings he had on him onto the table. Then his clothes were searched. Afterwards, he was instructed to return his belongings to his pockets and to sit at the table.

Max guessed it was about 9.15 when Stuart McAllister arrived. He introduced Max to the barrister who was presenting his written summary and would be on hand for further questions. Shortly after 10, they were called into the courtroom. Fearful anticipation swept over him as he walked through a door into a brighter room with a high ceiling. He was told to sit on one of the polished benches behind the barrister. He watched and waited. The clerk took three steps from his lower desk to the bench and passed some papers to the judge. Max didn't see the clerk's face as he turned, and even then, it didn't register.

The judge leaned forward a little while looking through the papers, rubbed his forefinger along the side of his nose briefly and then motioned the barrister to approach the bench. The barrister disengaged from Max's solicitor and went to stand in front of the judge and the two men spoke briefly. The judge tapped the papers several times with his pen, as if to point out or confirm certain issues and then appear to take in and expel a long breath. Then the barrister withdrew. The judge glanced at the clerk and, with barely a movement, the clerk began to speak.

'Would the accused please stand. State your full name and address,' and they went through a series of questions and responses. Max continued to stand as the judge went through the facts of the case, collated the reports and pronounced a prison sentence of two years. This was followed by the numbing words: 'Take him down.'

Max had two immediate responses to the sentence. The first was profound shock, and then, in some strange way, relief. It had now started, and he was on the long road to the end of this terrible mess. He felt a hand touch him on the shoulder gently, perhaps in some way conveying reassurance, then looking up, he saw the movement in the police officer's eyes and knew his time had come to go. Standing as straight as he could, he glanced to the visitors' gallery. He thought he had heard his mother gasp at the sentence and he could now see she had her hand covering her mouth. It was probably only Helen's support that kept her steady. The door was opened for him, and he looked at the long flights of stairs that he was about to descend. The sound of his and the guard's footsteps echoed off the cream painted brickwork walls. Each of those steps took him to a lower landing where he was turned into an interview room. It was here that he was strip searched and his wallet, lose change, keys and watch were taken from him and listed. This was the first of many acts that would make him feel naked before the crowd, and utterly vulnerable.

They already had his hold-all for checking and they explained he would be given back certain items when he reached the prison. After signing the list of his possessions, he was taken down a corridor and put in a holding cell. They told him they would be back later with more information. This small cell was bare except for a solid bed at one end and a stainless steel WC planted into the floor.

Again, the walls were painted cream over bare brick. He became aware of the dry, musty atmosphere. There was no window. He sat on the edge of the bed and looked around. The only signs he could see of human occupation before his were two sets of what looked like initials beside the door. He had no way to know or measure time; it was simply long time. The first minutes he just sat looking, allowing his eyes to wander the brickwork thinking idly he might spot a miss in the paintwork. Then, tiring of this, he flipped his legs up on the slab and put his hands behind his head, shutting his eyes. This quickly grew uncomfortable. A slow-motion film would have shown him in dozens of different positions. This time was his introduction and initiation to being locked away, away from everything. His one overriding thought was that everyone in his situation would have similar feelings. If he could maintain a sense of humour and not fall into depression, he would be OK. At some point, a mug of tea and sandwiches were passed through the flap in the door to him.

It was nearly three hours, he found out later, before the plate in the door slid back and a voice commanded him to step back and stay away from the door. He did this hesitantly, feeling like a dog might feel; unsure of what might happen next. He needn't have worried. Two police officers entered the cell and with the relaxed tones of people who do the same thing regularly, put cuffs on him. Just looking down at the steel bands that sat on the edge of the knuckle of each of his wrists confirmed his subjugation.

'Where am I going?'

'All in good time, all in good time.'

He was taken down the remaining stairs to an area where there was a lot of activity and a noticeable increase in the noise level. They went out through another steel door and onto a concrete loading ramp. Backed up to this was a police van with its rear doors open. Max later learned that the vehicle was nicknamed 'the sweat box'. Inside were four separate mesh cages with a solid seat in each. He was put in one, then it was locked. There was enough room to stand or sit only. This space was relieved only by a small window, but the intensity remained. Two more prisoners were loaded and locked into cages. For a short while, they were quiet, then, regaining their confidence, they started asking each other what they were in for, already attempting to find a pecking order. The engine started and the van moved. He stared out of the back window, watching people on pavements, looking at traffic lights and shop windows, realising that the mundane would become the memorable. Once on the motorway, the farm land stretched away from the road. Vast fields stood ready for muck-spreading.

Then the sugar beet drillers would take to the fields as the first of the planted crops plugged the land in endless rows. Passing woodland and scattered villages, the motorway eventually drew in suburbs as though on an invisible line of string. Soon after this, the van took a sharp, unexpected turn, throwing him against the side of the cage. His palm slapped the cage automatically to balance himself, and he immediately felt the print of the wire mesh on his skin. Startled, he realised it was slowing down and dropping a gear. Looking out of the window, he saw, for the first time, the walls.

The Lightroom

Chapter 6

Massive, towering. They dominated everything. Seeing those walls for the first time was like a blow to the senses. Modern, like a grotesque work of art, topped by endless thick wire mesh and rolls of razor wire. The centrepiece to the edifice that stood ready to swallow him were its huge doors, which swung open slowly. This was the moment that fear reached into him, sucking at his insides; drawing the very breath from his lungs. The light changed a little, losing its intensity, and it was like being in a section of tunnel. As the van crawled its way to a halt, those huge doors must have swung shut behind him. Although he couldn't see it, in front of them was a steel portcullis. A bell rang some way off and there was the sound of boots on tarmac. Two officers appeared; the first inspected the vehicle, while the other examined the delivery papers. With a casual nod towards the officers, an unseen hand must have touched a switch that started the grinding and winding, winching up the portcullis. It was raised only long enough for the van to move under it into the arrivals and delivery yard, then it returned slowly to the ground, closing with finality. By now, some of the van's occupants were stretching, talking, inquiring, and trying to bury their feelings beneath their own anxiety for what lay ahead. The rough language and false bravado were a smoke screen for the fear that was beginning to surface in all of them.

What Max didn't know yet was that this was Pye Prison, 120 miles North West of London. Mostly built in the early 1990s, it is a Category B prison, extended from the original red brick with a slate roof design, plus three further large blocks and other buildings. There were three wings on each, and although the prison was originally built for 600 inmates, it was now taking up to 750. The latest additions were taken from the van by two Serving Officers, or SOs as Max would later find out; lined up, and then taken through a steel door into the offices.

Their handcuffs were removed. Rubbing his wrists at the soreness, Max looked across the desk as the registration process started. One by one at the end of the room, they were strip searched behind a screen. First, he removed his top half holding his arms up. He and his clothes were checked. He was then instructed to put his top back on and remove all of his lower clothing. Squatting and leaning well forward, he was then checked for anal tubes. This was the degrading step that seemed to peel away the last layer of his dignity. He felt belittled and de-humanised by it. Then, moving as though on a conveyer belt, they were directed into the neighbouring shower stall.

Stripping and walking naked, feeling the cold tile floor beneath his feet, he stepped into the fall of water. It was just off warm. An officer instructed: 'Use the soap,' pointing to a block of green carbolic in a holding tray. The smell was sharp with a toxic edge, reminding him of the stuff used for washing clothes when he was a small boy. Standing naked afterwards, he was given a pile of clothes and a small towel. He dried himself quickly, in a hurry to cover himself. Grey was to be the uniform colour for him now. Tracksuit bottoms, T-shirt and sweatshirt; all stamped with the large letters: PYE HMP. The canvas slip-on shoes nearly fitted. He could feel the coarseness of the clothing next to his skin and the abrasiveness of the shoes. The breaking down of self, the conformity and the feeling of wiped identity was beginning. The clothes they arrived in were taken away to the laundry, to be returned at a later date. Moving into another office, Max sat on a red plastic seat in a row, all bolted to the floor. His small group awaited further registration. Everything here, he noted, was bolted to something fixed. Looking around him, not holding any eye contact for too long, he saw one of the group holding his head in his hands. His limbs were shaking; he was clearly very agitated. He had seen all this before; the man was probably a user.

When Max's turn came, he stood, feeling uncomfortable, then moved to the desk where his fingerprints were taken. The officer told him: 'Two steps back, stand facing me on the red line.'

As he did so, his photograph was taken against the white wall. It was that blank, staring, numbered photo that shouts 'convict' at the world. Health statements were registered with diseases and drug use, if any, then they were given prison and status numbers. A low-sided plastic crate slid monotonously back and forwards across the table with a scratching sound as their possessions were returned to them, minus anything considered suspicious. Money brought in was credited to their canteen accounts. Their induction followed. Max's group joined other new intakes, creating a larger group of around 25, and they were all seated in a lecture room. SOs officiated, backed by several trustees who were watching every detail, looking for any small give-aways that could become gossip – it was the staple diet in places like this. Before any details were given, anyone who had not been to prison before was asked to raise his hand. He was knocked back by the response, as only three people did so, and he was one of them. Soon, he would realise that re-offending was the biggest problem on both sides, with proper skills and education (and the lack of them) in the middle. The induction covered prison rules, healthcare, punishments, and jobs courses; and then, like kids being shown around a new school, they were taken on a tour.

Watch, listen and learn was the mantra. Clutching their bundles of prison-issue possessions, they walked through the roadways, which were all boxed and fully meshed with intermittent gates for crossing into separated exercise yards. These yards were partitioned by further mesh fences, topped by endless rolls of razor wire. Streetlight standards, to throw light on any dark night sky, were marked out at regular intervals. Cameras were everywhere. Inside, they were embedded in every ceiling, outside they were on poles covering every angle.

The poles were anti-climb with more razor wire. It was early evening and some of the yards still held people. Those by the fence line came close, and, linking fingers with the mesh, they winked and threw kisses and taunts at the newcomers. They prodded and poked, hoping for a reaction. It was like school, but with menace and the threat of violence stark and up front. Max felt other prisoners' eyes on him, weighing him for weakness at any opportunity. When they arrived at the canteen, the last meal of the day was already being served. They joined the queue, collecting a multi-partitioned tray of food, wholesome, and filling, but not imaginative. The final show was his cell. It was occupied, although not at that moment. Until 7.30pm, it was association time for communal and social activities on that wing, including pool, radio, TV, and general conversation. Seeing the thin, bare mattress on the lower bunk, Max dropped his bundle onto it.

'OK then, any questions,' said the Community Officer, who seemed keen to get away.

Max just nodded; he could find no words.

'Right then.'

The CO left, leaving the door to the hallway open. Max separated his bundle, taking the blankets and the thin pillow and making up his bed as best he could. Then, for want of something else to do, he folded all his remaining clothing in neat piles and placed them in a row under his bunk, putting the rest of his belongings in a locker. He used the standard issue stainless steel WC that was inset into the floor and rinsed his hands under the cold tap in the attached fitment that passed as a basin. Without thinking, he shook his hands vigorously and then wiped them on his clothes. He looked at his surroundings, mentally measuring the space that was to be his only refuge. There was a narrow window, just above eye level, with its vents open to a dark sky. A small TV and a few personal items appeared to be his cellmate's only possessions.

Max could see no books or reading material and he wondered what sort of man would be sharing this room with him. Having read somewhere that 25% of prisoners had the reading and writing skills of an 11-year- old, he wasn't expecting an easy time. He didn't have to wait long before a man in his late 30s came in. He was already nearly bald, slightly shorter than Max, plenty of muscle, but fat with it. Max's brain was racing and he let out the single word: 'Hello.' He didn't get an answer straight away. The man first hauled himself to the top bunk and dangled his legs over the side. He said nothing while sizing Max up, then said: 'We're changing bunks, mate.'

Max stood his ground, saying - without taking his eyes off his cell-mate: 'I like this one and I intend to keep it.' To this, he received a smile and then the other man just said: 'Fair enough.' A short while later, his cell-mate said: 'So, what are you in for?' Max tried humour first. 'Mistaken identity, I shouldn't be here really.' To which the reply came back fast: 'And I told the judge I didn't do it, but he didn't believe my story,' laughing at his own joke. The ice was broken. Roy was a habitual offender, having been out for just three months after serving time for a robbery. Then he stole a car and, when stopped by police, he had punched one of them - so back inside he went. The doors were locked at 7.45 and the TV went on. Max endured it until the lights went out at 9.45. As he lay on his back in the darkness, he thought of Roy above him. He felt easier now about his cell-mate, but could see no way for any friendship to develop. One day done. With good behaviour, Max had about 500 to go. He would count those days every night.

It is said that the first night inside is the longest. His sleep was broken by anger and fear, disturbed like a sea after a storm. The prison alarm went off first at 6am. A slow and increasingly loud piercing noise, in blasts that filled every ear on the block.

A few minutes later, after dressing, Max picked up his towel and wash bag from his locker, and, hearing the door release, he followed Roy's lead out to stand on the landing and await the first roll call and headcount.

Resting his hand on the rail, he shifted his weight, looking downwards through the mesh divider to the landings below. He watched one of the morning SOs listing each prisoner by the numbers they shouted out. It felt oppressive, looking at this over-filled space. Gradually, the noise started to build as, group by group, they moved towards the showers. Eventually, his landing was accounted for and he was on his way to the shower block. It was here that he was absolutely alert. He learned to avoid staying in the water longer than it took for a quick rinse off, and he never held eye contact. Any spark could ignite trouble, and it was always closer than he thought. There were toilets there as well but he never used them, preferring to use the one in his cell. Locked in again after returning to their cells, they waited for his wing to be released for breakfast.

And so it continued throughout the day - being counted and being locked, being counted and being locked. At 8am, work began for most; the kitchen staff had started at 5am. The prison was run on a very strict routine that underscored every official action. It was interspersed by prisoners' actions that were off-piste. He saw the first of this when one afternoon, during the exercise hour in the yard, two small plum-size packages came over the wall, propelled by sling shots. They were picked up immediately, after a few scuffles, and secreted away or perhaps passed around to confuse anyone watching, and then stuffed into cheeks, or anal tubes, and brought back into the wing. Drugs were always available. Most of them were just walked in every day, through the main gates with the prison staff. One evening, the barber who sat on his wing daily was off his head with someone Max didn't recognise. They were both smoking Spice, and they were soon on the floor of a cell near his, occasionally twitching, writhing, with their tongues lolling.

When this happened, sometimes they came round and it was fine, sometimes things got complicated and ambulances were called. Paramedics would do their best, but sometimes it ended badly. In this case, the next day a new man was holding the barber's clippers. Sometimes there was a dislocated fascination with other people's self-administered pain. In these situations, it was all about his own survival. It was the hard men who controlled the drugs that permeated through the very fabric of the prison organisation in unimaginable ways. The evenings seem longest. Maybe it was the darkness. The monotony of time passing. It was measured out in equal days, collecting like a dripping tap into a bowl of water. He had reached 18 days now. Keeping fit was close to an obsession for most prisoners and the gym provided that outlet. But not for Max. He had always hated the gym, preferring to swim or walk. Here, continuous walking around the yard was not advisable. Settling for a simple set of well-designed exercises - press-ups with yoga he called it – he completed his own routine for half an hour each morning. He enjoyed the flexing and tightening of the sinews and muscles taking the strain of his body. The second half-hour was spent sitting on one of the many benches for more meditative exercise. The first time he sat there, he looked, as everyone does, above the heads of the people in the yard, across the high, wire-topped outer wall. The low cloud compressed the horizon flat and squeezed the colour from the scene. His eyes moved to the belt of trees stretching their leafless limbs, both thick and thin, towards the sky. The rooks cried their repetitive call and were starting to gather high up in their clefts. It would be some time before he saw the bottom half of those trees, with their entire strength and beauty.

There lay the symbolic significance of his dislocation. Sun or rain, this pattern would become the basis to a habit that would hold. Max had worked out early how his canteen account functioned, who to see about buying things he needed and how the prison's postal system worked.

He had transferred money to his mother's account before he came inside, so that she could regularly top up his prepaid card with the prescribed amounts. The prison phones enabled him to have valuable moments of conversation in the evenings, but the calls produced mixed feelings in him afterwards. The lightness of emotional conversation was offset by a vague feeling of emptiness when the call had ended; an ache that needed time to soak away. Two brief phone calls had brought his first visitors. The first was his mother, who travelled by train and then a taxi. Sitting opposite him under the glare of guards and cameras, she was clearly nervous and trying to hold it all together. Leaning forwards, with her hands clasped at the edge of the table, she opened the conversation.

'Oh, love,' and then faltered. Starting again: 'Are you OK?'

He tried to reassure her he was coping well, but the strain showed in her face. She was swimming in unknown waters. The noise of people echoed around them while they talked, and Max was aware she was probably hiding her real pain at seeing him in prison. Worry carves a deep furrow and she was carrying this weight badly. Max was aware that the ripples from his actions, and the death of the dealer, went on and on to a shore out of sight, affecting people he would never know. A week later, his boss from the joinery came to see him. It was a surprise to Max when he was told who had arrived. Apparently, he had business in the Midlands, although Max didn't believe his story. He felt, rather, that it was a show of unity, as his boss recounted that he had also been in trouble as a younger man. He had buried his past deep, worked hard and climbed away from it.

The prison policy was that work occupies minds and time, so Max was given various options, and after an interview of sorts he was accepted for a job in education. His working day was spent in the large room next to the library in the old building, which still held boxes of items at one end, ready to go into storage.

Alongside two trustees, Max's role was to help inmates of any age advance their reading and writing and learn how to express themselves better. He did this by helping them to write letters and by listening to them read. The irony of this role was not lost on Max. He had struggled at school because of his dyslexia, which had not been recognised at the time, or diagnosed, and his poor writing and reading kept him at the bottom of the class.

He had learned to deal with it over the years, and always tried to avoid filling in any complicated forms in front of others. He empathised with those who struggled with the written word, and his time with these men led him to reflect on his own back story. At the age of eight,

Max's father has insisted the boy be sent away to school; and for the next four years, what he got was an old-fashioned education, heavily loaded with discipline. He had wanted to please his father and tried hard for the first year, but the reports always told the same story - he was usually at the end of the also-rans. He had never been bullied, but he realised that violence under some circumstances would work. The only way was to stand up for yourself and be counted when the time came. The day the entrance exam results came out for the next school, Max had been in the dormitory, sitting on the side of his bed, having opened the brown envelope downstairs. Reading its contents, he went to seek out some quiet spot, not knowing what else to do. Seconds later, the door opened and a group of young boys flooded in, not giving him time to arrange his defence. The chatter was all about the exam results, their average marks; but more importantly, which schools they were going to go to next. Max sat silently on the side of the bed, hoping somehow he might not be noticed. All too quickly, heads turned in his direction, to involve him in their euphoric scene. As his mouth opened to respond, his eyes filled with tears. The reward for bewilderment in the classroom and near bottom of all the classes had resulted in an average of less than half of that needed to go to any of their named schools.

What had gone before was irrelevant now. The boys just drifted away, but those moments made a mark on him forever. The sense of failure never left him. It lay like a seed inside his soul, resting, waiting for the damp warm moment when it could spring to life again. It followed him like a half-shadow, ready to damage him another time when he weakened. He had decided to build his defences - independence, aggression, success, wealth – but he knew that none of these would completely overcome his unsound footings. One school gave way to another, and his father had long disappeared out of his life. Finally, after grinding out the butt end of his school years, Max left the classroom with the realisation of how utterly unprepared he was for what was coming next. His future. A few short weeks at home and an agency found him a clerical job in London. The numbness of this beginning would jolt and shock him in ways he had not known before. He waited like a bystander for his life to roll out. Bag packed, a suit with two trousers, white shirts and assorted extras, he had set out to the station. After all the talk and advice from his mother, he was leaving on a train to London with the address of a hostel in Euston in his back pocket. His first steps to an uncertain future had begun.

He felt detached during the train journey, but that all changed with the noise and commotion of the vast station. His guts tightened a little as he started to make his way to the hostel on the underground, with only one mistake with the choice of platform. He made a note to use the following day - a Sunday - to do a dummy run to work, to be sure he wouldn't be late on his first day. At the final tube station, he emerged with his bag. Fumbling in his pocket, he produced the folded paper with the hostel address. The newspaper seller casually looked first at Max and then at the piece of paper he was holding and, without a word, just pointed with an ink-stained finger to a small side road leading behind a large department store. Perhaps, he thought, the seller had seen many before him come this same way. Max was signed in and he paid a week in advance before being shown his room. Looking round, he took in the high white ceiling and the two-tone, cream and pale green painted walls. Three beds, three wardrobes, three chairs, three bedside cabinets with a top draw - all matching. A mirror hanging strangely by a chain on an angle was the only adornment to the wall surfaces. Looking again, he realised that one set was unused. Putting his bag down, Max reached out and prodded the bed, seeming to test for softness; then, in one swooping movement, he flung himself backwards on to it. Crossed his legs, he put his hands behind his head and looked, smiling, at the white ceiling. The two young men he shared with came from the Midlands and, although from very different backgrounds to his, appeared happy to have his company. Things changed for him right from the start. Out went the pyjamas, he toned down his accent and - most importantly - he had a new haircut. A few weeks slipped by before he left his clerical job, bored to a standstill with it, and moved on to more money and outside work as a delivery driver's assistant. He liked the informality of it but, although he told himself it didn't matter what he did, he vaguely felt his mother would not approve. So, he just didn't tell her. Life was good. Friends, girls, and good times; they all came easily and so this transient life had its beginnings.

The Lightroom

Chapter 7

On slow days in prison, Max had plenty of time to recall events in his early life, playing scene after scene in his mind. He had drifted into carpentry after labouring on a building site, signing up for a day-release course at a local college to get his diploma. Eventually, he gained Level 3 and his boss let him loose with a saw on repetition work. Gradually, his confidence rose and he took on private jobs at the weekends. Finally, with a deep breath, he kicked off on his own. The freedom of working for himself, and being his own boss suited him well. Now, helping others here in prison provided another source of pleasure and, in a strange way, sense of fulfilment. There was one skinny kid – Eddy - with flat hair that fell straight from his crown, and a mouth full of teeth like a rocky outcrop. He looked much younger than his actual age - 25 - as he came hesitantly to Max's table. Sitting alongside Max, he said nothing for a few moments, then rubbing the palms of his hands slowly backwards and forwards on the table, he started to talk. He had a seven-year-old son who he rarely saw. He wanted to connect with him somehow, but didn't know how. If he could write a letter, perhaps lots of letters, to him, say something funny on a birthday card, without expecting anything in return, then who knows? He lifted his hands, widening his arms, and just shrugged.

'Can you write?' asked Max. 'How is your writing?'

'I can, sort of, but slow. It's the spelling and stuff.'

Max began: 'Writing is a form of expressing yourself, like speaking, but just because you can do one well doesn't mean you can do the other one equally well. It requires a bit of thought before you write.'

Eddy's eyes were fixed on him, a light was there. He was engaged.

'So, what do you want to tell your boy? Shut your eyes and imagine he was here with you now. Talk out loud, it sometimes helps.'

Eddy started again: 'It's not his fault, it's my fault things went wrong. I want to tell him not to follow me down the same street, to work hard at school, to make something of himself.' His voice trailed off.

'That's great,' said Max. 'Carry on, as if he were sitting here, not me.'

'I'd say - all these rows with your mum, all the bad feelings, none of it is your fault. I think of you a lot and I want good things to happen for you.'

Laying a sheet of paper on the table in front of them, Max passed over one of his pens. Eddy leaned on the table almost covering the paper with his body and wrote, hesitatingly, the first two words: *Helo Kyle.*

He straightened, chewing the end of the pen, deep in his laboured thoughts. Max wrote on a second sheet *Hello Kyle*, to include the second *l*, and then stopped. Eddy, noticing this, leaned forward onto the page again and sweated in another stroke of the pen. Slowly and painstakingly, he pushed a word at a time across the page with his finger. It took a while, the lines weren't too straight, and sometimes he asked about a word and practised it on another sheet of paper first, but the letter gradually grew to a stream of thoughts, conveying his message to his son. Eddy ended the letter with: *I will rite again.* Then he put his name underneath. Silently, while he was doing this, Max wrote the correct spelling in larger letters on the second sheet, underling the missing letter. Eddy raised his head, smiled, and returned to the page. Passing it to Max, he said: 'Can you do the envelope?'

Distracted, Max hadn't heard. He was watching a bluebottle pitch on the table then drive itself repeatedly towards the corner of a book. Its trajectory held him for a moment, before he turned back towards Eddy. 'I'm sorry, what did you say?'

'The envelope, can you do it for me?'

'Yes, sure, tell me the address. It's good to keep this going. Let's meet up again the same time next week.'

Of course, Max knew that writing the address on the envelope also meant putting the stamp on it. Eddy had now moved away, turning only to mumble his thanks. Picking up the envelope and writing the address, Max flicked open the folded sheet to see the writing again. What lifted him was the last line – *Eddy*. It had a single line through it, and the other word written alongside, was: *Dad*.

The job was good for Max. It helped him maintain or even improve his status, the measure by which small privileges were given. Years of practise had enabled him to overcome his worst spelling mistakes, and he felt comfortable helping these men, whose educational levels were way below his own. He learned that most prisoners fenced in their emotions, and some of those he helped seemed OK, even reasonable. Then he found out what they had done to be in prison. The fighting was savage. Sometimes home-made implements were used, and that unnerved him the most. Once Max saw a man, on release from morning lock up, spot a prisoner he had an argument with the previous day. He ran at him, launching himself, kicking, screaming and finally stabbing the other man. Nobody interfered. By the time the guards got to him and the paramedics arrived, the man was in a coma and blood was all over the place. The nutter was hauled off for solitary and not seen again, probably moved to another wing.

Even though there was careful segregation, sometimes things went badly wrong. The bullying and intimidation were the sporadic occurrences that came to the surface from time to time. There was an established pecking order. Max was careful to keep a still tongue; he stood up for himself, but was in no way rude, insulting or confrontational. These things mattered. He first met Tunksy on one his trips to the library. He had been taking a book from a shelf when several others fell to the floor. Max picked one up and an open, unguarded conversation developed. It was relaxed, jocular and warm. Tunksy was in his late 50s maybe; tall, angular, and he spoke without rushing.

From this simple meeting came the grains of friendship. His company was good for Max, he was sharp in discussions; he had an uncanny way of picking the corner of an argument, and peeling it back, only to spear Max with his point of view. Once, when they were talking, Max asked him why he had what appeared to be an elaborate coloured tattoo of a playing card on the inside of his left arm. Tunksy turned his arm over and, using his forefinger, pointed at it and said: 'This is a tarot card.'

Stopping to scratch the side of his nose with the same finger, he went on: 'Tarot cards originated in 15th century

Europe, and by the 18th century they were being used for divination in the form of teratology. There are four suits, each with 14 cards, including face cards.' Pausing only for a breath, he added: 'Also, there is a 21-card trump suit, topped by a last single card - the top trump - that trumps anything. And that's called: the fool.'

He tapped the tattoo again.

'Ah…. But why the left arm?'

'It was fate, I could have chosen the right.'

He gave Max a wink and a smile. Tunksy believed we make our own life chances, but, because of our failings, we squander them. Max found out from the many conversations they shared, that Tunksy had been brought up on a hard street. He was in for the second time for armed robbery. In prison, people took you how they found you.

It was after breakfast, on day 57 when routines had started to fit, that Max was told to box his belongings. He was being transferred. This was on the cards for every prisoner, but as it was earlier than unexpected, it unnerved him. He changed into his own clothes, and, keeping only the prison shoes, he boxed all of his possessions and was gone from his cell. Leaving his cellmate Roy and others behind, he left that landing for the last time.

Accompanied by an SO through the secure section of the prison, he reached the final bar gate. Before passing through to the offices, he was handcuffed. Raising his hands, he felt the weight of his shackles and started to wonder what lay ahead. With his first experience of being in prison behind him, now it was more curiosity than fear. The process of decision-making was no longer his.

Normal worries, such as where to sleep, what to eat and how to afford it, were no longer his responsibility. His world had shrunk to one main preoccupation: how to pass time. When the re-registration was complete, he was taken with others through the same steel doors to the delivery yard, where he stood briefly in the sharpening wind while the rear doors of the sweat box opened. As he was being placed in a cage at the back of the vehicle, he asked where they were going. This time, as the cage door locked, the response that bounced back was: 'Collections before we deliver.' Then the rear doors banged shut and were locked. He didn't hear the portcullis, but the van moved, then stopped again under the archway. He did hear the loud scraping sound as the main doors opened behind him. The engine revved and settled, and he knew his life was moving forward. Turning his head to the window, it was the prison that started to move away from him. It seemed an inordinate amount of time since Max had seen the beauty and strength of whole trees against a proper horizon.

He saw people on the pavements all talking, walking and fiddling with their phones. Just for a moment, he was transfixed. Amused, he settled back, shifting himself on the wire mesh seat subconsciously, knowing comfort would be beyond him. He felt the world was somehow rushing by him. Just like the view. The van made another scheduled stop and three younger prisoners were incarcerated in the other cages. The youngest had the loudest mouth, running off like a foul drain. In the end, when there was no response, he fell silent. It took two hours or so to reach their destination. Having gauged the position of the sun, he knew they were traveling eastwards. The land was flattening now with that slight haze of drizzle in the air. The fields of potatoes had been sown, occasional buildings and far away villages all fell away behind him, being stripped from his view. His body was taut with anxiety by the time they arrived.

Cottesloe Prison was comparatively new, built in the late 1980s in the middle of the flat lands of Suffolk. It was on the site of what had been the Great Hall on the Marcham Estate, which fell foul of death duties after the First World War. The family had accrued unimaginable wealth from British manufacturing interests and land investment. The home farms and forestry, although shrunken in size, were now part of the prison. The land was a rich, soft sandy soil; forgiving to the plough and farmer alike. Five hundred inmates were held in this prison and soon Max would be one of them. The outside doors opened like jaws and then snapped shut behind them. Inner gates opened, allowing the van to swing round and back into an unloading bay. Under the cover of bright lights, they were taken to the registration area, and so began a complete re-run of being absorbed into a new fold. Max was given his prison number and an improved status number, and, after the induction lecture, new clothes, food and several checks, he was taken to his new cell. The walk seemed less intimidating than last time, but his sense of fear grew when he considered who he might find as his cell mate. He was taken onto D wing, past the table tennis and pool players, who seemed to pay little attention to him, and finally to cell number 17, on a lower landing. The door was open. The cell was empty. At the doorway, the SO said: 'You will have a new cell-mate over the next few days, when the new intakes are allotted.' Turning, Max could see the SO was being friendly, and acknowledged this with the simple response of a nod and: 'OK.'

Testing the lower bunk for comfort he unpacked his crate and lay for a short while with his legs crossed at the ankles and his hands behind his head. How strange it was to be among so many, and yet be completely alone.

His real feelings would remain buried as deep as secrets and expressed only in these timeless, one-way conversation. Rising later, he sorted his few possessions, and took occupation of the space he had - just four metres by three metres. The bell for lock up went at 8.15pm and, after the checks, the bolts shot across at 8.30pm. Posted through each door with a shout shortly afterwards came the breakfast packs. He tried reading, but was restless. Standing, flexing his legs, he stood on tiptoe, realising immediately that he was starting his warm-up exercises for swimming. Carrying on, he looked through the cell window past the outer bars and into the blackness. The clock was ticking, it was just that he couldn't hear it. At 10pm the lights went out.

Waking, instantly alert, he was surrounded by darkness. Even in the stillness of the moment he knew it was the distinct, singular smell of tobacco from a burning cigarette. So near, so real, yet there was nothing. Lying perfectly still, his mind was sharp, gradually this feeling of knowing, faded to acceptance. It was a half-awake dream of an imagined presence. The first night had passed easily. On his own, tired but relaxed, he had slept until the alarm at 7am. Reaching to the floor, he turned on the small radio, and adjusted the volume slightly. He listened to the radio for a few seconds as the prison alarm slipped to a lower pitch. The news headlines came to him with digital clarity. The Prime Minister was in Brussels at a European summit meeting. Max smiled, thinking of the total irrelevance to his own life of anything he was hearing. He pulled on his tracksuit trousers and socks, stretching as he scratched himself. He turned to the basin to have a wash and at 7.45 he heard the announcement: 'Doors Open.' The steel bolts shot back in unison across the landings, and he heard: 'Roll Call'. And so it started, again. Later that morning, job allotments took place. He was told that, starting the following week, he would be one of two men, chosen perhaps for their higher trusted status, to work in the forestry section.

They would be taken by a prison driver to the site of a mobile saw mill and put to work, and then collected at the end of the day. They were warned that any infringement of this opportunity to work outside would result in heavy loss of parole as well as privileges. Max and the other chosen prisoner met up in the exercise yard on a blustery day and were taken through to the offices. Outside in the delivery yard, they climbed into the battered old Land Rover. The prison gates opened and as the vehicle moved away it blew out a long smoky cough before the engine settled to its tune. After about a mile, they left the tarmac, joining a deeply-rutted track made worse by the several wet months. The Land Rover slewed its way, first one way then the other, as the four-wheel drive engaged, fighting to bite. When the land rose a little, so it drained and the vehicle covered the last part of a mile in the true manner it was designed for. The small site was a clearing that had already been stripped completely, leaving only the low roots. Beside the track lay a long pile of cut trunks, evenly stacked in four- or five-metre lengths. The Land Rover pulled up and as they got out, a man in his 60s came towards them. He was tall, but stooped, and was wearing stained bib and braces overalls, streaked with dirt and oil. Max watched him nod an acknowledgement to the driver, a few words passed, he laughed at an unheard joke, then came over to them. The Land Rover belched more fumes as it left. The man had heavy grey stubble and wore a baseball hat with the curved frayed peak turned down. He took off his gloves to reveal large hands that had seen a lifetime of labour.

Smiling, he put out a hand in turn to both of them, introducing himself as Alfred Matheson, pointing as if to confirm his name on the side of the open truck and trailer. He ran through the set up. His son drove the small bob cat with large twin forks for lifting the poles and helped operate the mobile timber milling machine, which was capable of taking trunks of five-metre lengths and just under a metre in diameter comfortably.

Once set, it could trim, then cut, to any size required. Max and his co-worker Craig were primarily lifters and shifters, moving the cut timbers, stacking and racking them correctly on the trailer and clearing up. Alfred kitted them both out with fluorescent jackets, hard hats, work gloves and ear protectors. In the background, the thump of the diesel engine started up. The beats settled quickly to a regular rhythm. Matheson took two quick steps to a control panel, removed the glove from his left hand and pressed several knobs in quick succession. The rig reacted immediately to his command. With a heavy judder the hydraulic rams clamped the first trunk. Its ends were clean cut with a chain saw, and it was loaded and clamped by the bob cat. The arch of the saw moved down the trunk, seemingly floating, the blade effortlessly cut the exact measure with a screaming pitch, changing only when the cut was complete. The trunk was rolled and the process repeated until it was cut free of bark. When this was complete, the trunk was transformed to a block form. The saw was re-set, in order to cut the wood into planks. That day they were cutting 100x50mm in five-metre lengths, and so the machine ran for most of the day. Slowly and steadily, the pile grew towards a full truck. From the moment the saw started, it was the smell of the pine in the Douglas Fir that leapt up to Max's nostrils; a sweet, clean fresh smell, almost a calming balm that he would remember, and forever associate with this place.

Lunch and the afternoon passed and, by 5.30pm, they disassembled the mill, and the bob cat was loaded behind the truck. The Land Rover arrived and Max and Craig talked on the way back, the work having drawn them in. Craig was an unassuming man, softly spoken, diffident even, who had just one month to go before release, after serving two-and-a-half years for fraud. As a family man, this had tipped him over the edge during his first year and resulted in a severe breakdown, which he never really got over.

Craig's case brought into question the whole issue of crime and punishment, which Max would think over many times more in the coming months. Arriving back at the prison, they crossed the delivery yard quickly. About to shut the steel door, something made him look upwards, movement maybe. He focused on a self-seeded Buddleia shrub growing out of a crack in the top of the chimney stack. Clinging, growing from the mortar line, and bending with the wind, in all its adversity it would one day soon bloom into purple flower. Instantly, this gave Max the strength to hope for his future. Like the shrub, he would need to hold on in order to flourish. The last meal of the day was kept for them and they then parted to go to their own landings to shower before the lock in. Leaving the canteen, Max picked up email messages from his mother. He was amused for a second, at the irony. He had to write physical letters and she had to use email. A shock awaited him in his cell; a new occupant. The young Dexter was a surly kid, well-built, over six foot and smelling of tobacco. Max was pleased now that he had pencilled a 'no smoking' sign on the cell wall to avoid early confrontation. The lad talked quickly, throwing his words around. There was an air of confidence about him; clearly, he had been this way before. His speech was hard to understand - fast, guttural, from the street, but he was personable. Given some time, he hoped they would wear in together - like pebbles on a beach.

Max spent about four weeks cutting on the mill. Although it didn't challenge him in any way, he enjoyed being outside and working manually. The first few weeks saw the weather turn drier and the mud harden. The evergreen plantations had grown close, as though holding hands, cutting out the light. Little grew beneath, only seeds lay waiting in their shadows. On the way back one evening, Craig told Max that at his lowest, he had thoughts of suicide. It was the Samaritans that he had turned to; those understanding, gentle phone calls had saved him from the abyss, he said.

It was the boring monotony of confinement that made some among them want to bang their heads against their own perceived wall. Then, one morning, Craig wasn't there. He must have been released. Just like a bird, he had disappeared from view. The cutting and the poling eventually finished on two sites and the Mathesons moved on. Gone like a circus from the town field.

Max now followed an exercise routine in his cell in the evening, while Dexter was off on the prowl around the landings. It was the creeping boredom of filling time that drove Max down, like a slow drum roll, a rattling emptiness inside him. His concentration span for reading, writing or even radio and television seemed short some days, and so it all became self-perpetuating. He remembered how Craig's depression had burst out of him with silent sobs behind the trailer on more than one occasion. Max had gone to him once, thinking it might help in some way, but in this environment, that move was a mistake.

One evening, just before lights out, Max forgot to count the days he had now done. Later, although he didn't know it yet, he would start counting the other way. He had been transferred to a new group for fencing instruction. Four of them, all trustees, were an odd, mixed bunch, selected for the trust the prison staff had in them, and not their skills. There was a fraudster and an ex-lawyer. Both men had golden tongues, and soft white hands that in a previous life had lifted nothing heavier than a desk telephone. There was also an uneducated east London car thief, with a set of fold-over teeth and a character to match. The echo of all their voices in the countryside was like a bag of noisy spanners among well-tuned violins. Often stripped to the waist, sweating continually, they laboured. The long, hot summer sun burned dark tans onto their bodies. The softest hands shed their bloody blisters, that retuned later with earned callouses.

They dug post holes, using the long-armed post spades, and with the wire tensioner and the staple gun, whacked in those same pine posts and laid the barbed wire tight. And so, across fields and woodlands, the summer stretched out for them. It was on one of those afternoons, when Max was winding the tensioner with a final twist on the handle, when the barbed wire sprung from the housing, whipping back in the air. The strand caught him on the edge of his shoulder and the uppermost part of his arm. Lowering himself to the ground, he let out a hissing sound as the initial fireball of pain bit. Blood ran down his arm, thick and sticky. It seeped between the backs of his fingers and finally into the dirt. A shadow covered part of him and a voice said: 'I remember spraying a wing that colour once.' It wasn't a serious wound, more of an inconvenience. Standing again, using his T-shirt to apply pressure, Max drew a deep breath and then at the very top of his lungs, shouted the single word 'FUCK' as loudly as he could, while walking away up the slope. Frustration had overcome him. This whole fucking thing was more than just an inconvenience, his life had ceased. He was someone else now. Stopping well away from the others, allowing his head to drop down, he took a long look at the grass growing around and under his feet. Slowly he nodded, recognising the futility of his own situation. Even though he was out here, he was incarcerated. Then he turned and walked back to the others repeating his mantra out loud: 'One day at a time. One day at a time.'

The lacerations healed but, at the end of the summer, his shoulder was troubling him and he was transferred at his own request. After the doctor's report confirmed impinged rotary cuff, rest was prescribed as the best cure, and the move was easy. It was really a need for change, to stem the increasing feeling of despondency he felt each day. This senseless waiting, always watching the clock; it was useless time, like running in the wrong direction. From his work station in the library, he watched as the summer collapsed.

By October, the temperature cooled, the outdoor tan had faded, and the rain came. First, in gentle showers, shaken by the winds, then with growing intensity, beating its irregular slapping against the window panes, driven by those first storms. His visitors were few, but regular. His mother had been every month. Sometimes Helen came too. Occasionally, others came, gingerly with their curiosity in front of them. He wrote letters and received cleared emails, all these things helped, but they weren't the answer. The answer was out there, somewhere over the wire. Christmas was stark and bleak for him. To some inmates and screws, it was just another day, but there was no work for the prisoners; doors were open all afternoon, and there was turkey and roast potatoes. For distraction on his wing, he arranged a pool knock-out competition, having bought two men's magazines as the first prize. For some inmates with families, this was a wretched time. A depth of loneliness overcame some people at the turn of the year, and so it was that early January morning, when the doors unlocked with that familiar snapping sound, the echo still in the air, that they found Igor Barucz, hanging by some tied up cloths in a cell at the far end of the wing. He had tied the cloths to the window bars and twisted it round and round his neck until his life popped out of his eyes. A sad and unnecessary end to a human life. There was a splash of interest for a while after the clearance, before Igor was forgotten. The memory of him swallowed by the prison's routine.

On March 18 at 10am, Max was released on licence. He would have supervisory meetings, and there were some conditions attached, but he was free. He did look back, but only briefly, almost to remind himself of what he had to forget. The day was cold, as he slid into the back seat of the taxi, carrying only the same small hold-all he had taken in with him. He had chosen to go home on his own because he wanted to spare his mother both the journey and the memory of the place he left behind.

The taxi driver was civil and smiled at him just before they pulled away. The driver had probably seen it all many times before - the usual destination: the nearest railway station. Max was twitchy, looking at people as though they might see the mark on him, but no one took any notice of him. It was all so novel. Moving freely, making his own decisions. He bought a paper and two sausage rolls with a large tea, then moved to a bench to wait for his train. It wasn't long, and he was away. The journey was easy.

Coming into Liverpool Street station, he took the tube to Waterloo. The blandness of normality was intoxicating to him at every turn. He then caught the train south to his mother's. Spring was upon them, and Max took some long walks. The buds and young leaves had been quickly followed by daffodils, backed by wild garlic, with the scent lifting from the floor of nearby woodland. Then came the bluebells among the broad-leafed trees, their shimmering haze on a multi-green. Eventually, returning to London, he started clawing his way back to some sort of life.

The Lightroom

Chapter 8

Max got up and dressed for a working day. He whacked down a mug of tea, then started loading the van with his tools. Keeping them inside was a necessity, as theft and vandalism were rife in this part of London. He headed into the traffic, going west towards the house where a kitchen had been delivered for him to fit. He had been given pre-paid parking for this job, and it would be easier at this time of the day to find a bay. He was let in by young woman who gave him a smile, probably of relief that he had turned up, albeit a little late. Fortunately, the flat-pack kitchen, with all the fittings, lay in the hall on top of the new work tops. He checked the lists. The electrician had moved the cooker socket and cut in extra sockets, so he could first isolate the hot and cold water supply and then remove all the old units. He worked quickly and methodically and things progressed well as the day trawled by. By late afternoon, the new carcasses were assembled and fitted, wall units hung on neat and tight, all square and with level joins. All the doors were covered, ready to put on later. Using his big mitre jig, he cut the first work top then the second, bolting the join together tightly underneath before fixing it firmly to the base units. Running a hand along and over the corner joint, he checked it passed the litmus test. Slowly and very carefully, he measured the cut for the sink. He knew this was not a time for mistakes. First, using the cordless drill, he made the pilot holes. Then he steadied himself before easing the jig saw along the pencil mark line. A glance to his watch told him he had enough time to fit the sink with the taps, connect the hot and cold supply, plus the waste pipe, and be on his way. Sweeping the dustings into a corner with a broom, he stacked the cardboard packaging and stood back briefly to look at his work. A few hours more on Monday to fit the appliances and doors would finish his part of the job, and the tiler would then take his turn. He left the flat.

It started as a typical Friday night for him; stopping at the supermarket on the way home, then back to the flat to put everything away. He changed out of his work clothes and snatched up the small bag containing his swimming gear. He stepped into the street, locking the door behind him, and walked quickly down the road leading to the estate, keeping fully aware of anyone in close proximity. Once through and out on the main road, he relaxed a little. He was always aware of the noise around him, it seemed ceaseless. The sun was beginning to set, not with a pink hue on the cloud, but what seemed an angry scarlet, producing a majestic beauty.

The image was tinged for him in the knowledge that the colours were caused mainly by pollution. Turning the corner, he came alongside the brown-tiled front of the underground station, and immediately had to avoid two rough sleepers, begging. He was immune to their plight, but buried by his own. The warm air rushed to him as he descended and, hearing a train, he broke into a run, just making the doors. Looking around in the still busy carriage, he saw people about to start a Friday night out, but there seemed little joy. The pool was only two stops, and he was soon outside in the street again.

Walking in a moving mass, he eventually arrived at the Leisure Centre. It had only opened a few years ago, a clever glass and brick urban design with a good use of naked steel structures inside. He waved his card on the turnstile and went in. Same time, same people, same distance to swim. He enjoyed the easy laughs with the people he saw here regularly. But there was no depth of friendship – instead, just a thin layer of warmth. It was a strange bond within narrow confines. It had occurred to him on several occasions that no-one knew where the others lived and when someone stopped coming, nobody knew what had become of them. A move, an illness, or worse. These were friendships without obligation or closure.

The clicking of the turnstile was such a regular sounding noise, it always registered with him that he was just a number passing through it. A whirring, then a loud click as the double doors opened, and the change in temperature hit him. Walking down, past a row of lockers on one side and changing cubicles on the other, he reached his regular locker row. Like so many things in life, this was based on habit. Slotting in a coin, he unpacked items from the bag, putting things in the same neat order in the locker. It amused him that, quite often, there was no-one near him going in; but when he came out of the pool, the only other person in the entire changing room would have the locker right alongside his. Was this sod's law, he wondered, and who or what was the sod?

First he took off his shoes and socks, putting them on the front edge of the locker. The heat from the underfloor heating registered with him as he bent a little. Pulling both his shirt and top off together, they too went in. Moving to allow two women to pass, one of them turned back. He snatched only a glance, knowing he cut a good figure. Work and swimming had more than just toned him. Hearing a shout, he saw his two swimming friends.

'What kept you?'

Max called back: 'Save your energy, you'll need it.'

The banter flowed as they all got changed, talking over the cubicle walls, oblivious to other people. Then the swim began. The 'wet hour' was always hard; face down in crawl, unable to hold a thought, just counting the lengths and enjoying the continuous feel of the water passing over his body. A physical purge with a feel-good factor when it was over. A hot, reviving shower usually brought him round, and leaving the shower with a towel round him, he took everything from the locker into the changing cubicle. His coin suddenly slipped through his wet fingers and rolled gently through the floor grill and into the drain. He watched, realising he had made no move at all to stop it.

He felt, in some enormous way, powerless. He sat on the bench and his towel slipped a little. He stared at the grill, feeling suddenly that - for an inexplicable reason - he was about to cry. Something so small had nudged him nearer an unknown precipice. Eventually, he got dressed. These moods still swept over him from time to time. Sometimes they lasted days, sometimes longer. He had suffered from depression for many years, and he found it difficult to talk to anyone about it. Max hadn't realised when he was a child, that his father had an affair for years. He had a parallel life with another woman, living alongside a lie. When his father eventually left, Max had felt a rage burn inside his then young heart, and he carried it with him still. Time doesn't always heal, but it does soften. A shrink wasn't needed to work out when and why his most recent depression had started, but Max knew it was also connected in some way to the anger and lack of patience that was always with him.

This Friday night, he didn't join the others for a drink after the swim, but went home and stayed there, alone. The next day was not too good either, so he forced himself to get out and be among people. He saw he had plenty of time to catch a film at a small independent cinema he was fond of, and, putting on his jacket, left the flat. It was a dark sky coming in; low cloud with moonlight just touching the edges. As he crossed the main road, just making the bus stop in time for the electronic board registering the arrival of a bus that would do him. It seemed a waste of time to queue for a bus. People still did it, but it always became a free for all when a bus pulled up, with people pushing in at the margins. He got on, and it wasn't too busy. He swiped his card and found a seat upstairs next to a sullen teenager. They eyed each other with no interest or connection before turning away. For a few blocks, Max sat slumped, watching the neon night lights cut stripes across the inside of the bus. Ten minutes passed as the bus slowly made its way to his stop. As he got off, he felt rain on the wind and, crossing the road, the first spots touched his face. Quickening his steps, he headed down Milne Street and then through the door. He had arrived at his retreat. He could escape to another place, away from his thoughts.

This arthouse cinema was one of his favourite places, hidden up a side street near Clapham Common. The only sign that could be seen from the street was red neon script above the large black industrial sliding door announcing **No 11 Cinema**.

The point of entry incongruously was a pedestrian door, mounted in its centre. Once inside, it opened into a very bright, modern space cleverly designed with the use of brickwork and glass and adapted to give a sassy, but relaxed, atmosphere. Beyond the booking office were two screens and a small foyer bar with sofas and coffee tables. They ran smart advertising campaigns from time to time, creating the idea that the place was somehow secret and select. It clearly worked, as the cinema was always busy.

He walked out through the swing doors when the film had finished. It had been a sub-titled French drama: a questioning story based on a relationship and moral choices. The type of film that encourages questions. He enjoyed films like this and would sometimes go with others he met only at the cinema, but he was equally happy to go alone. That evening, he stopped for a beer in the cinema's small bar, and as he got his drink, he saw Niall and Lily, who lived in the same street as him, with some friends. They all stood discussing the film, before moving to a table to carry on talking. Max was asked if he would like to join them. After the introductions, the conversation moved on from the film to current affairs, and while the talk batted backwards and forwards, he looked at the other couple in the group. Their idea of casual dress was very different to his. The man was tall and rangy, and wore an Italian-styled grey suit with thin lapels, on top of a striped shirt and sharp brown shoes. He spoke quickly, moving his hands continually, perhaps to make himself appear more confident and knowledgeable.

The woman, as if in contrast, stood perfectly still when she spoke. Her voice was higher pitched than he might have expected. She wore a short dress and heels that brought her towards his height, and seemed to him to be more aspiring than upwardly mobile. They both held strong opinions. The man seemed happier when he eventually identified what Max did for a living. Maybe then, they could put him in a place, or order of things. He didn't like them much. They both seemed happiest when talking about themselves. So he focused on Lily, while Niall talked with the other couple. Lily's character made for easy conversation. She was funny, outward-going and quick to find humour; he liked that.

Lily did a lot of talking, and - as women friends tend to do - dug around, to find out whether he was seeing anyone at the moment. When Max smiled and shook his head, she mentioned he should meet one of her friends from work, saying it would make for a good evening. He was always keen to meet new people and open to suggestions, but he wasn't necessarily optimistic. Max bought the next round and then gauged it was his time to leave on a good note. Pushing back his chair, he stood and thanked Niall and Lily, and the other couple, whose names he had already forgotten, for their company. Without looking back, he walked past the foyer and out of the door, into the night. The temperature had dropped a little and having been inside for a few hours, Max felt it. Stretching a hand into a large inner pocket, he pulled out a thin scarf and a beanie and put them on without pausing. Reaching the main road, he decided to walk a couple of stops to warm up and quickened his pace through the still busy street. The aromas of the multiplying takeaways came straight to him. On the pavement, litter was everywhere. Vapours congregated; shoppers were still shopping, crowds of people were on their way somewhere - or nowhere, just like him - and behind each face, there was another life. Headlights from the traffic carved up the tarmac. Street lights and shop illuminations blurred together and the noise of the city still hung over everything. Looking up, he could see there was no room for the moonlight. A bus stopped near him and he turned and got on, heading for home. With his head very slightly on one side, he went over the evening's conversation and the events that had led to his meeting Lily a few weeks ago. As was so often the case with new people, he met them when something needed fixing. Lily had seen him loading his van one morning. Suddenly she was there, alongside him. He had not heard her approach or seen where she came from, and she introduced herself, pointing to her house and saying she lived at number 17. She explained they had a problem with an old floor and could he take a look for them? He said he would call in on his way home that evening. He wrote a note in his diary about Mrs Red Jumper at No 17 and set an alarm. He had forgotten all about their meeting until he turned into the street again at just before six that evening. Unloading his tools at his flat first, he went in search of a parking spot. Finding one down the road, he walked back past his motorcycle. His bike was still under its cover, like the others it was jammed up closely in a row, like military casualties. Number 17 was a bay and forecourt, a mirror image to his own. He guessed they bought it before the prices burst through the cloud base.

Someone must have seen him coming, as the door opened before he could use the knocker.

The man said: 'Come on in,' and, while backing into the main living room, introduced himself as Niall, explaining the problem seemed to be in the corner at one end of the living room. Going through, he shouted out: 'Lily' and she came through from the kitchen, drying her hands on a towel. 'Hello again,' she said, adding that they could smell damp, and had kept the heating on high to counteract it. Max laughed inwardly, thinking a lot of bloody good that would do. With Niall's help, he lifted a small bookcase away from the wall in the corner. He produced a small screwdriver from his pocket and gently lifted both corners of the carpet from the gripping runs. Then he rolled the carpet back about a metre.

Looking at the point where the skirting board meets the floor, there was a wide gap where there shouldn't have been. Using his weight, and with his feet together he bounced lightly and felt the give beneath his feet. He repeated this a couple more times along the side walls before telling them that two joists had definitely gone and others were probably rotten. Some of the floor would have to be taken up before he could be certain what needed to be done. While telling them this, he returned the carpet. He explained that he couldn't give an exact price for the work, as he did not know what he might find until the floor was up. At times like this, he gave a best- and a worst-case scenario; allowing a wide margin so that he didn't put people off, but always suggesting it was unlikely to be the worst case. This approach seemed to work well. Lily and Niall looked at each other, and Niall said: 'Just do it, when can you fit us in?'

This was a more common response now - people didn't question the cost, they asked how quickly he could do the work. Max assumed this was because it was hard for them to find reliable people. So the job was booked in for the following week. The room had been cleared at one end for him. Using a lump hammer and bolster, he found a shorter floorboard running across the room and took this up first. He didn't need the strong military map torch in his pocket to see what the problem was. The subfloor area was full of rubble at that point, right up to the undersides of the joists. Next, removing the skirting boards carefully with the same tools, he picked up his old claw hammer and took up all the floorboards at that end of the room. Niall and Lily could see from the other end of the living room the unfolding problems. Lazy builders had, at some time in the past, found a short cut and had jacked up joists and put loads of rubble under the floor. Now it had gone rotten. Fortunately, this was wet rot, as he could see no tell-tale signs of dry rot.

This was very lucky, as two air bricks on the outside wall had been covered by a low planter for a long time and the lack of air circulating under the floor, together with warmth from the heating, could have made this a very different story. He removed three joists that were in various stages of rot on the ends and then started to bend his back to the shovel. All of the rubble had to be bagged before disposal and the sub floor area cleared completely. He cut the rotten joists in half and stacked them in the forecourt garden, adding to them the growing number of bags of rubble. He was hot when this was finished, and the owners had gone out, leaving him a mug laid for tea with milk and biscuits by the kettle. The kitchen was an expensive, designer-created, industrial-looking room, all aluminium. Looking around, Max could see that everything, even the toaster, had been swept off the worktops and put away somewhere. As the tea was brewing, he made a quick call to Jay about collecting the rubbish, then picking up the key he had been left, drove to the timber merchant nearby, returning with what he needed. Settling to work, he cut two plates for the joists to sit on and toothed them into the two existing ones he had cut back. Fitting them tight and screwing them down firmly. Next, he cut the three joists from the newly-treated timbers. Because of their length, he brought these through the living room window, together with the new floorboards. The decision to use a hand saw and to put dust covers down helped to keep the mess to a minimum. The boards all went down right and quickly, as he knew they would; the skirtings were re-fixed and then Max cleaned up. Job jobbed. He left a note to say he would put the bill through the door the next day.

The next morning at 8, after delivering his bill, Max met Jay. He was only half an hour late, which was practically on time by Jay's clock. The battered old flatbed transit belched into view with Jay and his enormous black bulk seemingly jammed in behind the steering wheel. The truck heaved on its springs as it stopped.

The driver's door swung open on to the pavement with an agonisingly long creak and Jay slid out somehow into an upright position.

'Yo, Maxi man,' came his warm greeting.

They had it all loaded in minutes, among the other rubbish and up behind the scrap. With a handshake, he dropped Jay £120, and the money was zipped up in a belt under his shapeless, grey tracksuit bottoms. Jay opened the door and, using the steering wheel as a lever, worked himself back into a driving position. Slamming the door, Jay started the engine and leaned out of the window: 'You look after yourself, Maxi mate.'

With a laugh, he started the engine and coaxed the smoking machine down the road. Max watched for a moment, thinking that he had known Jay for many years, but he didn't have clue where he lived, or even whether he was licensed. None of it mattered, he was one of life's gentlemen, and had been there when Max needed him most.

Now, looking out of the bus window on his way home, Max thought again of the film he had just seen. The drama had centred on life's choices, whether to stand against the tide, and at what expense? So many parallels with his own life, and so many unanswered questions. And what of the man – Niall's friend - with the brown pointed shoes. How strange it is that we are constantly judged by others, but rarely hear the verdict

Chapter 9

This, of course, all happened in another life. First the fatal car crash, then the long haul to recovery; the return to work and the bouts of uncontrolled temper and depression. The drug dealer's death, the time in prison and then trying to find some purpose to his days. It was a route that had taken Max to the doctor's surgery to ask for help. He felt he was just treading water.

Everything changed when Helen died that winter. It was pancreatic cancer. She had not felt well for a while, and from diagnosis to death was eleven short weeks. In the first month, she withdrew quietly, then it all became too much for her and it was hospital. The last week she was in the hospice in the nearby city. She became so shrunken that Max was shocked when he visited. Then his mother called to tell him that Helen had passed away. Gone, that light, that spirit, that life, extinguished. His mother had been stoic till the end. Then she crumbled, telling Max that life was hard, but death was always brutal. Strength, she said, would come from moving on; while remembering what had gone before. People were always alive inside your head. The hospice had called his mother the same evening Helen slipped away. Helen had no relatives and Katherine was known to be her closest friend. The hospice staff explained they would arrange for the body to be taken to an undertaker chosen by his mother.

Absorbing this news, Max sat quietly to think about Helen. She had been such an important part of his life, and for so long. As his father had disappeared when Max was still young, he had only really known one parent, along with his 'aunt' Helen, who lived in Itchenor on the West Sussex coast. She and Katherine had become friends at school and stayed close all of their lives. Helen had run a Bed and Breakfast from her large, red brick Victorian villa and during the summer season, his mother would add an extra pair of hands.

It was always busy and Max's memories were of long, warm days lived outside. Helen engineered a meeting with a local boy, Stevie, whose mother she knew. The two boys quickly became inseparable and during those holidays they made tents in the garden with old sheets pegged over a line between the apple trees, and built dens in the orchard behind the house. One summer, he learnt to swim in the creek. Helen had patiently taught him off the slipway right in front of the house.

With snatched time between chores, and over endless hours, he started to improve and, finally, he could swim from the slipway up the creek, to the neighbour's old pier and back. This was the test that allowed him go out into the water on his own. His life then was so carefree. He could wander and adventure during the day, returning only when hunger drove him home. At lower tides, he and Stevie would mooch slowly, wearing shorts and wellingtons, along the edges of the creek, watching the oyster catchers and the egrets constantly working the food chain, with swallows and house martins gracefully turning above them. Sometimes, they would pick up bits of metal sheeting looking for crabs or search shallow mud pools with their fingers, hoping to find flat fish. Endlessly finding interesting objects, only to be superseded by the next. The best finds - marker buoys, occasional fenders, unusual shells, a treasured oar, hag stones galore – were all saved, taken back and presented. Then they were threaded on string or rope and hung on the side of the wooden lean-to, attached to the garage. The smell of those wooden sheds and garages never left him. Piles of nets, linseed oil, petrol, stored apples picked in autumn sitting on shelves lined with newspaper; more newspapers kept in piles for unknown purposes. They all collided to smell as singular as the very memory itself. Max took his first newspaper round, having asked at the shop for a job, and proudly announced to his mother that he had started saving for a dingy. He delivered to the big houses in the Almond Drive and Hook Avenue area.

It was hard and heavy work for a young boy yet to hit the growing years. He enjoyed, when he had the chance, talking to the adults along his route. It made him feel so grown up. One morning, an elderly man working in a front garden called him over after Max had said good morning to him. He took him to be the gardener, as he was wearing baggy trousers, held up over a bulging belly with red braces, complemented with an old shirt and a flat hat. The man removed his gloves, straightened up, and paid Max a compliment saying: 'I've been watching you delivering the papers. You look, you listen and you're earning, all good traits.'

Then the man asked what Max was saving for. When he told him, the man gave a thoughtful nod. This was how Max had fortuitously met Fred Parker, the owner of the large and sprawling house, which was on his delivery round. Over the next week, he was greeted regularly by both Fred and his wife and he engaged them both in conversation about their garden. It was clear that, without trying, he had charmed them both. What of course he didn't realise was that Helen knew many people in the village, including Fred Parker and his wife. The couple visited Helen when Max was out, presenting both their offer and their plan to let Max use an old dingy they still had. Predictably, his mother and Helen reacted with enthusiasm. The next day, Fred left a note on the door asking Max to call back after he had finished his paper round. He wondered if he had done something wrong. He left his bike leaning against the hedge and saw Fred and his wife in the garden. He followed them along the side of the house, through an oak arched door in the wall, which was blanketed with Virginia creeper. They walked on between several coloured hydrangeas and came to the huge lawn that gently sloped down to the edges of the creek. As they walked, Fred told the boy they had retired here years ago and they loved their garden with its fabulous views over the water. They reached a black-stained, timber-clad boat house. Sliding his fingers into a hidden ledge, Fred produced a key and opened the door.

The large space with a concrete floor was mostly empty, except for a small, upturned boat on chocks, partially covered with a tarpaulin. Max recognised instantly from its shape that it was a Mirror dinghy that had been winched up the slipway, through now bolted double doors. Fred pointed: 'The mast, boom, rudder and sail with all new rigging; life jacket - all here waiting to be used. We haven't had it out on the water since my last granddaughter got too big for it. What you don't know, I'll teach you, what do you think?'

Max had stood silently for a moment, unable to express the complete joy he felt. Then it poured out. Questions followed the big thank you, and more question followed that. And so it was, that a wider world of deep creeks and unknown inlets from the main harbour to other villages and quaysides opened up to him. He was being trusted and this gave him a sense of responsibility. He learnt to rig and sail quickly, gathering instructions from his mentor who liked to stand by a flooding tide, with a single thumb tucked into his oversized belt while waving the other arm wildly. Such comments as: 'Pull the sheet in tighter. Watch where you're going. Get low under that boom or you won't see tomorrow. Go about. No, other way.' Sailing towards the wind and tacking came easily to Max as he'd watched the dingy sailors pull the centre board and tack back to the clubhouse on a southerly wind near Helen's house. Eventually, after several outings, the shouts lessened and when Max finally turned to look, Fred had gone. The double doors had been opened and the winch line and trolley laid out in readiness for him. And so the days passed. The following summer, Stevie's parents moved away and the boys' friendship slipped like a line on a mooring. They both expected to see one and other again, but never did.

Over the next couple of years, Max's relationship with Fred flourished. By then the news round had gone, the way news rounds do, but he was still keen to help out in any way he could to re-pay the kindness he had received.

Fred was responsible for introducing him to carpentry in its rawest form when they set about mending a feathered board fence together. He was shown the way to use a claw hammer to remove the old, partially rotten boards, then he de-nailed the still usable top arris rail. Checking the length of the board needed with a tape, and writing it in pencil clearly on a clean piece of paper in case he forgot, he counted the number of new boards needed to fit the gap and wrote that on the paper too. They went to the workshop and measured and marked each one, finally using a set square to mark the cutting line accurately. He was shown how to cut them with a saw, taking great care when starting the first downward motion not to cut himself. Kneeling on a wooden horse to keep the new feathered boards from moving, his concentration made him sweat and his hands became clammy too. When this was done, they carried all the boards to the fence and, using a clamp, held the first one in place. Then, using flathead nails, he hammered them securely into place. Slowly, the fence repair progressed, with the two of them constantly checking the level of the top of the growing fence line until the last board was in position. Gathering all the tools, they returned them to their proper place. He thought it was fun, but clearly, he had an aptitude for this sort of work, even from this early age. On another day, he learnt the art of sharpening a chisel. He was fascinated by the angle of the chisel moving gently in a figure of eight motion on the oiled stone. Over time, this would make the tool as sharp as a cut-throat razor. Max honed this skill through many hours over several days, sharpening all the chisels he could find and then returning then secretly to their allotted places.

    The sailing club was a real family place. Adults filled the bar in the evenings and there were always people milling around during the day. Kids around his age would group around a large table in the inner hall night or day.

The noise and music level would rise and fall depending on their numbers. It was here that Max met Josie, his first girlfriend.

She was about the same height and age as him and wore her blonde hair long. It was the first thing he noticed about her. She had her chin in the palm of her hand while resting her elbow on the table. The boy next to her was talking to her, but clearly, she was bored. He smiled at this small scene. Unbeknown to Max, she had seen him when he came in, wearing his favourite old suede 'freewheeling' coat.

When part of the group started to go outside, he stood and turned for a last look to remind himself of how she looked, and she was looking straight at him smiling. Nervously, he returned the smile. They both stopped on the step and started to talk, then walk, then walk and talk – that's how these things happen. For a few short weeks, they were inseparable. They sailed together, walked together, kissed and fumbled around together. This teenage love burnt hot and bright like sulphur on a match; and went out almost as quickly. Max smiled when he thought how simple life had seemed then, and how lucky he had been to have spent so many summers on the West Sussex coast.

He recalled the last day he had spent with Helen. His mother had remarked that she was looking weary and could probably do with a visit, so Max had called her and arranged to go down to Itchenor the following Sunday. He remembered that day quite well, as when he had walked across from his flat to his motorcycle, he immediately noticed one of the saplings that had been planted as a replacement last year, was standing broken from the waist. It must have happened during the night, whoever had done this had also kicked at the wooden framework around the base that had served as a children's flower bed for the two little girls in a nearby upstairs flat. Max just couldn't understand why anyone would want to damage or despoil the surroundings they lived in. Those two girls wouldn't understand either. He bent to a knee, straightened the frame and re-bedded the plants, which looked like winter pansies. There was nothing he could do about the tree. He walked towards the motorcycle park area, and stopped short.

He felt instant tension and anger as could see a long slash from, perhaps, a Stanley knife though the bike cover. Fearing the worst, he covered the remaining ground quickly, only to find the cut had also gone through to the seat underneath. Standing upright, breathing deeply, he let out a low moan. 'Why?' And why him.

He was sick of it all. He went back indoors, returning with a large roll of duct tape and scissors from his tool box. Removing the cover, he conducted a messy repair to the seat and then did the same to the cover. Before putting the cover back on, he looked carefully over the guts of the engine to make sure there was no more spiteful damage. Once covered again, he hoped this would now blend into the drabness of its surroundings. Making his mind up in that instant, he decided he would use the van instead today. He got changed, returned all his gear to their storage places, and checked the time again. It was just gone 9 and as he was just kicking time; he decided to leave anyway. He took an old waxed jacket and his flat Harris Tweed cap and left, locking the door securely behind him.

As he approached the van, he pressed the key fob to unlock it and, without really thinking, lifted the door handle and swung into the driver's seat, then put the key in the ignition. Sitting back for a moment he was aware of the one spring in the seat that was tired, giving a slight lopsided feel. The van wasn't new when he bought it several years ago, but it had low-ish mileage, it was a clean runabout and it hadn't carried weight. With only 93,000 miles on the clock now, there was plenty of road run left in it. To him, vehicles were like a drill or power saw - there to do a certain job in a specific way, every time without fail. What it looked like was of little concern. He didn't want gimmicks, he just wanted it to serve its given purpose. When it was worn out, he would get rid of it and buy another one. He wasn't naïve though, he realised how powerful advertising helped the manufacturers to weld brand and status to their products, producing ongoing consumer envy. He wished, sometimes, that buying new things would do it for him; but it didn't.

Pushing his jacket away from the hand brake, he flicked on the ignition, watching the dashboard light up, started the van and pulled away from the kerb. Out in the main rush of traffic, he moved quickly, well, relatively quickly for London, towards the arterial road that would take him to the coast. Settling into his own private travelling space, he adjusted the heater, then picked a radio station that was playing classical music. He knew very little about classical music, but it soothed him. Getting near to the outskirts, he pulled off the main road onto a slip road leading him to array of shops. Parking the van in the lay-by, he stepped onto the kerb to cross the pavement into the convenience store. A lick of wind blew a paper bag across his path, and he watched it drift towards a pile of discarded items outside the shop. He went in; the bright lights over the well-stacked shelves confronted him. The hum of the refrigerated units reached him from somewhere deeper within the shop. He looked around and saw what he was hoping to find – flowers. From a coloured plastic bucket filled with water, he took four small bunches of freesias, hoping that Helen would like the soft scent and the vibrant colours that were just starting to appear on some of the stems. Paying with cash, he pulled a £5 pound note from the change and put it into the charity collecting box. Back in the van, he turned off the radio and took in, without distraction, the wonderful colours of the trees on the turn as they fled by him on this sunny autumn morning. Nature was showing him a glimpse of the eternal cycle of life. Another van slashed by him, jolting his senses back to reality.

The miles ticked on and eventually he saw the long flat marshlands of the coast come into view; the flatland he knew was teeming with wildlife and was a haven unto itself. He turned east and headed onto the downlands that would eventually lead him to the spire city. That tall spire dominated what was once a market town, and could be seen many miles away in any direction. Now it only dominated the skyline.

At the approach to a large roundabout just outside the city, the traffic thickened a little before thinning again. Another couple of miles and he spotted the little turning south by the Crown and Anchor pub. This stretch of lane led between trees that overlapped the road, making a wooded tunnel in summer. Now, their leaves had begun to cover the tarmac surface. The lane opened out a little with a flint and brick farmhouse with barns and old outbuildings along one side, fronted by a low flint-knapped wall glinting its greys in the sun. More fields were lying bare now - in summer this would be a sea of swaying barley. The first sign he was almost there was when he approached the last bend, and the masts of anchored yachts and dinghies stood above the bushes like a bunch of topped corn. He was early, so he pulled over to side of the road, got out and took a few paces to the front of the van. Leaning back on the bonnet with folded arms he faced the breeze and looked up the creek to a faraway view. He felt quiet and at ease with himself, wishing he could roll up these moments and keep them like a map to find his way back from the bleakness he felt in the city at some later date. Turning suddenly, he realised a man on a bicycle was slowing to a stop beside the van. 'Got a problem mate? Need some help?'

Max laughed, explaining he was just admiring the view, and then an easy conversation followed. Just two human beings, being human. He watched the man cycle away, and wave without looking back. Checking the time, Max drove the last few hundred yards before swinging in to park in front of the old clapboard sheds. Turning off the engine, he looked first to the long, overgrown state of the orchard behind the garage. It had been many years since he had been here; on the last few occasions he had seen Helen, they had met at his mother's house. He got out of the van, involuntary locking it with the key, and then having to open it again to get the flowers. He headed round the bend of the gravel drive to enter the back garden.

This part of the garden had been tended regularly it seemed, but to a price. Opening a picket gate in the fence and then starting to cross the lawn, he stopped immediately. He heard a noise that he had not heard here before; a dog barked, then again, and suddenly, with a rush from between the fading shrubs came a dog. He saw this big, bounding black beast coming to him with a tail that looked like it might work loose. The dog ran round him until Max crouched a little, holding out his hand as if waiting for a small child. First a sniff, then a lick, and then the dog nuzzled against him. After patting the dog and rubbing its ears gently, he straightened again and, with the dog beside him, walked up the lawn to see Helen standing by the back door, waiting for him. He gave her the flowers, then he stooped a little for a big hug and caught the very faintest draught of an unknown perfume. They went into the warm kitchen, closing the back door behind them. The dog had already gone in and was lying down in his basket by the edge of the table, watching their movements.

The first questions he put to her while she was putting the flowers in water, were about the dog. Why? And when? Helen suddenly became very animated, saying that looking after the dog for a weekend had begun as a favour for a neighbour a few months previously. This had stretched to a loan as its owner then moved to the Midlands, taking a new job and renting a house up there. She was secretly delighted, as what had started with uncertainty had grown into deep affection for the dog. The Labrador's name was Dag, he was just over three years old and moderately well-trained. Max could tell from the way she spoke about the dog that she was very fond of him. She said, too, that the dog had given her company in a simple and unexpected way. She turned back to the stove and stirred a large pan of soup, and while she was busy with this, Max sat at the long pine table. Dag came to him, as he dangled his hand beside the side of the chair.

He had read of the calming influence of animals, and Dag bore this out, even in this very short time. Looking around him, Max saw that things were just as they had been. The magnolia emulsion on the walls was slightly discoloured over the stove, the clothes dryer, with its pulley cords tied off on the raising peg on the wall, the painted dresser, with large glass paned doors above it, fronted an array of glasses and plates, all neatly stacked. In front of him were side plates and cutlery, plus a French loaf sliced up on a plate of mixed cheeses. Helen brought over two large bowls of steaming soup, each on a large dinner plate, and set them on the table. She took off her apron and hung it up on a hook on the back of the kitchen door and sat down. She pushed the plate of bread towards him and encouraged him to start. He was hungry, but posed questions as he ate, in order to gauge her responses. She was not as strong as she used to be and now had help in the garden and, one morning a week, in the house. This surprised him a little. She didn't look weak to him, so much as tired. The conversation topics varied between the occasional visits to his mother and vice versa, what she was reading at the moment, and her friends in the village.

Some couples had moved to flats or bungalows in the cathedral city, one friend had moved to an expensive warden-controlled flat, designed especially for the elderly, and now wished she hadn't. Helen said she had no plans to move and added, jokingly, that she was staying put for ever. He laughed at this, as it was so typical of her. They had a cup of tea together sitting in the wide sun porch facing south onto the garden, with Dag lying between their feet. It was then, in her direct fashion, that she asked him some deeply searching questions about his work and life in London, as well as his recent re-adjustment. Unlike his conversations with his mother, avoidance was not an option.

When they had finished talking, Helen suggested he took Dag for a walk across the dyke, it was a route he knew well.

Helen said she would have a short lie down while he was out. If she was still asleep when he came back, the spare back door key would be in the same old place. Max took the lead from the back of the kitchen door, and a whistle. Helen assured him the dog would come to the whistle: maybe not immediately though. The plastic whistle was threaded with a long red boot lace in a knotted loop and was soon hanging around Max's neck as he set off. Picking up his jacket and hat from the van, he put them on and, with the dog on the lead, made for the shore road. He was quickly unsure of who was taking who for a walk, as Dag was pulling him along with his enthusiasm. He soon came to the weathered oak footpath sign, pointing like a finger, alongside a bent five-tube bar gate. Opening and closing it behind him, he was on the path to the dyke, and felt it was safe to let

Dag go. Once off the lead, he didn't run far away, just mooched about, using his nose to scent the wind and the ground. They turned left on joining the next gravel track. It stretched away to a radio mast in the distance, perhaps a mile away. This was the start of a peninsular of land, reclaimed centuries ago. On the left of the path was a wide ditch serving as a natural drain for the dyke on the right. The drain was bounded on both sides by dense, tall reed beds, which bent gently as they were out of the wind. Without a thought, Max climbed the dyke; some fifteen steps to the top and then was ripped into by the full sea breeze coming in from the south west. The tide was high, slapping hard against the reinforced side of the dyke. He started to walk this narrow, elevated path, still keeping Dag in view. Away and behind him lay the squat Norman church tower, the quay and cottages of the old village of Bosham. It had been a thriving port in the 17th century, turning trade across the channel from its relatively sheltered position at the head of the main creek. Now, it served mostly leisure boats; many of them moored and going no further than their length of chain.

The village trade now was day trippers coming by cars from the main road off the escarpment a little way further back. Walking at a good pace to keep warm, with the dog clearly upfront of him, he looked again at the sea. It was very choppy, it seemed almost to be carving itself up. As he strode along, he was catching up with two people. When he got nearer, he saw an older woman, probably with her daughter. They both wore overcoats and scarves and were walking with linked arms. Then the older woman broke off to put her arm around the younger one with a hug of reassurance, or endearment, he wasn't sure, before returning to linked arms again. Next, he heard the distinct continual crunch of gravel from the wheels of a bicycle. He didn't need to turn his head as the woman slowly came into his side vision. Her bicycle was old, with a battered, woven front basket, held on by two small leather buckled straps. For some unknown reason, her soft green beret stood out large in his mind. He stopped walking by a thin shield of bushes growing out of the bank of the dyke and watched the scene unfold from his higher perspective, as though looking through a camera lens on a film set. When he stopped, the dog stopped too, before idling back towards him. The cyclist called out, the older woman turned, and the two women stopped walking. Then the cyclist, while supporting her bicycle, gave them a joint hug. It all seemed to happen in slow motion. He started walking again, passing parallel to them at a pace. They might have been talking, but he heard nothing, he focused on the radio mast in front of him, thinking only of the phrase 'the onlooker sees most of the game'.

He reached a narrow road used to service the mast, which was within a small fenced compound. Turning around, he snapped tight inside. He couldn't see the dog anywhere. Blowing two blasts on the whistle, he nervously looked around again when Dag emerged though a clump of bushes a little way off. Relief swept over him as he relaxed again. Finding a spot out of the wind, a slab with his back to the fence, he sat looking at the seascape.

He tried to remember there was only one day that had any real significance, and that was today. After a while he stood and straightened his legs. Feeling the cold wind again, he started the return walk on the lower gravel path. Hearing a squeak, he looked at the dog. Dag was chewing a tennis ball that he had just found, every time its jaws shut on it, the ball made the same sound. Max reached out with an open hand, standing still, and then gave the command: 'In my hand', more in hope than expectation. The dog stood still just a metre or two away, both of them measuring each other with a stare. He flexed his fingers in a beckoning motion, and finally the dog came to him.

Touching the ball gently with his open palm, while holding the stare, he gave the command again: 'In my hand,' and the dog dropped the ball, reluctantly, into his open hand. He praised the dog. Max realised Dag wanted him to throw the ball and, slowly, the dog realised that in order to get what he wanted, he had to do as he was told. As they walked on, he looked up at the cold clear sky to see the first of the young Canada geese in the familiar formation turn on the wing and head for the green fields beyond the big ditch. What a sight these birds were. Eight to 18 pounds fully-grown and with a flying speed of 50 miles an hour. As he turned at the gate on the road, the light was just beginning to go. The dog was on the lead now and pulling hard for his food at home. Moving to the side of the footpath, he passed a man coming the other way with a dog, also on a lead. They exchanged a quick hello. Max noticed the other man was training the younger dog to walk to heel by folding the lead, looped over the dog's snout, to act like a horse's halter and was holding the lead with just his forefinger. When they had disappeared from view, he did the same with Dag, achieving instant success. They walked up the rear driveway and turned towards the sheds with the log store behind it. Max slid his hand along the top inside edge until he located the key hanging on a cup hook and took it with him to open the back door.

The lock seemed to jam a little when he worked the key, on the second time it unlocked and opened, but the door catch didn't work properly. Going back to his van, he brought out a multi-headed screwdriver and returned to the house. It took no time at all to remove the rim lock and, turning it upside down on the table, carefully remove the back. It was a simple job, the return spring had jumped, bending the end a little. He clipped it back in its proper holding then realigned the body of the lock and screwed this tight as well, so the locking mechanism moved in a straight line, and finally returned the rim lock to the door. As he was finishing, Helen came into the kitchen and the dog got up from under the table and went to greet her. While she stroked Dag, he said: 'The door is OK now.'

'You didn't need to do that, but thank you,' Helen said.

They talked about his walk for a few minutes before he went to put the screwdriver back in the van. When he came back inside again, he felt the warmth of the kitchen and saw Helen busy making sandwiches. The old, familiar red tea pot was warming, standing ready to take the tea. Glancing at the large clock on the wall he knew he must soon be on his way. He looked under the table at Dag who was looking back at him and, without moving, started thumping his tail. The dog's recognition made Max feel good. Helen brought over a plate with two rounds of sandwiches, saying: 'Ham and tomato, cheese and pickle; you can take them with you, if you prefer.'

Max was grateful. He started on the top one as Helen poured the tea into two, blue patterned, bone china mugs with the milk jug placed at an easy reach for him. While he ate, she fed the dog and then talked of how a front was moving in, which would mean cold weather all the following week. 'You'll have to wrap up well if you're going to be working outside,' Helen suggested. Max was really touched by her concern for him, he was not used to anyone showing it. He finished the sandwiches and eased his way through a second cup of tea.

Finally, standing up, he said: 'I must be off.' He put his arms round her and held her for a moment before saying quietly: 'Helen, you're wonderful, thank you for the day.'

'You must look after yourself, Max, you're all we have,' said Helen, her voice dropping a little as she spoke. He took his hat and jacket from one of the spare chairs and moved to the door. Dag was watching every movement and got up to walk to Helen's side. Her hand swung down, and she just touched the dog's head, tickling it with a forefinger. With his hand on the door knob, he opened the door and the lock moved as it should. He pointed at the lock, giving her a thumbs up sign, and started to move through the doorway. Helen was now holding the dog back with her foot. After a few steps over the threshold, he turned back to face her again and smiled. He waved the spare key, saying he would put it back. She hadn't heard him; the door had shut and she was waving him goodbye through the partially glazed window. Cutting across the lawn and driveway, he reached the log store again, sliding his hand, he located the cup hook and hung the key up. Pointing his van key, he unlocked and then opened the door, slipping in behind the wheel. The jacket and hat were pushed over on the passenger seat and he pulled out a dark blue sweatshirt between the seats, which he put on for extra warmth. Starting the van and turning onto the lane, he began his journey back.

Max hadn't realised that the visit would be the last time he would see Helen in familiar surroundings. Nor how sudden her death would be.

Chapter 10

What Max also didn't know was that Helen had given his mother a letter several weeks before, not to be opened until after she had died. Its content was brief and factual. It was to be shown first, along with the Death Certificate, to Helen's solicitors, whose offices were in Wimbledon. There were instructions to contact them immediately and go and see them, taking the papers and two forms of photo identification, in order that her final wishes could be carried out. Katherine did this, making an appointment as soon as possible, and taking the train to London. She was met by a man, younger that she expected, who offered his immediate condolences and then ushered her to a downstairs office just back from the reception. It was sparsely furnished and obviously only used as a meeting room. The solicitor looked at the identification documents, then photocopied them. Helen had no living relatives, her older sister having died many years ago, and the solicitor explained there was a codicil to the will. This stated that Helen's body was to be removed from the place where she died and to be disposed of by cremation with no service of any kind. No attendees and no flowers. He produced a copy of the part of the codicil containing these instructions and placed it on the desk in front of her. The will also said that Helen wanted her instructions to be carried out by her close friend, Katherine May Bentham. He then produced a small bunch of keys, which he placed carefully on top of the other piece of paper. Looking down, Katherine saw a small, beige parcel tag with the number 3 on it. Someone had used a very short piece of crimson ribbon to attach the label to the key ring; it was probably the ribbon used to bundle deeds together. She was still looking at the keys when the solicitor said: 'These are the keys to Mrs Howard's house and, as you will see from her instructions, it is her wish that you and your son Max visit the house and take any item, or indeed items, that you so wish, as keepsakes.'

He had been further instructed that the will itself should not be read by anyone until the wishes contained in the codicil had been completed. Feeling overwhelmed by all of the morning's events, Katherine just said: 'Thank you.'

The solicitor asked: 'Do you have - ?'

Then he coughed politely as though to clear his throat, before continuing: 'Any bills and expenses will be reimbursed to you, or if you prefer the bill can be forwarded onto me at this office and it will be paid from funds from the estate.'

Again, Katherine responded with just: 'Thank you.'

The solicitor, using his thumb and forefinger, reached into his waistcoat pocket and withdrew a neat, black card case. Using his thumb, he flipped it open to withdraw a crisp, white card before returning the case to his waistcoat again. As he placed the card on the desk facing her, using two fingers apart, lightly touching the edges of the card, he slid it alongside the keys. Katherine couldn't help thinking that he was trying not to dirty the card in any way. 'If you have any questions later, or should you wish to speak to me about any of these points, please do contact me.'

With a well-practised smile, he stood up and came to her side of the desk. She opened her bag and carefully stored away all the items he had put on the desk for her, together with her passport and driving licence. He opened the office door, and then showed her from the building. It wasn't until she was on the train that Katherine looked at the card. Fingering it lightly, she saw in bold black letters the name Norton Vaughan Solicitors, and beneath this, his name, Charles Peterson, with his office and direct line numbers. Turning it over, she saw the reverse side was blank, then replaced it in her bag. Sitting back, she wondered at Helen's detailed organisation; it was so like her. In the near empty train, alone with her thoughts, the tears came quietly. She wiped them away.

Raising her head, and with a deep breath, she looked towards the faraway view through the train window, but didn't see it. Once home, she called Max and told him of her visit to the solicitor's office. All the details tumbled out in a rush of emotion, like a quick downward random scale on a piano. 'I'll be down as quick as I can mum, and we'll talk then,' said Max.

'Thank you.'

Katherine's next job, which she did immediately, was to contact the newspapers and place an advert which simply stated:

Helen Josephine Howard of Itchenor, West Sussex died on February 13, after a short illness, aged 64. No one could have wished for a better friend. A great many were lucky to know her. There will be no funeral service.

Max arrived at about 5pm. Katherine heard the motorcycle's thunderous revving as he touched the accelerator before switching off the engine. As she opened the front door, he was just taking his helmet off. Opening her arms, he walked into them. That evening, they went to a nearby pub. Not a gastro-pub, fashioned by an interior designer; more of a local place that sold beer and happened to serve food from a few tables set aside from the bar. To Max, this was a proper pub with grub. The wines were well chosen and the beer well kept, and wholesome, fresh food was served on white plates. There was none of this chips in a mini dustbin and substituting plates with pieces of timber or slate. Max had found the menus in the gastro-pubs were embossed and embellished so much, it was impossible for the food to live up to expectations.

Their table was booked for 7.30, which was a good move, as the pub was full. This was just what he had hoped for, as he felt both of them should be among the sounds of people. It was just the sort of place Helen would have liked. They were shown to a small, round table with a heavy wrought iron ornate base.

Moving the chairs a little, they gave themselves a view of the room. At the bar, Max ordered a large glass of white wine, and, glancing at the beer board, picked a strong, golden beer. The barman fetched them, saying: 'That beer is perfect today. Clear, clean, full hops back taste, I'll open your tab.'

'Would you like my card?'

'Not necessary.'

The next day, they decided to go down to Helen's house, with Katherine driving. The sun was shining intermittently through banks of soft white clouds, with the slightest touch of cold in the air. They left the final stretch of dual carriageway, and passed several fields. Max recollected the fields he had viewed from the prison van, and hoped that experience would gradually melt into the shadow of his memory. The masts came into view and then the village of Itchenor. Parking in the road rather that the rear driveway, they walked to the front of the house. The half tide was ebbing, leaving the pale green seaweed exposed on the mud. Amongst the gulls' cries, they could hear the distinctive slap of the halyards in the alloy masts on the moored boats further out in the deep channel. Taking the keys from his pocket, Max opened the front door, and bent quickly to pick up a large pile of mail, which he put on the hall table. Then he stepped aside to allow his mother to enter. He decided, before crossing the threshold, to say nothing until she reacted. He saw, or rather took in, that the winter hadn't been kind. The garden was messy, a section of the fence was down and part of side gutter was on the ground. They looked around this soulless house that held so many memories, but now it was without its familiar echo. It was as though Helen would be back soon – there was a letter on a table, a dishcloth idly left on the drainer, a coat and hat on the back of a chair. But she wasn't coming back. This was the end. The dog, Dag, had gone back to his former family. Max decided to go outside, and walking towards the orchard, he changed direction.

Pausing at the garage window, he raised a hand above his eyes to shield them from the light and, leaning forward, peered inside. Helen's car was parked to one side, with a wide, empty space alongside. Everything looked untouched. He straightened, and for no reason, shivered a little. He went back inside, to find his mother in the kitchen, holding a small wooden box that she raised in her hand and said: 'We all played bridge with these.'

He smiled at her, then glancing around the kitchen, he stopped at the double-handed coke bucket between the sideboard and the Rayburn. That had been Dag's spot. Max knew what he wanted. He went to the sitting room, took two steps to the wall, and took down an oil painting about the size of a tea tray. It had been painted in 1901 by W L Wylie, portraying a gaff-rigged sailing boat, beating its way in a stiff breeze up the creek. It was the way the wind filled those sails, and the surging spray. It conveyed the details perfectly. In the background was a row of cottages and an empty plot alongside where Helen's house was now. He had stood in front of this painting many times as a boy and, inspired, had loved learning to sail his own boat, with Fred as his instructor. After this, they locked the house and drove back. That same evening, Max returned to London.

Towards the end of that week, a letter arrived from the undertaker, along with their bill, which Katherine paid. Then she sent these papers and a covering letter to the solicitor, so he could see the instructions in the codicil had been completed. She also listed the items they had removed from the house – just the bridge cards and the painting. About two weeks later, two identical, heavy quality manila envelopes came through her letter box, one addressed to Mrs K M Bentham and the other to Mr M Bentham. Katherine sat at the kitchen table, holding the envelope end onto the table and pondering its content. She suspected it was again from the solicitor.

She rang Max. He was busy, laying some new decking on a job, but he broke off to talk to her and she told him about the letter. He suggested she opened his first and tell him what it said. His mother read it verbatim:

Re Helen Josephine Howard (deceased)
Dear Mr Bentham,
This is confirmation that this firm has been appointed executors in the will of the above. We note from the will of the late Ms Howard that you are recorded as one of the beneficiaries to the estate.

Please will you confirm that this is your correct postal address and that we may contact you at this address during the administration of the deceased's Estate. If you prefer to be contacted by email please let us know. We require two forms of photographic identification to be produced at this office by yourself before matters can proceed further.

It was signed by Charles Peterson.

Max was surprised. He noted the solicitors' address and said he would make contact and arrange to see them. Katherine's letter was similar, but shorter and without any reference to identification being required. A second letter arrived a few months later, addressed to each of them. The wording was straightforward and brief. It said that the majority of the Estate was held in one property, and that after probate had been granted, the property would be sold. At a stage after this, when the Estate had been finalised, they would be in a position to make a distribution to all of the beneficiaries. Max just put all this to one side. The year dragged on, he had plenty of work to keep him busy, and it was not until the next April that another letter arrived at his London address. He read the letter carefully and then had to sit down.

His right hand was unsteady as he re-read this latest information from the solicitors, soaking up the words slowly. He was informed that matters relating to Helen's estate had been finalised, and the house had been sold. A cheque for his beneficial interest of £438,215.73 was enclosed. Attached to the letter, with an oversized coloured paperclip, was a copy of the grant of probate, the will, and copies of the final accounts. He was asked to confirm receipt of the cheque as soon as practicable. Max put the papers on the worktop, then placing both hands palms down and drawing a deep breath he felt its cool surface. Standing, straightening, he got up from the stool and walked round his small living room. This wonderful woman had brought his boat in for him. He knew this legacy was absolutely life-changing. Anything he wanted to do, or anywhere he wanted go, was now open to him. Taking his phone from his pocket, he pressed his mother's number. Katherine, although equally surprised, was more down to earth. 'Money won't change my life, but it can change yours. This amount is not enough for you to do nothing, but it is enough for you to do something.'

He was still feeling shaken when the call finished. It transpired that planning permission had been granted for three, large, detached houses on Helen's orchard and the whole site, together with the house, had been sold to a developer. He later saw, on examining the solicitor's accounts, the remainder of Helen's estate had been left to three separate charities, with a smaller sum to his mother. Max spent the rest of the month finishing jobs that he had taken on, because he didn't want to let people down. But his heart was not in it any more. He was restless. One of the projects was building a hall cupboard in a wide, but shallow, recess in a converted flat. The flat's female owner had picked up two goodish Victorian doors with moulded panels, which were for the front of the cupboard. To balance it, he was going to fit two narrower panels, then run it into the edge of the staircase at one end.

The woman had been specific about the height and widths of these shelves and the length of the rail. The woman, probably in her late 40s, had told him to help himself to tea or coffee, and had been about to leave the flat as they were talking. It did occur to him that she must have been up long before him that morning to look as she did when she set of for work. Pushing through the morning, the frame was in and the shelving started. Growing hungry sometime after midday he returned to the van for his sandwiches. His hand was barely on the handle of the van door, when he could see, quite clearly, that his lunch box was not on the front seat. Expelling a long breath of frustration, he muttered: 'Oh you bloody fool. It's still on the worktop at home.' He turned and set off to a corner shop that he had passed on his way in that morning. It was further than he remembered, and there were no sandwiches left. He came back with a pork pie, a carton of milk and a newspaper. Back inside, he made a mug of tea and sat at the kitchen table, unwrapped his pie and took an over-sized bite. Then, chewing, he unfolded the newspaper and lay it on the table. He skimmed through the headlines, and looked briefly at political story that he would read in more detail when he got home. Then he turned to the middle of the paper and was drawn, probably initially by the colour, to a large photo. Turning it around, he saw the picture was of a tower on a conical hill, taken at dawn with the background of the sea and a rising sun bursting the horizon. The caption spoke of delivering the golden promise of a new day. It was the Dorset coast. Max leaned back in the chair; he was totally captivated by the picture. Then, using a finger, he carefully drew an imaginary circle around it. Several pages and a few more stories later, he saw a headline 'Journey's End' and a picture of a former railway carriage. The text underneath explained that the carriage, with a wooden extension and a sun terrace beyond, plus an overgrown plot of ground, was due to be auctioned. It was in the middle of the Dorset countryside. Both pictures had sparked his imagination.

Pushing the chair back to the table, he folded the paper and put it next to his van keys. He put the packaging from his lunch in the bin and put the cup in the small dishwasher, then returned to the job in hand. Working steadily, he almost finished the guts of the wardrobe, but he then wound down like a spring from a clock, and stopped. It was 4.10 pm. Clearing up quickly, he left his tools in the wardrobe carcass and propped a note by the kettle: 'Back same time tomorrow to finish, would you like me to run a sander over the doors to clean off the paint that didn't come off in the caustic tank?'

Then, as instructed, he shut the front door with the second key to double lock it, posting the keys through the letterbox. He picked up a pizza on the way home and, after showering, changed into clean clothes. Organising supper was straight forward: plate, pizza, microwave; then a handful of rocket leaves, knife and fork, eat, done. Choosing a glass, he whipped off the top of bottle of malt beer and poured it slowly into the glass to avoid frothing it up. Moving to the sofa, he took a slow pull and placed the glass on the table in front of him. Without realising, his tongue snaked the froth from his top lip while he reached for the newspaper. He looked again at the photographs and a quick online search helped him locate the tower's location. Horton tower was built by a gentleman landowner by the name of Sturt in 1750. Sturt was the Lord of Horton Manor, as well as the MP for Dorset. It was said at the time to be the tallest non-religious building in Britain, standing 140 feet high. What its purpose was - if it had one - was less clear. It might have been used as an observatory, but more likely it was just a folly for the owner to admire from his estate. Looking carefully again at the picture, he studied the surrounding countryside, wondering what that coast line would be like. Placing the paper on his knee, he turned to the piece about the former railway carriage and then used his phone to search for property auctioneers in Dorset. Up came Pittock and Reid, an old family firm, and he saw that their next auction was May 28 - three weeks away. Their auction list included more than a dozen properties, and he went through them all carefully, focusing on two houses that were both worn out, but with apparent merit. Leaning back again, Max considered whether the random act of picking up a paper when he had gone to buy some lunch could be the spark that lit the tinder. The next day, he was back to work on the hall cupboard at 7.30, as requested. Again, the woman was just leaving. Speaking in a rush, she said: 'Thank you. It's going well,' and she turned around on the landing on the stairs.

The last he saw was a corner of her briefcase swing behind the newel post. 'Oh,' she popped her head above the banister rail. 'If you could do that sanding thing, it can only help, thank you.' And she was gone. Max worked steadily, finishing all the shelving, then using the trestles to lay out the doors and the larger sander, which he ran over the stiles and frame of both sides of both doors. He first used a medium, then a fine, sandpaper and gathered most of the dust in a bag on the plane. Finally, both doors were hung with small white china knobs and fastening bolts. Leaving his bill, he gathered his tools and headed home. All that evening, he couldn't get the idea of Dorset out of his mind. He decided, as it was nearly the weekend, he would go and have a nose around on Saturday, perhaps find a place to stay and make a weekend of it. The following day, he rang the agents and fixed two appointments to view. Very early on Saturday morning, he set off; first taking the main roads south until he made the London ring road. It was just after 7 as he joined the M25, and then he turned on the news. As the van settled at the speed limit, the engine noise swamped the news reader and he turned it off again. Transferring to the M3, he started the long run west. He had estimated that around three-and-a-half hours should cut it, and he planned to stop in about an hour for a good fry-up, which would set him up to meet the day. He had put his destination in the sat nav, but didn't think he would need it until he was a good deal closer. The miles churned.

Eventually, he reached a roundabout that took him onto the minor roads to the approach of a small, busy, ancient market town, built between two rivers. Driving down its main street, Max noticed the artisan bakery, three character pubs, a superstore, and several smart-looking clothes retailers. Pulling up at the traffic lights, with the old Market House, now a three-star hotel, on one side of him and the market square on the other, he waited for the lights to change and then crossed the long, narrow stone bridge leading to the flood plain marshes. The road rose a little, and he passed straggling cottages and nondescript housing spreading back from the main road in patches, before the view opened up. He was like a boy on holiday, full of expectation at every turn of the road. In front of him, a low wave of hills stretching across the horizon suddenly appeared and then, gradually, the heathlands with their grey, sandy soil gave way to fields and trees on the lower slopes. The tops of the hills were only grass with occasional stunted trees leaning heavily to the power of the wind. Slowing on a bend, he saw a sign with a narrow, single-track road leading to his destination; nine miles.

Rather than sticking to the direct route, on impulse he turned, dropped the gears and slowed, noticing the start of heavy weeds growing down the centre of the lane. The van wound its way along the valley, then, at a sharp corner, it started to climb steadily, traversing the hill with a lengthening view of the valley at each opening in the hedge. Pulling in a few times for oncoming cars to get by, he passed isolated working farms on the mud-spattered road, and a pair of holiday cottages wedged in a cleft on the hillside, before emerging on the very top of the spine. This would lead gently down for a few miles to his destination. In a dip on the top of the hill was a car park, small and sloping slightly, and he pulled in, parking away from three other cars. Walking up a stony path between some bushes, he came out on the very backbone of the hills. The land rolled away steeply on either side. Away to the east lay a huge harbour, its large bowl continuing through multi-hues of blue. There were a couple of islands and a patch of full sun picked out the far-off town, giving it a Mediterranean look. Swinging a half circle, he took in the most beautiful countryside of fields reaching out as far as he could see. It was as though he had opened a picture and walked into a world of warm colours and sounds. He felt he was standing in a holiday brochure. From somewhere came the sound of a light aircraft disturbing his thoughts. It didn't come close, and the sound of it had already started fading to a very slight buzz. Squinting, he looked up, but saw nothing. Looking back towards the lane, there was a gradual downward gradient as the hillside pointed the way to the sea. He could see part of a small town surrounding the edge of a bay. This was his destination. He walked back to the van, plugged in the sat nav, and drove on. The two houses he had come to see, both built of local stone, were quite different. The first one, in front of him now, was an end terrace house, one of a terrace of three. It was older than its neighbours, perhaps listed, and had a small triangle of ground at the side of it, big enough for a shed but he doubted it was large enough for a garage. As he was early, Max leaned closer to the front window and saw the house was empty. Standing on the opposite side of the road, with his hands in his pockets, he examined first the chimney stack with its flashings, then the slate roof and gutters. The old cast iron gutters were neatly holding two slipped slates. The roof was nail sick and the chimney's guts were very likely perished by a century of coal fires. All this was seen within not much more than a glance. Pulling his hands from his pocket, and about to cross the road, he was approached by an elderly man with an equally elderly, small dog. 'Needs a lot of work that one, hasn't had a bob spent on it since I was a boy,' he said, laughing and showing just a clutch of crooked teeth. The man shuffled off. Looking back down the road, Max saw a young man walking towards the house. He crossed over to meet the earnest young Flashman in a black suit, carrying a folder and keys – obviously the estate agent.

An outstretched, sloppy handshake opened their meeting and an auction catalogue was passed over, and then, after a juggling of keys, they entered the house. Following the agent round, Max took in the old lathe and plaster ceilings and tired, well-worked fireplaces. The ground floors were rotten, with fungus and spores spilling from the back of the skirting: the tell-tale of dry rot. He could see and smell damp, there was no bathroom and a sub-standard, lean-to kitchen and yard. It needed a full-scale modernisation; Max was unsure he wanted to take that on. Standing in the small sitting room, getting ready to leave, he looked at the single cross beam, examining the large rash of holes, as big as the end of an old-style key. 'Woodworm,' the agent said. 'It's to be expected in any house of this age.' While he was talking, Max fished from his pocket a small electrical screwdriver: 'May I?' Without waiting for a reply, he inserted the tip into one of the holes and, using the end of his finger, pushed very gently. The three-inch spike disappeared. Tapping the beam once to a hollow sound, he smiled at the agent, but said nothing. He knew it wasn't woodworm, it was far worse, it was death watch beetle. Max and the agent then left for the next property, which was only a few roads away. The guide price was higher. It was a two- bedroom cottage, basically sound, with no suspect cracking to the outside walls.

It had solid timbers and had been re- roofed at some stage, probably not long ago. All the exterior woodwork needed some attention, and the kitchen units suggested it had been modernised about 30 years ago. At the bottom of the plot, stood an old garage that wore a coat of corrugated iron, covered with lichen giving off a tired, rose red colour. Ivy smothered part of the flank wall, overgrown shrubs grew close, leaning on the extension with their branches, mingling with the compact, now wild westerly garden. It was in a state of false decay, because Max knew that, given a few weeks, he could really do something with this house.

Back inside, using his small screwdriver, he levered up the corner of both fitted carpets downstairs, to reveal flagstone floors. This all looked so very tempting, in many ways. If that auction gavel fell to him, this could be his new starting bell. Revealing no particular interest in either property to the estate agent, Max shook the man's hand and they went their separate ways. Seeing the agent drive away, Max walked to the end of the road, listening to the gulls' cries, and realised that this house was only two roads back from the sea.

Watching sea birds curling on the thermals, rising sharply with open wings, he turned the corner onto the promenade road. A sweeping, sandy bay was in front of him, flanked by cliffs. It was sheltered from the predominant south westerlies by high headlands. The tide, with hardly a ripple, was near full and barely lapping at the sand. This was a swimming heaven. Overdue for something to eat, he walked back to the cottage slowly and after prowling around outside again, he knocked on a neighbour's door to explain his interest. The conversation revealed a background with no horror stories, and Max then walked through the next road north where he saw The Quarryman's Arms, a small but comfortable-looking free house. Moving in a wide arc, he came out nearer to the town itself, with its early summer tourists mooching lazily in unplanned zig–zags. Pushing further into the busy town, he passed an old man, stiff-hipped and leaning with arthritic hands on a carved stick.

Sitting, waiting for a bus was a queue of elderly people, clucking animatedly at each other. Crossing the road at a running pace, he reached the café on the corner of the high street. He held the door open for a woman with a baby held securely in a sling in front of her, and a curly-haired child close behind. Choosing a table towards the back of the busy café for a view of the proceedings, he sat down and waited. The place was decorated with a beach and holiday theme, and there were fishing nets, an oar and all manner of things hung from the ceiling, including a lobster pot in the corner.

The walls were covered with large photos of sailing boats of all sizes, as well as youngsters' sailing dinghies. The pictures were all cleverly framed. Max must have been miles away, because suddenly a young woman was in front of him, ready to take his order. Apologising to her with a smile, he ordered the extra-large Spanish omelette with chips and salad, with a diet cola. Putting his hands behind his head, he stretched, not looking at the activity around him, but vaguely watching the moving traffic outside. He was enjoying what was a beautiful day. Before returning to the van, he went into a newsagent. Just inside the door, he stopped, looking at the headlines on various newspapers as he normally did; but he didn't pick one up. He felt to do so would break the spell. Looking around, he saw what he originally came in for - an ordinance explorer map of the whole area. This was the walkers' map, the one with every public right of way, bridleway, footpath, unmade cart track; it was all there. Taking his choice to the counter, Max was surprised by the warm greeting of the older woman behind the counter. It was only a simple: 'Hello. Can I help?' But it was the way she said it. The tone, the inference of her voice that she really meant what she said. He just stopped.

She took the offered map and note, then placed the change in his still open hand. 'You must be on holiday, I hope you have a lovely time.'

'In this area, you can't fail to can you?' he responded, smiling back.

Then he left the shop. It was the genuine interest in her customers that had surprised him. She had the time, perhaps that was the difference. In London, there was no time. People were just too busy to care about much. Walking with a hand in his pocket in a new direction, his fingers touched the coins as he registered an ice cream sign. On impulse, he stopped at the window, lingering over the choice. He came away with a Dorset banana cream. Just off the pavement, there was a bight of ornamental gardens with two benches. One was only part occupied. Leaning in slightly, Max said: 'May I?' Pointing at the end of the bench.

Back came a croak: 'Be my guest.' It was the usual race to lick the ice cream fast enough before it ran though his fingers, but not so fast that it would shorten and deplete the pleasure. Later, starting to move away, he heard the old man say: 'Hey, you've forgotten your map.' Turning and stepping back, he took it from the outstretched hand: 'I'd have been lost without it! Thanks.' The old man let out a noise that started as a chuckle and turned into a cough, which then absorbed all of his attention.

The sun had gone from the day and the sky had clouded over, but Max didn't think rain was coming. Cutting up a side street, past a small block of garages with fading peeling colours, he stepped off the foot path for a young mother with a pushchair. The muttered 'Thank you' was low, as though she was pre-occupied. More likely, she was just plain tired by the burden of her day. The side street only went so far, before thinning to a narrow passage with a muddy floor between two terraces. Pressing on, he emerged in another road of larger houses. He guessed they were artisan dwellings of the late Victorian era, well-kept and now owned by more prosperous families. Seeing a park at the farthest end with open gates, he went in. There were several pitches, with a roped off cricket square fronting a rather magnificent pavilion designed in another century. It had a full veranda, arched with brocade iron work topped with a small clock tower.

Max chatted to one of the dog walkers crossing the park and was told that both the pavilion and the bandstand near the other gate had been totally restored two years previously under a grant. All manner of music was staged on the stand throughout the summer. Leaving by the far gate, he made his way back to the seafront and crossed over to walk back along the beach, leaving only his footprints before the now receding tide. Max was pleased he had used his phone to take videos clips and photos during the day, especially of the second house and the road it was in.

Now he decided to make the most of the evening light and drive up the coast and through the villages to find somewhere to stay. He would return to London the next day. He drove out on the western coast road, thinking that the only thing he hadn't found in the town was something he didn't like. The road was long and uphill. The first village lay like a splash on either side of the road, with the cottages all built in the local, heavy grey stone. They were slotted in awkwardly in a jumble of shapes and sizes. The pub was doing its best outside, but couldn't hide the closing down sign in the convenience store next door. As the village slipped away, he passed a quarry on one side with cut and graded stones from slabs to briquettes in a large yard, then there were fields, greener and lusher than any picture. These stretched in front of him while the road snaked across the fields towards the sea. The next village, Combe Wallin, was about seven miles from the last and it clearly had a heart. There was a village square, with a double fronted pub facing it, surrounded by bigger cottages. All part of a widening circle of community. Parking close to a high, stone garden wall overflowing with honeysuckle along its full length, Max noticed a path with an arrowed sign *'To the rectory'*. Behind him was a tea shop, now closed and still, with a side garden and one-piece benches and tables. It was nearly 6.30 as he went into the pub in the square and asked if there was a single room for the night. They only had one single, and as it was early in the season, it was available. 'That's mine then, I'll get my bag,' said Max.

Standing perfectly still, the hot shower teamed down on him, running off his head and shoulders. With his eyes closed, he breathed in the memory of the day. Clean clothes on, phone plugged in to re-charge, he shut and locked the door. Food was his first thought, as he went downstairs into the short passage that emerged in the bar. It was a wide area, originally three or four rooms that had been opened up to provide a good-sized restaurant area. It was rapidly filling up, with an increasing buzz.

He immediately liked the surroundings, which included a large, open fireplace and a sofa with an array of small, comfortable, upholstered chairs. The interior had been designed with skill. At the bar, he collected a pint of local strong bitter and picked from the menu a large steak with asparagus and a salad. Finishing his food, and emptying his glass, he returned to the bar for another pint. He then walked over to a man, about mid-fifties and in a wheelchair, who was sitting at the back of the bar area on his own. Max had seen the man earlier, and he appeared to be quietly observing the movements in the bar with a small glass of beer beside him. 'Hello, may I join you?' The man in the wheelchair lifted his head and with some sort of a smile said slowly: 'Now that would be a pleasure.'

'My name is Max.'

'Well, Max, thanks for coming over. I'm Jeff. Sorry, I can't shake hands,' nodding towards his limp arms. 'Please, sit down. You here on holiday then?'

'Sort of, it ends tomorrow, then back to London. What about you, do you live here?'

'Yes I do, but it ends soon for me too, maybe in a few months.' His voice trailed off. To keep it going, Max said: 'So, where are you going back to?'

'I am not going back. I'm just going. I've got cancer, bone cancer. I get brought in here every so often to taste the beer. One day soon, I'll be horizontal on a wheelchair and then I'll only be able to smell the beer though the open window. For now, I like to look at the small details, everyday life that people often miss.'

Dropping his voice, he said: 'See the woman over by the corner? She's got an arse as wide as a small mattress.' Max practically blew the top of his beer. Jeff carried on: 'They had an all-you-can-eat for a set price here last week. She kept going back for more. It would have been easier if she had just taken her chair and put it alongside the hog roast. Having stuffed her face, she then went outside for a fag.' He stopped briefly. Max felt uncomfortable, he was unsure where this was going.

'You see,' Jeff delivered his message. 'I would really like to live. She doesn't seem to care. I have no choice in the matter, but she does.'

Max waited for him to take a wobbly sip of his beer. Then he saw a young man was striding across the bar towards them. 'Sorry I'm late, dad, we should go. Mary's got food ready.' With the briefest of hellos, he started to turn the chair towards the door. Jeff spoke one last time to Max before he left. 'If there is anything you want to do in your life, do it now, you don't have time to waste.' And he was wheeled away. Now was the right time, Max knew. Time doesn't 'slip' or 'tick' it is simply there while we travel through it. Our lives, our plans projected forward. He thought of the travellers' proverb: tomorrow is promised to no-one. So it was now.

Auction day. May 28

The auction started at 11am promptly. A semi-circular advertising banner, backing the rostrum, shouted the auctioneer's name and the company logo in large letters. It spanned the low stage, with the auctioneer in the centre and tables on either side. The PA system was lit up, several people, perhaps solicitors, were seated at the tables, working on last minute preparations on their laptops. In front of them in the conference room were about 60 chairs, mostly taken, divided by a central aisle. The deep spaces at the back and the sides of the room were filled with more than 50 people standing. The noise of chattering grew into a solid wall of sound. Max had taken his place, half-way down one side of the room, with the intention of watching the bids from unknown faces. He had been to a London property auction already, to understand what went on and how the auctioneer worked the room. This audience, although half the size at the London auction, appeared just as lively. He guessed who the auctioneer was, from the strident and confident manner in which the man moved among his peers.

Finally stepping to the rostrum, then clearing his throat with a backward cough, the auctioneer clipped his microphone onto his suit collar. Saying nothing at first, with a loose grip on either side of the rostrum, he surveyed his audience. Standing upright, he produced his gavel, holding the stem through his fingers. Its head protruded below his fist as he rapped it firmly on the side of the rostrum, then he said in a brisk, commanding voice: 'Good morning, everyone.' And with only the slightest pause while the sound fell away in the room, he launched in with: '14 interesting lots covering the full spectrum today. Telephone bids are being taken on my right,' waving his hand in the direction of his team, already holding mobile phones to their ears.

With his introduction over, he offered Lot one. 6 Lower Common Lane, a bay and forecourt with three bedrooms. 'Who will start me at, shall we say - 125?' This was below the guide price, but not necessarily the reserve. There was silence, it stretched into the quiet, and then it broke. 'Thank you, sir, 125 I have 125.' And it started. He used both hands outstretched to mark the bids, pushing them up £5,000 at a time, taking in the new bidders skilfully, although to the room it appeared at random. Reaching £155,000, it dropped to £1,000 bids before being knocked down at £162,000. And so the lots rolled, with the noise level rising and falling between them. This time was real, and Max became more tense as the lots passed, fingering the catalogue periodically to check the lot number.

When the monitor announced his lot, the catalogue picture came up on the screen and the auctioneer started again. 'Lot 9.' Max could feel the compression in his chest and a clamminess had crept up on him. 'Number 4, Wilson's Terrace, Carlisle Road. Where shall we start, 175?' Immediately, a heavy, florid-faced man in a red shirt put up his big hand. Max sized him up as a builder dealer. 'Thank you, sir.' Again, the hands went up and so did the price at £5,000 a touch, until it passed the guide price of £195,000 to reach £215, 000.

As the bidding dropped to £1,000 for few more bids, and then stopped, the auctioneer shot out a straight arm and pointed to a couple towards the middle of the room. He said: 'I'm here to sell. This property will be sold. I have £219,000. For the first time.' Max tried to look relaxed and waved his catalogue at the auctioneer. 'We have a new bidder at £220,000.' Looking to the couple who were busy whispering, the auctioneer took two more bids, then it faltered. He leaned forward with a wide smile and said: 'I have said before, never stop dead for a late bidder, he's probably just trying it on.' There was a small burst of laughter in the room and more whispering by the couple. The auctioneer carried on: 'To make it easier for you - £222,500?'

The man nodded, though the fight had gone from him. He was spent. The property was knocked down to Max at £223,000. A woman approached Max with the auction contract, leading him to a table in an anti-room as the auctioneer's voice faded a little. Sitting, Max realised he could only just write the deposit cheque; his hand had started to shake. Giving the name of the solicitor at a local firm who had done the due diligence for him, Max was then told completion was on, or before, four weeks. He stood, shook hands, and left the conference room with the papers. He felt exalted but worn out.

Chapter 11

During the return trip to London the reality sunk in. The high from the massive adrenalin rush was long gone, Max was now left with his plans to close his life in London and transfer to a new beginning. Excited by what he had achieved so far, he pulled over to the side of the road and phoned his mother. 'Wonderful news, I'm so pleased and excited for you. Helen would be, too; this is a new direction. I'm sure it will go well for you.' Questions and answers went backwards and forwards, and the call finished. He then contacted the solicitor, giving him the details and asking whether it was possible to have a two-week completion, rather than four, to get an earlier start. 'That shouldn't be a problem. I'll email you a completion statement for your funds transfer before the end of the week.'

'Thank you.'

Max slipped back into the traffic flow. He prepared a simple plan in his mind. All his tools, clothes and other small things would fit in the van; all large items would be sold through an online auction site. Anything else was on the pavement for a free take away; what was left would go to the tip. He already had a brace to package his prize possession, the painting of Itchenor, and this he would drop off at his mother's for safe keeping for a few weeks. Driving on, his mind settled to the hum of the tarmac for a while, before flicking back to Jeff, the guy in the pub in a wheelchair. It wasn't so much that he had accepted the cancer, rather, he was somehow just dealing with it. Jeff was now facing the dreadful unravelling of life. It was coming earlier to him than some, and he was at the start of what we all know is coming, but rarely acknowledge. The statement from the solicitors arrived by the end of the week, and funds were transferred. By then, Max had given his landlord a month's notice on his periodic tenancy. Two weeks later, he and the flat were packed, cleared and cleaned, and down the road. This time he didn't look back.

It was midday when he picked up the keys from the agents and then inspected what he had bought. He didn't miss much; it was just as he remembered. After moving his personal items to the back bedroom, together with an ex-Army camp bed, he moved all of his tools to the downstairs back room. Then changing into his old clothes, he stepped into the warm sunshine and began work, slashing back the honeysuckle and then cutting everything right back and re-shaping all the overgrown shrubs. He managed two trips to the dump to rid himself of the cuttings.

Two surprises were revealed. The first was an old Edwardian iron two-seater garden bench. Under it was a small herringbone brick patio with a path, which led to the side gate. Given a pressure wash, he would then add a soft border of pea shingle to lift the natural colours. He wired back the honeysuckle in an arch above the seat. This would later provide a fragrant canopy of shade. Small adjustments were made to the side gate, and the bolts could then be shut securely. Finishing up and washing with cold water, Max told himself it was going to be like camping for five or six weeks, until he got himself straight. That evening he called on both neighbours. On one side were Mick and Sharon and their little daughter. They were near to his age, pleased someone was moving in, and said the noise wouldn't worry them. On the other was a single man called Doug, perhaps in his early 40s. He was a self-employed electrician, and the two of them got on instantly. So much so, Doug came round to look at the fuse box that needed to be upgraded and connected with new, thicker earth wire, and agreed to do job the next Saturday morning. Max had located a builders' merchant on the industrial estate at the back of the town and indoor work would start in earnest the next day. By the end of the third week, the house was a very different place. He just worked and slept. The take-away food soon lost its appeal, but the end was in sight.

At the weekends, he went to the Quarryman's pub to eat and had got to know old Brolly the plasterer, who agreed to skim three rooms and the ceilings for Max, after more sockets and spot lights had been fitted. All the radiators were changed, Max flushed the system and fitted the new boiler, which would be connected and tested by a registered gas fitter at a later date. The new kitchen had arrived and would only take a couple of days for him to fit. Next would be the new bath, shower and tiling. All the old tongue-and-groove pine doors were removed with their hinges still on, and were stacked in the back room ready to be taken to a local caustic soda tank for stripping. Later, they would be re-polished to a warm high shine. Sundays, he worked in the garage. Using his bench saw to cut the joints and work with the timber clamps, he glued new, replica casements for three of the widows. One window needed a new sill, but otherwise all the frames and sills were sound. It was all shaping up well. A school-leaver looking for a holiday job was keen for a couple of weeks' preparation and painting work; and so by the end of six weeks, practically everything was done. Carpets had been laid upstairs, and the new bed – Max's first real item of furniture - had arrived the following day.

It was then he decided to have a sort of gathering of his neighbours, his new friends from the pub and the people that had helped him or worked with him along the way. He invited them all for an early evening drink that Saturday evening. During that morning, he went in the van to an off-licence, one of those by-the-case dealers on the back edge of town, and bought two cases of wine - one red, one white - plenty of beer and a selection of soft drinks. He also hired a box of glasses and took everything home. He then set off to walk to the weekly farmers' market in the high street. That was when he saw her first. She had her back to him, as he remembered. It was the Labrador with her that caught his attention; black but with a slight reddish-brown tinge on her back legs. He stopped, watching. The dog reminded him of Dag.

It was on a slip lead with no collar, sitting quietly, patiently waiting as the woman talked. It must have been well-trained, as Max could see the lead was slack. The dog turned and observed him too, before turning away with indifference. Max then saw the woman side on, as she stepped on to the street. She was in her 30s he guessed, dark hair and tall-ish. Splashed with bright colour. Then, she disappeared into a passageway leading away from the market. He was still for a moment, thinking of what he had seen. What was it that caused him to stop, was it the colours or her movement?

The noise from the street brought him up and he walked on in the other direction, trying not to become fixated on what he had seen. Back with the task, he chose all sorts of snacks, including game pies, unusual small sausages, olive bread and a variety of cheeses. When he got back, he set up his trestles in the back room, with a panel door on top to serve as a table. He covered it with a clean sheet, and put the glasses and paper plates ready. Sharon, next door, had agreed to heat the sausages in her oven and, after taking them round to her, Max filled his new fridge with bottles of white wine. A small barrel of beer was tapped ready in the kitchen. On the table, propped up for everyone to see was a small, coloured sign that said simply **Thank you everyone, for all your help.** This sign would later be hung in a black edged frame, as a reminder, and with a far deeper, personal meaning. It was a warm summer's evening and practically everybody who had been invited came, including Pippa Taylor, Max's local solicitor. Everyone seemed to mix easily as he wandered around filling glasses and offering food. The sounds of many different voices and laughter in his downstairs rooms and the garden made Max feel good about himself. It was a simple social occasion that finally breathed new life back into an old house. The last people drifted away about nine and he began to clear up. Later, when it was done, he toured his house room to room.

The polished pine doors with their Norfolk latches and the flagstone floors lifted the character of the place, and the new kitchen and bathroom fittings only added to its appeal. One day soon there would rugs, a sofa, a table and chairs to fully complete the picture. Making a last cup of tea, he retreated to bed. He plugged the phone in to charge, and, turning it on, just caught the local news and weather forecast for the next day. It gave a high tide at 11.52am, the winds would be very light, projected at 3 knots, with sunshine most of the day. His first swim in the bay was overdue. Leaning over the side of the bed, he thumbed the phone off, and turned off the tall angle poise light. Lying in the darkness, he thought of his mother's visit a few weeks back. She had been downcast, seeing the place at its worst, but now he could send her a raft of photos to show how much progress he had made and to encourage her to make another trip down. Last time was a blustery Sunday. They had a great day, lunch in a village pub, a short walk on the hills, then back to Hawkston for her to catch the train home. These images thinned, and he fell to sleep.

Up early next morning, he made breakfast and ate it quickly. Heading out for a circular walk, he picked up a newspaper at the newsagent in town. Scanning the cards in the corner of the window, he passed over the first few then stopped at: *Curtains, blinds and loose covers made to measure by professional seamstress.* He went back inside and borrowed a pen, as his phone was back at the house. Resting the newspaper with some difficulty on one hand, he wrote the number on the edge of a page. Just about to move away, he locked onto a small card outlined in red ink near the bottom of the window. In a flowing, neat, fountain pen handwriting, it said:

Spike needs a home. 3 year old mid-sized Lurcher. Will you be the lucky one?

Call in at 17 Archer Road or call this number.

A dog? This subject had been trailing Max for some time. It was a thought that reappeared every time he saw someone with one. Archer Road was familiar to him, too. Tilting his head backwards with his mouth slightly open, it came to him. It was a sign he had passed at the other side of town on a footpath. Why not, what harm could it do to see the dog? After handing back the pen, he retraced his earlier walk with a small detour to the footpath sign that cut through to Archer Road, arriving outside number 17. It was an Edwardian villa with a short, sloping front garden, leading to a front door that had lost its gloss some time ago. The steps were steep and uneven. Putting out his hand, like many before him, for the sturdy, rounded rail, he climbed and pressed the china button within the brass circle in the brickwork. While he was watching the breeze stirring the whips on the willow tree in the back garden, the door opened and out bundled the dog. Max felt his wiry coat pass through his fingers before a man, perhaps a decade older than Max, stood at the door. He pointed deep into the hall, and the dog sloped away.

'I saw your advert in the shop. May I talk to you about it?'

'Oh hello, yes, you're our first. We've made some big decisions lately and finding a good home for Spike is top of the list. Come in.'

Opening the door wider, the man said: 'Let's go in the kitchen, my partner has just gone next door, he'll be back in a mo.' As they moved to the kitchen, and started talking, the dog came close to Max again, nuzzling against him. Dropping his hand, he scratched the dog's ears gently, while the man – who introduced himself as

John – sat in a chair near the table. Max, looking through the window, saw another man appear through a hole in the hedge. As he came in, John said: 'Rhys, this is Max, he's here about Spike. An ex-Londoner like us and keen to have a dog. I'll make coffee.'

And so, the three of them talked the situation through.

It became apparent that John and Rhys had kept hold of a London flat that belonged to one of them when they first met. Although they loved being in Dorset, John had been offered a new job back in the capital and they had decided to move back. Neither felt the move to the city would be good for the dog. They agreed to call round for a chat and a drink the next evening. They wanted to see where Max lived and to sort out the logistics. They shook hands. It was clear Spike was going to be well cared for. As Max walked down the road, he checked the time; it was coming up to 11am, so he put a pace on to get home. He located his swimming bag and, taking nothing in his pockets but a £10 note and some coins, he left by the back door. After locking it, he took the few steps to the garage and, reaching up behind the honeysuckle, he placed the key in the gutter. Walking out of the side gate, he turned from the alley crossing the road. He looked back only briefly, aware that Helen's legacy was the spanner that had turned his life around. Further down the road, he waved at Mary sitting in the same place as she always did - in her sunny front bay watching people pass; too old and worn out to walk with them now, but still keen to wave as neighbours walked by.

As he emerged from the sheltered back streets out onto the sea front, he immediately felt a warm breeze on the side of his face. It was dead on high tide as he went down the steps from the promenade onto the beach by the wall. Finding a spot, he took off his clothes, and, with his trunks on, holding his goggles, he turned to face the sea. He hesitated when he heard the voice for the first time of the man who would soon become his swimming partner. 'Are you swimming down to the buoy and back?' asked the man striding down to the water's edge. There were many times during the last year that Max had dreamed of this moment, but could he still do the distance, he wondered. Max nodded, and, as they waded into the water together, said: 'If I slow down, don't stop for me.' He was slow, and the other swimmer did stop and wait for him.

They rounded the buoy together and Max had to slug it out on the half-mile return leg. He made the beach bent over and gasping for breath. Tom introduced himself. Still doubled over and gasping, he just managed the single word: 'Max.'

Straightening, Tom laughed: 'You're OK - just unfit. You'll need more practice for the carnival swim.'

'What's that?'

'Ah, I thought you might be new here, as I've not seen you at the beach swim club. You've had a layoff, I reckon, have you been injured?'

'Well, not exactly. But I'm ok now.'

'The big race is further up the beach, one mile plus from the breakwater to the town beach. During the summer months, I'm out swimming every Tuesday and Thursday here at 6pm; high tide, low tide, any tide that half-mile buoy and back is swimmable; well, unless it's a big blow. See you Tuesday maybe?'

'OK'

Then, with a handshake, Tom was gone.

Returning home, Max changed into his working clothes, grabbed a drink and went into the garage. He turned on the light, preferring not to keep the door open, because of his tools. At the far end, turned over, was a Victorian swing top circular table just over three feet across and four matching church chairs, which he bought the day his mother came down. Removing the badly stained top, he placed it on a blanket so as not damage it. Starting with a medium sand paper, he rubbed the table gently in a backwards and forwards direction only. He was sanding away the surface of grime, collected over a hundred years. When finished, all the blemishes were gone, and he carefully set about the same procedure with a very fine wire wool on the double rolled edge, so not to damage it. Standing back, he could see the soft orange-red colour and smell the scent lifting from the mahogany, even after so much time.

Feeling pleased with the result, he went back to the house to make a cup of tea. Returning, he examined the hinge lock. It was loose in its seating, so he re-plugged the holes, then re-fitted the brass hinge lock solid. Taking more sandpaper, very fine this time as there was less to remove, he started on the pedestal. When this was finished, he cleaned up using the vacuum cleaner he kept for work. Putting on gloves and using a cloth, he applied a thin coat of light shellac, which was then wiped and partially removed with a clean cloth. This brought out more of the colour. Satisfied, he repeated this on the pedestal. Lastly, using a mop head fine brush, he applied the French polish. After a short while, he wiped it to a shine with another clean cloth. This brought through the magnificent colour of the wood. Leaving this to dry overnight, he would later give the table a light coat of beeswax and polish it until its lustre returned. Checking the chairs' stability, he took them outside to reduce the amount of dust, and gave them a heavy polishing. After locking the garage securely, he went in for a shower.

The next day, he decided to take up Vic Buckingham's offer. He had met Vic in the pub, and Vic had told Max to come by his workshop anytime and have a chat. He reminded him again when he left the drinks party. Max put on some clean clothes and came down the narrow staircase stepping up a single step to the kitchen. He chose a bright flower pot style mug for tea, feeling it matched his mood, and then put on two eggs to boil. While waiting, he phoned the seamstress whose advert he had seen about making blinds for his house, and left a message. As the alarm for the boiled eggs went off, the heavily-buttered toast was already on the plate. Moving with his breakfast to the back room, he crossed the stone floor as he took the first draw of tea. He had quickly grown to appreciate this east-facing room at this time of day. The morning sun eased its way over the window sill, stretching its light into the room. He quickly became used to its warmth and this became his favourite place for breakfast.

After clearing away and washing up, he left everything to drain, put on his heavy shoes and went out of the back door, locking up behind him. It had rained during the night leaving a changed colour on the path slabs. The privet hedge brushed against his shoulder as he turned to the side gate. It sent a spray of water to his chin. He stopped, then smiled to remind himself of this small burst of nature.

Turning past the gate, he walked leisurely down towards the town centre passing several other people. Many of them greeted him with 'Good morning' even though he didn't know them. This was a new concept for Max, and he was getting used to it. It was only a 20-minute walk to where he thought Vic's workshop was. Eventually turning into a side street with slash of flat-fronted Victorian cottages on either side, he saw the alleyway on the left was only as wide as a man could reach. Facing him was a large single storey building, built of concrete blocks with a low span asbestos sheet roof. The mid-brown faded folding door held a small sign and an arrow pointing to the continuation of the path at the side of the building. A useful yard was at the rear, with a block wall topped by bent, but secure, railings. Vic was clearly no gardener. Max could see a tired, but usable, long bench and oversized self-seeded forsythia bush through the railings. Time had raced over what had once been a garden. A set of folding wooden doors, the same faded colour as the one he had just seen, was in front of him. Resting his hand lightly on the door, he lifted the broken latch and went inside. He took it in with a ranging glance. The lathes, a long, carpeted bench, gas, glue pots, bench planes, tool cupboards overflowing; bunches of door braces hanging in different sizes; timber in wracks hanging from the ceiling. There was beech, mahogany, pine, oak and more. Oak building pegs that had been turned traditionally were stacked in a corner - all hewn from this man's soul. The smell in the workshop was a joy to Max. It was a complex mixture of soft fragrances from afar, clinging to the very fabric of the building. Vic was at the far end.

He turned, or rather looked over his shoulder, and called out 'Hello mate'. Then putting down a part-made beech chair leg, he flicked a switch to cut off his lathe. Waving an arm a full 90 degrees, he said: 'Welcome to my corner of heaven.'

As Vic reached over to a sink that was out of sight to Max, he could hear the tap going, filling a kettle. In the background somewhere a radio was playing chamber music softly. Vic was a short man, somewhat round and ruddy, unshaven and wearing a long, brown 'Arkwright' coat over jeans and a sweater with highly polished, brown Doc Martin shoes. The polished shoes seemed odd, but gave a hint that this man liked order amongst what was, to the untrained eye, disorder. His gait was an unusual shuffle, seemingly on the front of his feet. Vic soon advanced with two mugs of strong, unsweetened tea. Max had liked Vic from the moment he first met him. He was open, welcoming and helpful and Max hoped, perhaps in time, he would gain his friendship.

What he wanted today was to ask Vic if he could rent the part of the workshop he didn't use. After handing over the mug, Vic said: 'So, old son, what are you after?' It was much easier than expected. Vic was only too happy to let Max use the rear lean- to store, on the basis that he would strip and repair the roof properly. There was power, the floor was sound, and the door and doorframe were solid. Vic didn't want any money at this stage, because that would involve the expense of sorting out a lease and he didn't know if the two of them would really hit it off.

'Sort of suck it and see,' he said. Vic was canny, it was more about the repair to the building.

'Six months, rent free, in exchange for a new roof - all expense down to me,' Max put forward. Vic, grinning, put his hands behind his back and raised himself on his toes slightly, then eased back saying, like a man who knows his horse is a winner: 'Three months.' It was a done deal, even before Vic had finished speaking. Future rent was agreed at no more than it cost to rent a large garage, and there would be a contribution for the electricity. The space was as big as a double garage, and Max would use it when he found some work. They shook hands. Max would later realise that, when it came to money, Vic and cash had a special relationship. It would take Max a full week to strip the tiles, felt and batten the roof, then re-tile it. There were spare tiles covered with overgrowth in Vic's yard, and these would come in handy. After fitting new lead flashing, Max would run new cables from the junction boxes and fit new sockets and strip lights for safety. One bonus was that, underneath all the rubbish, all down one side, was a sturdy work bench. Weather permitting, Max decided to start the following day. Walking home, a greyness tinged the cloud; not rain, but the colour had slipped away from the sky. Stepping off a pavement to cross the road, a fast-food bag moved in the gutter. Then he heard the contents rattle in the breeze. He joined the promenade road with its backdrop of hills, reaching like an arm of protection around the bay. Pausing at the stand-alone Tourist Office, with its full glass front, he leaned forward to look at the small poster for the local independent cinema, The Lightroom. It was in what looked like a converted chapel in Fore Street.

About to step back, something made him look through the glass and beyond. He was being watched - by a black dog lying down with its head on its paws, completely relaxed, but alert. It was probably the dog that made him go in. Once inside, the door self-closed; the office was apparently empty.

The dog had just enough time to stand before a woman rose from behind the counter with a large pile of brochures in her hands. Max realised, when he saw the dog more closely, that it was probably the same dog he had seen in the Farmer's Market on Saturday, and its owner was now in front of him. As she greeted him with a straight forward 'Hello', she tried to place the brochures on the desk top, but they spilled from her arms, several falling at his side.

He bent to pick them up and the dog, sensing a game, was all over him, licking him. It broke the ice when she laughed, the dog nuzzled him again. 'She likes you, I can tell.'

He quickly took in that she was maybe a few years younger than him, but not by much, and was very attractive. He spotted that she wore no rings.

'Anyway, how can I help?'

'I saw the poster about the independent cinema. I've just moved here from London and I'm very keen to find out more.'

If he had reached for a light switch in the dark, he found it first time. She explained that she helped out at the cinema, and for the next 15 minutes the two of them talked about films. Then the door opened and two couples came in. Max hovered while they collected information, had a quick conversation with the woman, and then left. It seemed somehow that his moment had gone.

'Well, perhaps Betsy will find you on the beach sometime,' she said.

Keeping eye contact with her, Max replied: 'I hope so.'

He thought, why wait for another chance?

'Would you like to come out on Friday, so we can talk some more? We could have a drink, something to eat? I'm Max, by the way.'

She looked directly at him for a few seconds, caught off balance.

'I'd like that, but I have to check something when I get home.'

She wrote her number on a piece of paper and passed it to him.

'Could you ring me later?'

He looked at the piece of paper and read her name and number.

'OK, Roma, I'll ring after 7.'

She smiled, and then he left.

Deciding to walk through the 'new and not so' emporium, he practically fell over a pair of almost new two-seater, square edged, grey cushioned sofas. Looking at them and thinking over the price, he sensed the salesman at his shoulder.

'Very nice, they've just come in, good quality, and without a blemish.'

'Well,' Max said. 'There is one blemish,' pointing to the price tag. 'If I were to ask, how much for both, delivered round the corner to Carlisle Road?'

'Oh, um, I'm sure we could do something, there,' he said. 'I think we could lower it by £10.'

Max, enjoying the game, responded by turning away from him and saying: '£20 and you'll make a sale.'

'Done, when do you want them delivered, yesterday?'

'As soon as possible, I've nothing to sit on.'

The salesman said he would deliver the sofas himself after closing up the shop around 6pm. Paying with his card, Max left the store, feeling that things were moving fast. As he arrived at his front door, he took from his pocket the piece of paper as well as his keys, then went in. On the mat there was a delivery note saying that a parcel was under the seat in the garden. This contained the self-adhesive signs he had ordered for the side of his van. He checked them, they looked good.

THE JOINERY SHOP - *all works undertaken*
Underneath was his phone number and email.

Later, the two sofas were delivered and in place and the door knocker went for the second time. It was John and Rhys with Spike. John said they just wanted to make sure Max lived where he had told them he did and that he could be trusted with their dog. They came in, and briefly looked around the downstairs rooms. 'Can I get you a glass of wine, or maybe coffee?' asked Max. They looked at each other, as if waiting for a mutual response. Then John said: 'Coffee would be great, thanks.'

While Spike sniffed his way around the kitchen. Rhys went through what food the dog was used to, and how much, and wrote down details of the vet he was registered with. Max explained that, as he worked for himself, he intended to take the dog with him whenever possible, and he would rarely be left alone. John returned his empty coffee cup to the tray, and looked at Rhys as if to encourage agreement. John touched the edge of the table and said: 'We don't want any money for Spike, we just want to know he's in a good home, and we're happy with what we've seen.'

'OK, that's great,' said Max. 'But if you won't take any money for yourselves, would you be happy if I wrote a cheque out to the charity of your choice?'

They agreed, then Rhys said he would call the vet to say that Spike would be living with Max from now on. They would bring the dog back, with his basket, lead and toys, the next day. They weren't moving for a few weeks, so they were on hand if there were any problems or Max changed his mind. John started to get a bit emotional, but Spike seemed indifferent. Having sniffed all around the ground floor, he went into the garden for a leak. He was a beauty. Shortly afterwards, with more handshakes, John and Rhys left.

At 7.30, Max called Roma. She said she would love to go out on Friday, and he took down her address as 4, Pickering Farm Cottages, along with the postcode. He said he would call for her at 7. Looking up the postcode, it was a wild spot, about three miles to the north west of Eartham. The pub he had in mind – The Bear and Ragged Staff – could be full on a Friday, so Max called and booked a table straight away. Spike arrived the next day and quickly made himself at home. Max walked him in the early mornings, finding the dog was trained only in the essentials. It thrilled him to see the dog turn on the speed. He came with Max everywhere, happy to sit on a blanket on the front seat of the van, or in the back. Two full days on the workshop roof saw it felt and battened and nearly tiled out.

One more would see the lead flashing fitted and the tile ends mucked in neatly, with the broken gutter re-fixed to the down pipe. A neighbour appeared while he was working, asking if he could have the pile of broken tiles to fill in a fish pond and barrowed them away.

Friday came. Leaving on the Hawkston Road, Max almost missed the little lane with the sign to Seven Acre Wood. Turning into the narrow, uphill road, he eventually reached the cottages which lay end on in a stone lane of their own. Leaving the van with Spike in the back, he walked across the lane to Number 4. The house looked as if it hadn't quite taken the winter in its stride. Reaching out, Max knocked loudly.

The Lightroom

Chapter 12

Roma remembered clearly now. Standing up, the brochures and leaflets had fallen from her arms. Just about to curse, she realised someone had come into the office. Looking up, she saw a man already stooping to help pick up the leaflets. Oh heavens, the dog was all over him. Holding out her hand, she had taken the pile that he picked up and thanked him. Trying to sound relaxed, she had asked how she could help. He was maybe a few years older than her, she guessed, wearing jeans and a dark blue T-shirt. He had the strong outline of a man who looks after himself. He was polite, relaxed and obviously keen on films. Maybe she'd monopolised the conversation, because of her own enthusiasm, and just as she had grown curious about him, several people had come into the office and derailed it all. She thought he was going to leave. And then, he had asked her out. She knew she had been hesitating, not nervous just unsure, perhaps. Friday was her last day in the tourist office. It was just filling in for a few days really, some extra work during the school holidays. Her main job was teaching at Hawkston Junior School and she often took on temporary jobs for the odd week during the summer vacation. Her university friend, Alice, was the owner of The Pier café and she was going to help there in August. Well, that was the plan. So here she was tonight, wearing clean jeans and a long-sleeve T-shirt, hoping she had been right to say yes. Flicking her hair up with both hands and checking herself in the mirror, she started down the steep centre stairs. Before she reached the bottom step, there was a loud rap on the door. Betsy started barking in the back room.

'Quiet Betsy.'

The barking eased, the dog must have wandered back to its basket.

Roma opened the door and Max was standing just off from the step. She watched him withdraw his hand from his jeans pocket, holding his keys by the ring in a bunched fist.

'I hope you won't mind, but I've come in the van. Comfortable though. My dog Spike is in the back.'

'That's fine by me.' They walked towards the van.

'You didn't tell me you had a dog too?'

'We didn't have enough time.'

He opened the passenger door for her, then reversing to turn, the engine revved and the van juddered over the stone lane.

Once on the tarmac, he started to explain the circumstances: how the dog had only just come to live with him, and how it was working out. Spike came up close to the mesh to inspect the newcomer, and she put her hand flat on the mesh and said 'Hi, Spike.' The dog sniffed and lay down again. Max drove down the lanes to the main road running west for a few miles, before turning at the sign for the *Bear and Ragged Staff.* Giving a quick point at it, he said: 'I've booked a table at this pub. I hope that's ok?' A few minutes later, he pulled the van into the car park. The pub was an old coaching inn, built of local stone, with a slab stone roof and low beamed ceilings, decorated with a warm easy country style.

'Can I get you something to drink before we eat?'

'Oh yes, please. A glass of red wine would be lovely, thank you.'

Before turning to the bar, he looked straight at her and said simply: 'You look lovely.'

Then, ordering a large glass of wine and a pint of the gold, he opened a tab and turned back to Roma. Once settled at a table, and having ordered their food, she answered his questions about how she came to be working locally.

She talked of her grandparents' decision to move to the UK when her father was very young, and, as soon as he was old enough, he had joined the Navy. They had moved, as a family, many times because of her father's career, and in his 50s he had taken a post at the military base further west. They had bought a house in a village called West Combe, where her parents planned to stay when he retired. While Roma was at Birmingham University, her father had a massive heart attack on the base and died where he fell. Her brother, six years older than her, was cutting out a career in the US and when Roma got her Maths degree, she headed for London, the lights and the money. Three years in, working for a bank in Canary Wharf, surrounded by wall-to-wall suits, produced little but a slow burning dissatisfaction. It was a newspaper article that did it. She changed to Teach First, spending just over four years teaching at a secondary school in Haringey. This placement was the challenge that she needed and expected. Those four years had their highs and lows, but it was the education system and the deadwood that eventually drove her down. During these years, her mother met someone and moved to Bristol, selling the Dorset house and severing the tap root there. After a longish relationship of her own had evaporated, Roma's old friend Alice had side-tracked her when she came down to stay for a summer holiday. That was just before Alice opened The Pier café, a few years back now.

Max talked too, telling of a happy childhood and his summers on the West Sussex coast. He talked briefly about his hard schooling, his decision to train as a carpenter and his London life. But he missed out the pain, the depression and his time in prison. These experiences lived in the shadows of his memory. He talked of the people he'd met since his move to Dorset and the genuine warmth he felt for most of them. He spoke about his love of swimming and, of course, films; touching on politics. He told her of his hopes of establishing a business locally and maybe getting a dinghy.

The evening went quickly, they enjoyed each other's company and they left the pub close to 11, arriving back at her house along the same stony path under a dark, moonless sky that promised rain. Walking to the door, she took her keys out and said: 'Would you like to come in for coffee?'

'Thank you, but not this time. I've really enjoyed getting to know you and would like to see you again, perhaps we could take the dogs out for a long walk somewhere.'

'I'd like that.'

There hung the moment.

He turned, almost too quickly, and walked to his van. Stepping back, she saw the van lights move, then they quickly disappeared. Standing still, her thoughts were overtaken by another sound, that of Betsy pawing the door. She let the dog out, putting the latch on the door, and waited. Betsy crossed the lane and went into the field, slipping into the darkness. Roma took a deep breath and began turning over the evening in her mind. She had two glasses of wine to his one pint for a start. Had she talked too much? He was so easy to talk to, he asked questions, he was attentive. She liked his voice and the way he looked directly at her when she was talking. There was an unknown depth with a quiet confidence about him, suggesting great inner reserves. They shared interests. She was a good sea swimmer and they had both dabbled with sailing. When he talked about himself, he clearly was his own man, a thinking man too; but there was something she sensed or felt was missing. Then it came to her, he had talked far less about his past than he did about the future. Betsy walked past her into the house, and Roma followed her in.

Max's drive home turned out to be eventful, and his chosen route led to a chance meeting with someone who would become a firm friend.

That evening, Theo had been very lucky, but his easy going, happy demeanour had just evaporated. He was returning with stock he had bought for his antiques shop from farther west. His estate car was heavy on the roof and low on the springs. Having taken a short cut, linking the two main roads on the last leg of his journey, he was hoping to be home around 11 when the car developed a gearbox problem. It would no longer go into gear at all. Just coming out of a corner and changing up, he discovered there was no up, or down just extended neutral. Pushing in the clutch, he allowed the estate car to cruise to a stop, not quite reaching the overtaking bay.

He was stuck in the middle of the narrow lane with his hazard warning lights on. It was then that he saw lights approaching and was concerned for his own safety. He was out of the car now, waving his arms. He needn't have worried, as the lights slowed and a small white van pulled up behind him. The rain had set in and his only protection was a thin anorak and a peaked hat. The driver, who looked about his own age, got out of the van, pulling on his coat. He advanced towards Theo quickly, leaning forward as if to make less of himself. As he reached him, he straightened. Theo could see he was tall, well-built, and dressed in a proper wet weather jacket. 'Can I help? What's the problem here?'

Theo explained what had happened, with worry stained on his face. 'Well, let's have a look. Open the bonnet, I'll get a torch from the van,' said Max. He was back with a large, very powerful flash light. Leaning right over the wheel arch, he pointed it downwards into the tightly packed engine. He straightened again, abruptly removing his heavy waxed jacket and rolled up the right sleeve of his T-shirt to the very edge of his shoulder before working his arm downwards through the engine's tangle. Grunting with the exertion, he suddenly cursed, and slowly withdrew his arm. It was smeared with oil and there was a nasty graze running from the elbow down towards the wrist, leaking blood over his thumb. He smiled benignly and said: 'One more try, this time I'll be more careful.'

After a couple of minutes, he withdrew his arm again and, smiling, said: 'That's a temporary fix. Start it in second gear and leave it there until you're home. It's the ball and socket joint that needs to be renewed.' Without looking at his arm, or even mentioning it, he rolled down his sleeve, and put his jacket back on. Then, lowering the bonnet, he snapped it shut. Although the rain was easing a little, Theo was wet and cold. He was quick to say how grateful he was and immediately offered to pay Max for his help. Shaking his head, Max said: 'The time will come when you can help someone else.' Then he held out his hand, introduced himself, and asked how far Theo had to go. 'Oh, only to Combe Wallin, a few miles west of here. What about you?'

'The other way, I've just moved here. Best of luck, and don't change gear.'

Theo laughed, then said: 'Give me your phone number, you must come over one evening, I'll ring you.' Max gave him the number, thinking he'd heard that line a few times before. Theo got back in his car, started it gingerly in second gear as he was told, and, giving it good revs, he waved and moved away. With his headlights blinking over the hedgerows as he approached the crossroads, he swung the wheel and only dropping a little speed turned right, breaking gently as the road sloped away. Another look in the mirror told him that Max had taken the lower road and was immediately lost from view. Within 15 minutes, Theo was pulling on to the forecourt of *Barn Antiques*, a large barn alongside a small, but well cared for thatched cottage on the edge of an oversized village. It was originally for farm workers, but with mechanisation, second home-owners and holiday lets, the village population was very mixed. Opening the dark timber doors, he drove the car into the shed and then turned off the engine and went into the house.

When Max got home, he went for a short walk with Spike. Then he locked the doors and went upstairs to bed. His last thought was of Roma.

He rang her two days later and, as she was not working that week, they decided to meet for a walk the next day. Starting early, they bundled the dogs into the van on that August morning, then drove across the hills and parked, wedged on a shallow bank, just off the edge of the road. They let the dogs out of the back and let them run free. As the red flag was down, they could walk across the ranges. It was past 9 now and the morning sun was well up, leaking heat into the day. Just back from the sea was a wide band of shingle with scattered gorse bushes and low heather, interspersed with patches of stunted Holm oaks stretching for a couple of miles down the coast. It started with light walking on paths between gorse and wild blackberry bushes, progressing to heavy deep shingle with wider spaces. They had to lift their feet higher to clear the many ruts left from the tyres and tracks of the army vehicles that used this land for military training exercises. Max looked at Roma as she walked a few yards in front of him. She allowed the slip lead from the dog to dangle to the rhythm of her stride. The summer skirt she wore was a bright floral pattern, and her T-shirt was electric blue. They walked on, with the dry grass waving lightly at their calves. They slowed as they approached the shade of a clump of trees. She turned, looking at him, smiling, and pointing at their dogs. It was the way a smile started on her face that he noticed, a tilt of her mouth then the intensity of her eyes overtaking it. Out of the trees and pushing on through the shingle and the low heather, the wild flowers were just about losing

The Lightroom

their colour to the burn of summer. Then they climbed the first of three long, high banks that, in the past, must have been used as barriers to small arms fire going seaward. The view was always striking here. Standing out were intense light patches of bright sunlight that sat on the sparkling sea. More walking took them to the shell strewn beach and the sea was literally lapping at their feet. Stopping for a moment, he looked at her and said: 'These are the days of our lives, and when the moment is gone, you know it's gone forever.'

A power boat passed, parallel to the shore, with the widening arc of its wake seemingly tugging at its flapping ensign as if to hold it back. The constant hum of its diesel engine dominating the flat stillness of the early part of the morning. Someone was standing still, with hands on an unseen wheel, and it could have been the sun glasses the man was wearing that Max focused on briefly. Then his eyes swept the seascape, taking in the anglers' boats anchored further out, lying flat on the last of an incoming tide. As the boat skimmed further away, the crunching of the shingle beneath their feet became the loudest sound again. They were happy to be alongside each other with unspoken words. Pointing, he said: 'Here's the perfect spot.' Taking her hand, he supported her as they walked down the shingle bank. Then, lying back with the shelving bank as a back rest, she moved closer to him, tucking her head near to his shoulder. Reaching, without looking, he threw a stone in the opposite direction of the dogs for them to chase, then another the other way. Sitting up later, he leaned towards her and said: 'I want to give you something.'

He held out a downward facing, closed hand. 'It's one of nature's oldest treasures. It is just like you. When you hold it, it's warm, it has a perfect shape and it is intrinsically very beautiful indeed.'

She sat up too. Holding out her hand, he put in her palm a small, light brown pebble. Closing her hand, she felt its shape first, then, slowly opening her fingers, she looked at him and said: 'Thank you, I'll keep it safe.' After holding it for a while, feeling its warmth, she pushed the pebble deep into a pocket. Lying back with her eyes shut and feeling the sun warming her face, she thought that what she had just heard was probably one of the most beautiful things that had ever been said to her. Eventually, she stood first, offering him a hand: 'I'll pull you up.'

'You'll be lucky.'

She then offered both hands and he playfully became a deadweight as she drew him up until he passed the tipping point when he suddenly reached forward and took her in his arms, and gently kissed her. The dogs came from the shade as they climbed the shingle. With their feet sinking with each step, they cut across the top of the beach, passing patches of sea cabbages and joining the grassland that eventually led to the start of the sea wall. At that point, the tide had, over decades, cast up the shingle to the top of the groin posts, leaving them stranded, like buttons on a waistcoat. With the point behind them, the groins with their shuttered, linking boards grew more exposed, the lower ones were not yet covered by the incoming tide. Roma touched his arm and pointed to one of the posts nearest to them at the highest edge of the beach. Tied lightly was a bunch of fresh, red roses, gently coming out of bud into flower. Descending the granite steps, just a few feet brought them to the post. They both saw the two small parcel tags with reinforced holes on red ribbon fluttering like butterflies in the wind. This was an act of remembrance from a mother and daughter. They noticed a heavy, rusting nail driven into the side of the post, perhaps to hang a towel, maybe they had lain out of the wind, behind that very groin after the summers' swimming. Roma's face twisted, and, in some small way, she felt their loss. Walking away up the steps again, the dogs leapt past them from the beach. They crossed the sea wall, taking a track leading across the golf course. They slowed to watch a golfer. The stroke was played with a swinging lurch, producing a thinning shot that found its way effortlessly to the deep brine-filled ditch. They pressed on down the long, looping footpath between the fairways, eventually leading back to where they had parked the van.

Two days later was his first visit to The Lightroom cinema with Roma. The converted chapel was a total surprise.

It had been created by The Design Span Partnership – two young architects, busting with ideas that enlivened and inspired those that visited the building. Roma was overspill in the office and helping to take the tickets. The cinema was almost full that evening. The film was shot in the flat salt lands in central Spain, a tense award-winning drama that lived up to its critique. The sub-titles were second nature to him now. Afterwards, Max helped clear up and then she drove her car, with Betsy, to his house.

He cooked supper, they drank wine, the dogs slept on the carpet, and she stayed, as they both knew she would. The next morning, he let the dogs out of the back door while making tea, then carefully carried the two mugs upstairs to the bedroom.

She was sitting up now, hugging her knees, and resting her chin on them. He placed her tea on her side of the bed before sliding into his side again. 'Why do I like you?' she asked. Looking down at her outstretched legs, she tilted her head back towards him. 'Probably because with you, there's no pretence, no games. The men in my past usually wanted to change me, or tell me what I should be doing with my life - but not you. You really listen, you're interested. It's just so easy.' Then she moved her head to the other side, awaiting a reaction. He just smiled at her. She carried on: 'But, what about you?'

Max didn't answer straightaway. He was looking directly at her as he thought about what had happened to him in the past few weeks. He had made several good friends since moving to Dorset and he felt accepted here. He could see that Roma was the catalyst that could make his life even better and help him build deeper relationships. He knew that men and women make friends differently. Women seem more open and find all manner of personal subjects to discuss immediately. They bridge their differences. But men are more defensive, slower to come forward, maybe their egos, maybe their competitive nature, get in the way. Sometimes it takes longer to iron creases in that will last.

Most people want to be part of something, to belong. It is in the very nature of our being. Still smiling, he said: 'I know exactly why I like you.'

They lay together for a little longer. While she was in the shower, he was thinking over the parts of his life that he had yet to tell her about. But now didn't seem the right time. Over the next couple of weeks several things happened. His mother drove down, bringing the painting, which was ceremoniously hung in the large alcove away from a direct fall of light. He loved the way the skill of the sailor and the set of the sails were captured on that blustery day by the artist's hand. Katherine had been very impressed by Max's hard work on the cottage and even mentioned how the new blinds, toning with the sofa, added an extra touch. He took her out to Barleys, a local pub-restaurant, and they ate on the veranda overlooking the bay and walked home along the beach. His mother stayed overnight and left after breakfast the next day. He had wanted to tell her about Roma, but somehow it still seemed too early.

Tuesdays and Thursdays, swimming with Tom had become a habit now, and had developed into an hour or two in Barleys after the Thursday swims. Max was determined to do well in the carnival swim and the regular practise saw him improving rapidly. The signs on the side of his van had produced a few small jobs, and the advert in the parish magazine brought a belt of inquiries from very different sources. He wanted to take only joinery work, rather than site work. He believed it was important to respond quickly to all inquiries and, if possible, see the job quickly too. Today, he was early for an appointment to give a quote at the Bilson's home. He parked the van and sat thinking for a moment. Gathering his clipboard and pen, checking his tape was on his belt, and patting Spike, he then swung his legs round, stepping on to the pavement. A short walk through the churchyard would bring him to the Old Rectory. Passing the heavy iron gate and the side door to the church, he joined a gravel path that ran around the building.

Dancing in the bushes a little way off were a small flock of goldfinches. He stopped to take a proper look at them, but they flew away. There was an oak bench at the edge of the path in front of him. As he was still early, he sat and looked at the shape and lie of the headstones; some part-covered with lichen; the much older ones were flaking after long years of changing seasons. The grass had been cut recently, but only a few graves were tended. Many others were overgrown. All these names, all these people, they had just melted away; their deeds, their actions, their misdemeanours – all forgotten. Only their gene pool survived to mark their being. A woman walked past him and he glanced in her direction before standing up and walking through the lychgate. Crossing the road between the parked cars, he walked on to the driveway of the Old Rectory. In front of him was a magnificent, classic four-square Georgian house with a central hall, stairs and landing, built of red brick and with a Welsh slate roof. He loved the way, the lazy way, the old wisteria seemed to cling to the front wall. The house looked tired though. Using the lady's hand door knocker, Max rapped once and waited. He noticed the worn threshold and the small thin split in the weather bar at the bottom of the door. Before he could take in the well-stocked gardens, the door opened. A man in a suit introduced himself, apologised for being in a hurry, and rushed over the driveway to a Range Rover, quickly to disappear. At his shoulder stood a tall woman and, with a confident and relaxed voice, said: 'Hello. I'm Tessa, do come in.' She wanted an estimate to overhaul or replace 11 box sashes and sills to the main house and repair the sagging dining room floor.

While he was measuring, she had kindly brought tea in a floral-patterned bone china mug, and then stood at his elbow talking. They had not long moved in and the house was still full of endless unpacked boxes. Children's toys, bicycles, sofas - all had yet to find a place. So many possessions piled up, Max idly wondered why people needed so much stuff.

After finishing measuring up, he told her he would phone later with a price for the work. He seemed to have made his mark with her and was confident that the price he would give would be accepted. He waved as he left and went back to his van. Before he pulled away, Max sat, thinking, for a moment, with his hands resting on the wheel. There was a risk of unsettling Roma by not telling her about his past, and it could cause her to question his motives. This worried him. If he wasn't careful, not telling her soon might have a major outcome on their growing involvement. Later that evening, he sat quietly after supper on the sofa with Spike tucked under his legs. These were the small moments that join up an ordinary life. The comas, the pauses in our space of time. Leaning back with his hands behind his head, he looked at the painting on the wall in front of him. As a child, he used to imagine he was the skipper shouting to his crew as the boat barged its way over the choppy water. Those

The Lightroom

summer holidays that lasted so long were now just a flash within the pan. He flicked open his laptop and drifted through the first half hour of a film. At almost his cut-out point, the phone rang. Reaching for it, he thumbed the film off. It was, to his surprise, Theo.

'Hey Max, I said I'd phone. I owe you, when are we going to meet up? What about the weekend? Anytime, name a day, if there's someone you'd like to bring.'

'Yes, great. How about Saturday evening?'

'OK, do you know The Bowman? Let's make it 8pm.'

'Fine, and I will be with Roma. See you at 8.'

The call ended, and within a few seconds his mobile spun on the table as it vibrated with another call. 'Hello.'

'Max, it's Tom. Sorry, I've got a late surgery tomorrow. I will have to skip the swim, and I can meet you in the pub around 7.30. But you've got to show your metal and do our usual distance on your own. No short cuts!'

Finishing that conversation, Max then called Roma to tell her about the evening with Theo. Hearing her voice made him feel he wanted her the more. Thursday was a blur of work throughout the day, then a hard swim and into the pub to meet Tom. Friday went the same way, but it was on the way to the weekend, and, after returning from a good day at 'the factory', he stepped out of all his work clothes, leaving them where they fell. He turned on the shower, and as he waited briefly for the hot water to run through, he absentmindedly scratched himself a couple of times before plunging into the heavy force of water.

Tilting his head back, with his eyes closed and holding his breath, he allowed the water to run over his face, before it fell to his body. When he could hold his breath no longer, he tilted his head forward again, breathing normally, and so altering the passage of water across himself. Hot water on the skin was, to him, much more than the simple act of washing. It was a moment of deep revitalisation. After soaping, shaving and rinsing, idly he raised a hand to cut the flow of water and stepped out onto the mat. Towelling himself thoroughly, he replaced the towel on the rail, and then trimmed his sideboards with the razor. He went back to the bedroom naked, stepping over his pile of clothes while rubbing a hand across his face to check for any misses from the shave. He chose his clothes carefully, putting on a blue Oxford shirt and a clean pair of jeans. Taking a thin, dark blue woollen jumper from the drawer, he saw two small holes on the front near the neck line. Instantly, he felt frustration and disappointment at the waste. Moths, there seemed no cure that really worked. Shaking off his irritation, he left the jumper in the bedroom and took the first step on the stairs. As an afterthought, he returned, picking up the pile of clothes and took them downstairs to the washing machine Sitting on the lower stairs, he pulled on a pair of shoes and laced them quickly. He then reached for his keys from the small, polished mahogany plaque with three Victorian curtain hooks mounted on it.

Vic had made this for him as a moving in present. Spike was already at the door. 'Back, you beauty,' he commanded, and the dog moved behind him. Slipping the lead over the dog's neck, he walked out into the warm summer's evening, locking the door behind him. He drove to Roma's house to walk the dogs and have supper with her. It was after 6pm when he pulled up on the open ground at the end of the lane. She must have seen him arrive, as when he opened the van door, Betsy bounded forward to greet him and Spike. Roma was at the doorway with an apron on, shielding her eyes from the lowering sun with an open palm. Then she waved. She was in the process of removing her apron as he reached her.

'I'm almost ready, I just need my walking shoes.'

'I need to talk to you.'

She frowned at the tone of his voice for a moment, then went back inside. Surrounded by the dogs, she sat on the edge of the sofa, leaning forward as though only expecting to perch there for a short time. He sat opposite her, then sagging back under the weight of the topic, he opened his hands and allowed his arms to fall beside him. His face tightened before he started to talk.

First, he told her that he was hiding nothing from her, but explained that he, like everyone else, had baggage. He felt it only fair that she should know from him, and out tumbled his story of prison and how he had come to be there, and how, through pain, he had been flattened by depression. He asked her to consider carefully and hoped that she would see him for the man he tried to be. She listened to him without interruption, shocked and surprised, before saying: 'Everyone has baggage,' she paused. 'Mine is just much lighter than yours. I'm not interested in your past so much; I know you are a good man, what I want is to share in your future.'

Standing, they moved close together and – as of then - they were stronger.

He looked at the dogs. Betsy was lying still, watching them with her head on her paws, and Spike was sitting alert, with his ears at right angles to his head, tilted slightly as if to say: 'Yes, OK. Get on with it. I'm ready for my walk.' Max and Roma walked past the parked cars, followed the path between the bushes and went over the style into the large field. The ground rose in front of them as the gradient increased. Pausing, she took his hand and squeezed it gently in reassurance. The final push to the top of the hill was hard, but then the view opened up for them. The first blush of sunset might have been in the sky as they stopped, but not for long, then turning, with the dogs somewhere near, they made their way back to the cottage. In the tiny kitchen, Roma fed the dogs then carefully washed her hands in hot water before rinsing the fish free from the salt. Baking it in the oven the way her mother had done, she cooked it with olives, garlic, capers, tomatoes and several spices and herbs. It was topped with buttered potatoes. Max pushed the sofa forward and lifted the drop leaf to the table and then placed the two folding chairs from the wall at the table. The mats and cutlery were passed to him from the kitchen with cold wine and glasses. While Roma chopped some more parsley from her herb trough, he poured two large glasses of wine, then waited for her to join him. Taking a first mouthful, he allowed the cool, dry fruity taste to wash in his throat while he thought about her cottage. In reality, it was a one-and-a-half up and a one-and-a- half down, with a scrap of a yard in an unpretentious condition, one good size smaller than his own. The tired furnishings and fittings provided the reason for the low rent, but as the twelve-month lease was nearing, an increased rent couldn't be ruled out. Picking up his glass, he had a second take of his wine. Again, it relaxed him by a fraction. There was an easy solution. Should she move to his house? Wait and see would be the answer to that easy question.

The supper was brought to the table with the flourish of a magician, the flair of colour held in the dish with a good dash of parsley.

After eating, he cleared away the dishes and dropped the leaf of the table, topped the glasses again, and both of them moved onto the small sofa. Lounging there together, close in their shared warmth, they watched a film before letting the dogs out, then going to bed. In the morning after breakfast, wearing old working clothes, they went to help the elderly couple at the end of the terrace, who struggled with their corner garden. Roma enjoyed helping out by cutting the grass and planting while old Joe pottered in the makeshift green house with his cuttings and seedlings. It gave her the chance to work a garden she didn't have, as well as to repay them for looking after the dog while she was in school. Joe had introduced her to the vegetable garden too and Max was quickly put to work weeding it. Around midday, Maria came out with sandwiches and cold drinks. They carried an array of old chairs over to the table under the lilac bushes and sat together in the shade to eat. Roma recognised it was arthritis in their hands and hips that let Joe and Maria down, making life so much harder for them.

After lunch, Roma and Max went back down the lane to her house. While the dogs lay in the yard with the back door open, they went upstairs to wash and change out of their gardening clothes. Max pulled the blind down in the bedroom and climbed under the covers. Shutting his eyes, he felt he could sleep. She gently moved her body close to him and he felt the warmth and shape of her. Instinctively, he knew this was where he belonged. He took her in his arms and they lay together. It must have been the leaves near the window, moving in the light breeze that did it. The strong afternoon light was almost shut out by the closed blinds, apart from the thin gap down one side. The shadows of the leaves outside danced on the wall in front of them, and the beauty of this silent light show had them transfixed. Soon they slept, and on waking, Max had forgotten this small event. The sun was still there, behind the blind, but it had moved and the angle changed.

He was alone now, but could hear Roma moving around beneath him in the rooms below, and a tap running for a short time, perhaps to fill the kettle. Then he heard her steps on the wooden floorboards and the scrape of a chair. The quiet, solid sounds of company. He lay still, thinking how this woman lifted his soul. It rested him just to look in her direction. Without any conscious effort, she banished his darker thoughts and cut the nettles from his life.

They went out that evening to meet Theo at the pub, as he had suggested. They took both dogs in the back of the van and drove the four miles through the narrow lanes. With high hedges obscuring the views, secret glimpses were revealed only over styles or gates as they passed. The lane twisted its way over the countryside like a snail track on a carpet, finally reaching the junction on top of Salt Hill. Turning north, they came to the pub car park. It was just after 8 and it was nearly full. *The Bowman* was an old stone, listed building, built about 180 years ago, and it had a micro-brewery from the new adjacent oak clad barn, skilfully designed to sit at ease with its older cousin. The successes of this two- pub chain were crafted beers and excellent food, served on long, scrubbed tables in basic surroundings. Drivers, day trippers, walkers - all were welcomed with a log fire in winter; and a large garden, with its own wandering chickens, in the summer.

'Better leave the dogs in the back of the van, I think,' said Max. 'It's going to be a bit crowded in the pub, so they will be happier here with a bowl of water and plenty of room. The sun's gone now, and they've got fresh air with the side window down.'

Max pushed open the stiff, latched door of the pub, and they crossed over the coconut matting. Roma leaned against the inner door, and turned to smile briefly at Max, as they walked into the warmth and noise of a Saturday night. Theo, who was sitting at a large table at the far end of the bar, got up and moved towards them with a grin on his face.

'Hello Max.'

Then, turning to Roma, he introduced himself and shook both their hands. He waved an arm for them towards the table where his sometime partner, Tilly, was sitting. That dark, wet evening when Max and Theo had first met seemed long ago now. Tilly and Roma soon discovered they shared a love of books and of seafood, and they discussed novels and authors over crayfish salads. Theo's character slowly emerged. He was a charmer, a likeable rogue with an eye for the main chance. The very large burger with fries he had ordered didn't stand a chance. He held his knife and fork in his fists, like he wanted to do damage, stabbing the air from time to time to reinforce a point he was making. Max liked him, he was a genuine bloke. The evening flew away amongst anecdotes and the wine. As the server brought their coffee over on a tray, Max noticed a man walk behind him. He was thick-waisted, in his 40s, wearing black trousers, white shirt and a tight-fitting black jacket. It was a similar uniform to that worn by the prison officers. Looped from beneath the waist of the jacket hung a thick, chrome chain which disappeared into the man's pocket – obviously keys, like the warders. For that brief moment, Max was taken back, the cold hand of the past had just re-visited him. It was Roma who brought him back to the present, touching his arm.

Smiling at her, he shook himself down. Memories like those were best left undisturbed. Theo paid the bill, and they left the pub with the firm intention of meeting again. Driving a little way, Max, who had been careful to stick to one glass of wine, slowed the van to a low grass verge just off the road by a footpath sign.

'I'll let the dogs run. Walk with me in the moonlight. The stars are out and it's such a clear night. Come on.' He took Roma's hand and they walked into the field with its striking stillness. Tilting their heads back in awe of creation, they marvelled at a never-ending sky. It seemed they were standing under the open vault of heaven.

It must have been the following week that Max took Roma to his local, *The Stonemason's Arms,* and she saw a sign for a forthcoming karaoke night. She suggested they should get a party together for it. After a few beers, his throw-away response had been: 'Why not?' but it was said, perhaps, to be lost in the line of conversation. Roma and her friend Alice must have started pulling together a group quite quickly, because when Max next heard about the event, they had it all planned. On the night of the karaoke, both the bar and an adjoining room were crammed. Girls dressed to their heels; men with crisp, white shirts hanging loose, and the old guard, standing bemused by the fruit machines. With the bar staff at racing pace and coloured strobe lights flashing across the room, they had all come to sing – the fearless, the nervous and those loosened by the drink. The opening set was an older, short man and he massacred an Elvis ballad with the ease a scythe cuts through corn. Then came the soulful tone of a young girl with a broken voice. She sang so well, giving a near perfect rendition of Leonard Cohen's Hallelujah. Max leaned against the tall fireplace, behind several rows of people; listening and watching the performers at what he considered to be a safe distance. Reaching up amongst the empty glasses on the shelf above the fireplace, he retrieved his pint. He noticed Roma, with her arm briefly around the shoulders of an older woman wearing a pink leather jacket. She was the other side of 60, with a mane of blonde hair, mostly extensions. She and Roma were laughing as they took the microphone together and burst into the opening lines of: *Waiting for my Number One.* Max was transfixed, watching them. Their movements expressed their joy at singing and being on the stage, and then it was over. In that brief moment, the spotlight was theirs, and the applause that followed their performance was loud and well-deserved. Max wondered how people could get up there and sing. Did they practise at home? Did this give them extra confidence? Even the idea of it terrified him.

Finding his way to the bar for more drinks, he watched the performers as he waited. The music went on, topped only by the solid barrage of the continuous sound of the crowds at the bar. It lay like a backdrop to the singers and their music. That massive sound of voices, welded together, and interspersed with laughter. He heard a glass slip and shatter harmlessly on the floor, and the barrage of noise dipped a little, but only for a moment. The bar tills were banging open and shut continuously, and these sounds were lost amongst the rolling wave of music and conversation pouring out through the open windows and doors, onto the street, past the smokers and vapers, over the forgotten glasses and, finally, to dissipate to nothing more than a murmur. There were hugs from strangers, with the easy mixing among unknown neighbours, and then the remnants of their group spilled out onto the pavement and went their separate ways home. Roma looped her arm with Max's as he pulled her to him, and she touched her head against his shoulder. There was a final wave to Alice and Paul, and a reminder that they would see them the next day, and they walked the short route home. As he raised his arm to put the key in the door, he noticed, with the mildest touch of irritation, two beer cans had been deposited neatly side by side in the corner of his forecourt. After letting the dogs out in the yard, they went upstairs.

The Lightroom

Chapter 13

The Bank Holiday weekend was probably the busiest one of the year for the town. The carnival procession was a blinding, continuous train of noise and colour that wound its way through the streets. Bands, clowns, musicians and jokers were all weaving their tunes among the enormous crowd that lined the pavements. Alice briefly saw it go by as some of The Pier café customers rose like a wave to the window to watch it pass, before returning to their tables and their food. The funfair, on the top sands beach, was in full belt, with music cascading down the slope of the promenade. To the east, the swim had started on the high tide. More than 100 swimmers fired away from the beach, going out to a turn marker offshore, then to the long straight heading for the finishing line at the rowing club. The swimmers, accompanied by dozens of brightly coloured safety canoes, looked like dots on the surface of the sea. Afterwards, there were trophy presentations on the beach. Neither Max or Tom won a prize – their reward was to finish well up in the pack. A couple of weeks later, the summer was still clinging on by its fingertips when Max and Roma took a double canoe out on a Sunday morning. Paddling lazily along the bay, he sheltered her from the sun by putting his T-shirt over her head and letting it hang down her back. Talking, drifting slowly, they trailed a line over the back of the canoe with feathered hooks, then forgot about it. Later, with a splashing sound, they hit a shoal of fish. The line was dancing as Max touched it. Pulling gently, he saw the first twisting, turning, green and black markings of mackerel showing above the water. He took off four fish and lobbed them into the canoe, where they lay, jumping and banging around in the bottom of the boat. At home the mackerel were gutted and rinsed in the sink, and they still had the smell of the sea on them as they were placed on the barbecue that evening.

Roma and Max sat on the garden bench under the honeysuckle arch, eating, drinking wine together, and talking the evening away; just as ordinary people do. The sunset and dusk fell, and the bats came from the eaves of a neighbouring roof in ones and twos; flying short, low, jagged circles, turning sharply on the wing in the half light. As the evening faded, the bats disappeared. Then, as the air grew cooler, Max and Roma went inside. That evening, she spoke to him about the lease on her cottage coming to an end. She said she was unsure of what might happen next. He listened, then simply said: 'Would you like to come and live with me here? I'll sort everything for you.'

The silence to this was brief, before she smiled and replied: 'I would like nothing better than to be with you.' He moved to the sofa alongside of her. Taking her hand, he said quietly: 'So, that's that then,' wishing that everything really could be this easy. Over the next couple of weeks, Roma ended her tenancy and moved in with Max.

The first week of September, the schools went back and Roma's pattern of life shifted. She was enthusiastic to get back to work and had lots of new ideas for her classes. Max's list of work projects lengthened. With the help of some more specialist jigs that he had bought, he had set up a bespoke ledge and brace door supply and fit service. This bolted on well to the growing box sash manufacturing and repair business. He had a finisher from college working with him for two days a week and Max felt the time was right to take him on full time in the workshop. This would free Max up for other things. Late September saw the last of the season's sea swims with Tom before they transferred to the indoor pool. That evening the breeze was coming under the clouds in the south west, but there was a window. The sea still had that gentle swell, backing up to the beach. Tom's car swung into the car park; his timing was perfect.

It was 6.10pm as he parked in the bay with his usual habit of encroaching the white lines. His reasoning was that it stopped others parking too close and saved his paintwork. Tom's greeting was wide across his face. Stripping down, they both changed into in their trunks, putting all their clothes in Max's locked van. Then, kneeling, he pushed his hand behind the back of the front offside tyre, putting the key on the rim. They walked across the road then down the gently shelving beach, stumbling a little on the stones until their toes touched the cold edge of the sea. It was the same story each time - a bit of banter, walk in a bit, more banter, then when the sea temperature registered on their 'thermometers', their heads would lower and, with arms outstretched as if to salute this mighty spirit, they both dived beneath the first wave. Front crawl is a spiritual thing, it's like a re-birth. They felt the power in their arms, the water; their movement. It was just after low tide. The water in the bay was shallow, so they headed out maybe 150 metres, falling into a comfortable unison, side by side a few metres apart. The tide was just in their favour. It seemed to take a while to reach a flag pole on the promenade, the half mile mark. Still they swam on. The sailing club eventually came and went as the light began to thin and the first chills swept their bodies. Then the wind slid over them, moving the water in its wake, shaping it with an invisible hand.

They passed the scattered beach huts with their bright coloured paintwork, all shut up against the closing day. The beachfront was quiet and free from promenaders as Max and Tom pumped on, with the slipway and the lifeboat station ahead. Then Max stopped. He sensed, more than heard, that Tom had also stopped. He waved an arm westward as they lay on their backs for a moment, gazing in wonderment at the screaming red sun splintering the clouds on its way down. They swam on, and within a few minutes they were both stumbling again, this time up the slipway, past the last evening walkers. Dogs barked in the car park - it was Spike and Betsy with Roma, holding out two towels.

A last glance back at the sea and they saw the moon had risen in the east to complement the setting sun in the west. Changing quickly beside the car, the two men shivered as the breeze touched their bodies. Tom then drove them all back to Max's van, parked at the other end of the bay. With a wave and laugh, he drove off as Max and Roma, with the dogs in the back, pointed up the van for home. In quieter moments, Max would think of those summer months as waiting memories. There were long, hot, good days, filled with people. People that filled previous voids in unknown spaces deep within him. There were always the days when he wanted to push all his lonely, painful memories from his previous life into a corner and set fire to them. He wanted them to blow away on the wind of time. But they clung to him like a dragging, sucking morass, and he tiptoed round the edges from time to time, for fear of getting some stuck on his shoes and to walk back to the present with them.

Max's old Triumph had lain in the garage, covered by a couple of old blankets. It had needed a separate trip to bring the bike from his mother's home down to Dorset, and it was the last of his possessions to arrive at the cottage. Taking the blankets off carefully, scattering bits of sawdust to the floor, revealed the dirty beast in all its glory. There was road mud spattered from the sump to the chain guard and the wheels were dulled by a winter's grime, all before he 'went away'. Looking it over, Max spotted a small dent in the black tank near the emblem. He placed his hand on it, as though to sooth or even suck the dent away. To him, the dirt and marks were visible signs of use, deepening its character. Swinging a leg over the bike, he moved it off its stand, checking it was in neutral and manoeuvred it into the centre of the garage, returning it the main stand. Removing the seat with a long star screwdriver, he exposed the electrics.

Then he lifted the recharged battery into position and, after tightening the clamp, he connected the positive lead first, then the negative.

Flicking the key, the lights on the speedo jumped up at him; a burst of the starter turned over the engine, firing it to the roar he recognised so well. With the doors opened, he allowed the bike to run on the choke while he found an oil tray and slid it beneath the sump. Having by then warmed the engine oil, he turned off the engine and removed the sump nut with a spanner, allowing the oil to drain out. Next, using a belt spanner, he loosened the oil filter, then, using his hand, he unscrewed it over the tray as the surplus ran over his hand. Wiping his hands on an old towel, he waited until the dirty oil slowed to a drip before screwing in the new brass plug and washer, tightening it with the spanner. At the final twist, he felt the rising change on the edge of his thumb. He knew he had pinched it just alongside his nail. The swelling was not quite pain, but a single word slipped from between his lips. Beneath the thin coat of oil would lie a blood blister. Very carefully, he screwed in the new oil filter, tightening again with the same belt spanner, having made certain that the new O ring for the filter was properly oiled first. Finally, opening the oil chamber, he filled the bike with semi-synthetic oil to the required amount, checking this on the small glass at the bottom of the casing. The dirty oil was funnelled into a topped container for disposal later. For a moment, in his mind he was already riding the long dipping coast road running west up from Coombe Wallin. It was the dragging of the bottom bolt on the concrete as one of the doors caught the wind that brought him back. After closing and locking the doors, he cleaned his hands with cream, wiping away the surplus. Max went back to the kitchen where both dogs lay motionless on the cool stone floor, watching him. He washed his hands thoroughly with soap and hot water, and turned on the radio hoping to catch the early evening news while he fixed supper. Roma wasn't due back for a while yet.

Looking though the cupboards, he took red lentils, onions, and tomatoes and then located a couple of chicken breasts in the fridge. He decided to make chicken Balti for them both.

The next morning, he woke early as the light was starting, unsure whether it was the coming of the light that had woken him, or the strong, steady sound of Roma asleep on her back, breathing rhythmically like an incoming wave to a beach. In a state of complete alertness, but without moving, his thoughts became ordered. His mother was taking the early train down to spend a short day with him and to meet Roma for the first time during her lunch break. How would it go? As the strengthening light started to sponge up the darkness, he turned very carefully from his back to face her, trying not to disturb her in any way. Then, he whispered slowly: 'Would you like a cup of tea?'

The only sound he heard in response was: 'mm.' Gently levering himself out of bed, he went downstairs, put the kettle on, opened the back door to let out the dogs and returned with two large mugs of strong tea. He needn't have been concerned in any way about his mother meeting Roma. It was clear they immediately took to one another. It was only a quick lunch at The Pier café and then straight back to school for Roma. With a hug and a wave, she passed the railings and walked away from them, across the crowded playground to the school doors. Max and his mother walked back slowly to his house. They put the dogs in the back of the van and then drove over to the workshop, so she could see how his work was shaping up. There was a note under the door from Vic saying he had taken in a delivery for him. Then they drove the two miles or so to a small, gravelled car park high up on Swinhoe Hill. They talked as they walked to the top of the hill, with the dogs running free around them. The sun had retreated to a clouding sky, but the vantage point was still clear and the panoramic view was laid out before them, with the coastline reaching to the horizon. With her arm linked to his, his mother said: 'You've built another life here, Max. I'm so happy for you.'

Later, he took her back to Hawkston railway station, and stood on the platform as she got on the train and took a seat by the window. They waved together, that long moment that quickly goes. Then the train left. Walking back to the station car park, for no particular reason, Max decided to take a detour through to the high street. Taking a short cut behind the bus station, he looked across the untended grass in an alcove at the rear of the station's arcade of small shops. This angular piece of unused design failure was roofed and covered on three sides, sheltered from both the elements and most of the prying eyes of passers-by. He spotted the two empty supermarket trollies first, backed by the perished brickwork. A paper coffee cup stood upright alongside various discarded bottles and, next to them, was a large bundle topped with a dirty duvet. A man sat against the back wall, wrapped in a floral blanket and holding what looked like another cup of coffee in both his shaking hands. He appeared to be vacantly staring out at the light rain that had just started. Max had seen this helpless, hopeless look of a man shelled by drugs when he was inside. This deeply complex scene made him reflect how this man had his freedom, but precious little else. Society often seemed to fail those that needed the most help. Following the pavement into the bus station with its walkways, he passed the graffiti-stained walls, fading posters in cabinets and the putrid smell that came from years of endless people pissing in dark corners in the late hours, washed not quite clean by disinfectant.

The bus station was a long, two-storey building, typical of the '60s. It had cheap, mainly pebbledash, sectional panels; poor low-cost brick interfacing, with a side of sagging upstairs windows, only housing boxes and general storage.

The open side of the station was railed off to stop pedestrians walking near the buses, but no one seemed to take any notice. People dodged the vehicles as a tame fox might dodge lorries in a brickyard. The buses pulled in or out, blowing their clouds of diesel fumes at the high street and pedestrians alike. The queues were mainly elderly people with bus passes, waiting in an orderly fashion as their youth had taught them. Meanwhile, incongruously placed electronic time tables regularly blinked their messages. At this time of the day, the numbers were swollen by the nearby school turning out. Reaching the crossing, Max waited for the lights to change.

Witnesses said it was a selfless act. It was heroic, at great personal cost. They said: 'The two boys were larking about. One was pulling at the other's bag. Then he just let go. The boy stepped backward into the oncoming traffic.'

Another said: 'The guy sprang forward. He managed to swing the boy out of the path of the cars, somehow.'

They had all seen the man then leap away from the cars. He seemed to lose his footing, maybe it was the kerb. It was the way he fell, there was no sound. He just lay there motionless. People came forward, but the traffic didn't stop; there had been no vehicles involved. A middle-aged woman bent over his head, then shouted at a man nearby: 'Quickly, call for an ambulance.' Turning back to look at Max, she said to the people around her: 'Under no circumstances should we try and move him.'

Max saw a coloured kaleidoscope reach like an umbrella surrounding his sight, while a warm rain touched his skin. The noise of voices, jumbled and far away, reached him. It was easier just to let go. Let go. The words were hanging before him. Regaining consciousness, but lying completely still, Max drifted. He felt lost and dazed. People were all around him, making noises, but where was he and who were all these people? Why were they making so much noise? The sound of a police siren filtered through to him. Then there were gentle voices asking questions. A neck brace was fitted. There were green uniforms beside him.

He was being lifted into an ambulance and someone was talking to him all the time. He had no idea what they were saying. Concentrating, he knew he had fallen. He couldn't think why. A splitting headache rained over his eyes. He then understood he was being taken to hospital. There was a small voice far away, it kept saying: 'Don't worry. You'll be OK, you'll be OK.'

He was unaware of the paramedics carrying out basic tests and observations, checking his responses and co-ordination. Nor was he aware the ambulance was being driven at speed through the afternoon traffic. After being examined at A&E, the doctors were concerned. They sent him immediately for a CT scan and he would be closely monitored. He felt exhausted and he let the tide of it all take him. He was put in a bed and he lay between the cool sheets, resting for a moment, then he fell to a quiet dark place.

It took him forever to climb out of the dark. Eventually, he dreamed of a weight pressing down on him. Max opened his eyes and realised it was Roma's hand resting on his.

About the author

A H Pilcher has written several novels. The first to be published, in 2020, was *Arc of Doubt*, which received considerable media attention. *The Lightroom* is the second to be published, and is set in West Sussex, London and Dorset. Humphrey was born in Hampshire, and lived abroad for several years in his twenties, including some time in Australia, where *Arc of Doubt* was mostly set. He now lives on the south coast of England, where he is a regular sea swimmer and dog walker.

The author would like to thank his editorial team at Backleg Books, who helped him through many re-writes; and also his researcher and proof readers, who provided invaluable support. Thanks also to the design team at Macaulay Design.

Printed in Great Britain
by Amazon